WHAT
SHE
NEVER
SAID

A THRILLER

CATHARINE
RIGGS

THOMAS & MERCER

Published by Thomas & Mercer, Seattle

www.apub.com

Amazon, the Amazon logo, and Thomas & Mercer are trademarks of Amazon.com, Inc., or its affiliates.

ISBN-13: 9781542042130
ISBN-10: 1542042135

Cover design by Shasti O'Leary Soudant

Printed in the United States of America

To Chuck and Peg
Thank you

There are six things the Lord hates, seven that are detestable to him: haughty eyes, a lying tongue, hands that shed innocent blood, a heart that devises wicked schemes, feet that are quick to rush into evil, a false witness who pours out lies and a man who stirs up dissension among brothers.

Proverbs 6:16–19

I. PRIDE

Pride goes before destruction, a haughty spirit before a fall.

—Proverbs 16:18

The Angel

Some might call me a cold-blooded killer. I beg to disagree. I'm more like a kindly saint. A patron saint of crossings. One part Saint Christopher, two parts angel of mercy. Add a dash of Mother Teresa, and the recipe is getting close. I have a calling, and I'm good at it. I'll keep it up until I'm stopped.

"Will it hurt?" The bedside candle casts a shivering shadow across Loretta's sunken face. Tracing my fingers along the glass syringe, I gaze into her liquid eyes.

"Not for long." I've administered a few insulin overdoses. It doesn't seem like a bad way to go. But I never lie to my disciples. That would be morally wrong.

"It won't be worse than the bone cancer?"

"It won't be worse than that."

"Then I'm ready."

I tug her pink slip from my pocket and set it on the nightstand. "First, I need your secret."

Tears slip along the folds of Loretta's crumpled cheeks. "I don't have one."

I fight off a quiver of irritation. "You're forgetting our agreement?"

"Of course not. But I can't think of a single thing."

"Oh, Loretta. I'm disappointed. I can see the secret in your eyes."

She plucks at her satin bedcovers until a lavender scent blooms. "What kind of secret do you want?"

I shrug. "Your choice. It can be happy or sad. Scandalous or glorious. I'm not picky. It's totally up to you. But it must be something you've never revealed. A defining moment in your life."

Loretta is quiet for so long I wonder if she might back out of the crossing. But then she speaks with a trembling voice. "All right then. It's something that happened on my fourteenth birthday. I've never told anyone—not even my husband. I'm still so terribly ashamed."

"Go ahead," I say, nearly drooling. This side of me isn't quite so noble. Less like a saint and more like a tick.

"It was a hot summer day in Michigan." Her voice cracks as she speaks. "My friends were busy with chores, so I walked to the lake on my own. When I entered the forest, I heard a rustling behind me, and . . ." Her words drone on from there.

Closing my eyes, I sip on her secret. Her words are like a melody— the mournful notes of a dove. When she finishes, I have tears in my eyes. "Thank you," I say. "That was beautiful."

"Beautiful? But it was such a terrible moment. So unspeakably dark."

"There are times when dark can be beautiful."

Loretta takes a choking breath. "Yes, I suppose you're right. And I do feel better somehow. You promise you'll never tell?"

"I promise."

"Good." She lifts an arthritic hand and swats vaguely at the air. "You'll stay with me?"

"Until you cross."

"Then let's get moving. I'm ready to see my Charles." Loretta folds her hands across her chest and takes a quivering breath.

"Peace be with you," I whisper, and then I inject the fatal dose. A half hour later, I head to my office, where I retrieve my crossing journal and write the seventh entry in my book.

RUTH MOSBY

One

My goal each day is ten thousand steps. A Fitbit monitors my progress. *One. Two. Three. Four.* This morning I'll reach six thousand steps. Only four thousand left after that. It's nice the days have grown longer. I'll walk the harbor loop after work. *Five. Six. Seven. Eight.* I speed up the slope of Orpet Park through the grove of moth-eaten oaks.

At the summit of the steepest hill, I catch a peek of ocean gray. The islands are invisible today, shrouded in waves of lowering fog. June gloom. That's what the locals call it, although we've barely stepped into May. Locals? I *am* a local. Or should be after thirty-some years. But oh no. Not in Santa Barbara. You can't be a local unless you're born here. Ridiculous but true. Sometimes I wonder why I stay. But at my age, where would I go?

Cresting the final hill, I catch my first glimpse of the mission bells. They're a sad reminder of my walks with Carlyn and the chats we had every day. She thought the Queen of the Missions was a sign of God's blessing on our tony beachside town. I wonder what she thinks of God now. I wonder what she thinks of me.

I continue past the mission lawn, verging on parched and dry. The agaves look weathered and dusty; they're wilted at the tips. A handful of elderly tourists snap photos of the iconic scene. Their foreign chatter disrupts the calm, so I cross the street to the rose garden and follow the rutted trail. A lone dog shoots into view, and I slow my rapid gait. The golden Lab jumps, twists, and barks, nabbing a Frisbee in his mouth.

"Morning," his master calls to me, a smile gracing his youthful face.

"Morning." I lock my gaze on my running shoes. How did he miss the **DOGS ON LEASH** signs staggered every twenty feet? Or maybe he didn't but somehow believes he's above the city's rules. I make a mental note to call animal control and continue on my way.

I pick up my pace for the final ten blocks, feeling better than I have in weeks. Turning down my narrow driveway, I cringe at the sight of my neighbor standing on his porch.

"Morning, Ruth," he calls.

"Morning, Zach."

Zach limps down his steps and through his drought-stricken garden, a frown rumpling his grizzled face. He's dressed in board shorts and a tattered T-shirt, mended flip-flops shielding his feet. "You hear those kids partying last night?" he asks.

"No," I lie. "Was it loud?"

"Hell yeah. I can't believe they allow short-term rentals in our neighborhood. We've got to put a stop to that."

"Well, kids will be kids." I fail to mention I called the police at ten sharp. That's when the noise ordinance kicks in.

"I'm going to complain at today's city council meeting. Want to come along?" The breeze shifts, and I catch a whiff of spoiled milk. Zach has taken to strategic bathing, which results in an occasional stench.

"I would, but I have to work."

"Bummer. There's a better chance if we complain together."

I nod, thinking he'd have a better chance if he made an effort to clean himself up. When we moved into the neighborhood decades ago, Zach had been a handsome man with an easy smile and a mop of thick black hair. A homicide detective whose pretty wife, Tina, taught art at the nearby elementary school. The perfect neighbors on a perfect street of tiny Craftsman homes. Then their son died in a tragic accident, and Tina passed soon after that. A broken man, Zach took early retirement and nearly drank himself to death. He's in recovery now and has replaced the booze with an obsession for neighborhood affairs. "What about my petition?" he asks. "You plan on signing that?"

I bite my lower lip. "I'm not sure."

"Construction begins next week."

"I wish I could, but . . ."

Mumbling under his breath, he eyes me with a frown. He's also taken to talking to himself. Is dementia creeping up? "But what?" he asks.

"I don't think it's wise for someone in my position to take a political stance."

"Your position?" He rolls his eyes. "You work at an old folks' home."

"I work in a *life-care* community."

"Same thing."

"No, it's not."

His frown deepens into a crevasse. "So, you're okay with those homes coming down?" He nods at the four vacant bungalows located directly across the street. They're slated for demolition, to be replaced by a ten-thousand-square-foot mansion with an Olympic-sized swimming pool. Our future neighbors are a flashy young couple with toddler twins and an army of well-groomed staff. Seems our former middle-class neighborhood is attracting the fashionable Hollywood types.

"I'm not okay with it," I say, "but what can we do? The planning commission has made their decision. We're not going to change their minds."

"But if we don't take action, it won't be long before people like us can't live in this town."

"At least we'll make a mint when we sell."

"You're not thinking of moving, are you?"

"Of course not." Although I might if the price is right.

Zach sniffs and takes a swipe at his nose. "I just wish we could stop these assholes. They even complained about my new picket fence."

I hold my voice steady. "They did?" Last month, Zach replaced his aging fence with a synthetic version that lists from side to side.

"Hell yes. City says my fence is four inches too tall, and I've got one month to replace the thing. Where the hell am I going to get that kind of money? My pension only goes so far." He searches my face with his electric-blue eyes. They're the only part of him that haven't aged.

"That's terrible," I say, dropping my gaze and backpedaling down the driveway. "Got to get to work. Have a nice day." I hurry through the gate, swimming through waves of guilt. What if Zach finds out I turned him in? He'll be angrier than a cornered wasp. But by the time I step out of the shower, I've pushed away all my self-doubt. Is it my fault his fence is too tall? For God's sake, rules are rules.

Two

I slow my Prius near the gilded gates that safeguard Serenity Acres' front entrance. I'm behind a line of thirty cars—it's the daily changing of the shifts. The back service entrance is under renovation, resulting in this ridiculous traffic jam. The results had better be worth it. The delay adds minutes to my commute. I glance at my cell phone, hoping against hope my daughter might think to check in. But I'm dreaming. She's way too busy. But I won't let that get me down. When the security guard waves me through, I note a freshly inked tattoo on his neck. Visible tattoos violate company rules. I'll be giving his supervisor a call.

Winding my way through the tree-lined drive, I look for further infractions to report. They're often difficult to discern as the beauty masks the flaws. The campus is a stunning location, a series of two-story Moorish-style buildings topped with traditional red-tile roofs. But the whitewashed walls seem a little grimy today. I'll ask facilities to give them a touch-up. And I'll want answers on why the lawn looks so shabby. Did someone forget to mow?

It's not that I'm being unreasonable. We have certain standards to meet. Our guests demand perfection for their million-dollar investments, and I don't blame them in the least. The arched windows are washed weekly, the tiled floors buffed until they gleam. The gardens are clipped to perfection, and the blossoms are removed before they fade. The nine-hole golf course is fed by a private well; no sign of drought makes an appearance here.

I pull into my favorite spot in the far corner of the staff parking lot. I get an extra five hundred steps that way. Checking my Fitbit, I smile. Six thousand three hundred. Not bad. When I reach the backside of administration, a rumbling fire truck and ambulance await. Although emergency services visits us daily, no sirens disturb the peace. We keep illness and death at a distance; it's part of the illusion we create.

Inside the climate-controlled building, I wince at the hint of rotten fruit. Smells are the scourge of all eldercare facilities, but we're supposed to be above that here. I make a note to speak to the head of housekeeping and continue to my office door. There awaits my first appointment, slouching against the plaster wall.

"Good morning, ma'am," she says in a tired voice.

"Good morning, Selena. Please come in."

After stepping through the foyer that leads to my office, I flick on the overhead lights. I hang my jacket and set down my purse, pleased to begin my day. Taking a seat behind my mahogany desk, I'm enveloped in a calming sense of control. My office is my home away from home, decorated to my taste. The walls are peach, the furniture plush, the artwork united by pastels. The lighting is soft, the air nicely scented, my desk polished with natural lemon wax. An arched window looks onto a brick-lined rose garden that blooms throughout the year. This is the place where the big contracts are signed, so it's important to set the right tone.

I nod at the padded guest chair. "Please take a seat." Selena drops with a sigh. "How are you?" I ask.

"Good," she replies, exhaustion dripping from her pores. I try not to focus on her puffy brown eyes threaded with webs of red.

"I appreciate your stopping by after your shift," I say, pulling her counseling memo from my drawer. "You must be tired."

"Very." A caretaker here for over a decade, Selena has gradually moved up the ranks. She's a plump woman in her late thirties, the night supervisor in assisted living. A hard job, but not the worst. I rattle the memo in my hands.

"So, let's get straight to the point and get you home. You were late to work six times last month. Two times this past week."

Selena works her weathered hands together, keeping her gaze fixed on her lap. "I'm sorry . . ."

"Is there a problem?"

"Yes, ma'am."

"Which is?"

"I've been on the night shift for two years now."

"And . . . ?"

"I have three children."

"And . . . ?"

"And . . ." She takes a deep breath, and her words spill out. "I'm tired. That's why I'm late. I'm tired all of the time." She straightens her shoulders and looks me straight in the eye. "I'd like to be transferred to the day shift."

I drop the memo and drum my fingers on my desk. "Impossible."

"But there's a position open in the champion's unit."

"I'm sorry. I'd like to help. But there's no one to cover your night shift."

"But I'm so tired in the morning, and when I get home, it's not like I can sleep. I have to get my three *niños* off to school, and . . ."

And? I want to help. I really do. But it's not easy to find coverage for the night shifts. "What about your husband?" I ask. "Can't he help?"

She shifts nervously. "Carlos is in Mexico. He was deported last month."

"Oh."

She leans forward. "He didn't do anything wrong. He was on his way to his gardening job, and ICE stopped him." She sniffles, and I hand her a tissue and wait while she pulls herself together. "If only he'd fixed that broken taillight," she continues. "I told him over and over, but he never listens to me."

"That's too bad," I say, meaning it. Deportations have been picking up in the area, which is disruptive to our staffing.

"I don't know what to do." Her eyes glisten with tears. "He's so unhappy. California is the only home he's ever known." She wipes her eyes with the back of her hand. "His parents brought him here when he was a baby. But now the government says he can never return." Her voice cracks. "Every night my *niños* cry themselves to sleep. They want their papa back. I promise them someday soon . . ." She gazes at me with hope. "So you see, I'm needed at home at night. At least for a little while."

For a moment, there's a crack in my armor. A shaft of light pierces through. When Doug left me years ago, my life fell apart in a snap. I went from school volunteer and mommy shuttle to a harried working woman. I couldn't figure out the juggling at first. It seemed impossible to me. But through hard work and determination, I eventually came out on top. No reason that can't happen for Selena. Absolutely no reason at all. "Your paperwork is all in order?" I ask, picturing the contents of her HR file.

"What do you mean?"

"You have a green card?"

"No," she says proudly. "I don't need one. I was born in Santa Barbara, and so were my *niños*. This is our home."

"Oh." I think on that for a moment. "So, why didn't you sponsor your husband? I mean, shouldn't he have applied for a green card years ago?"

"Yes, but . . . he got in trouble when he was a teenager. He was hanging around with a bad group of boys. It wasn't anything terrible. He only took one beer."

"So, he never tried?"

She shakes her head. "He was worried his old arrest might come up. And then the years went by, and we didn't think about it anymore, and then . . ." Her tone turns pleading. "So you can see I need a better schedule. Can you help me with that, please?"

I slide the counseling memo across the desk. "I'm sorry for your troubles. I really am. But we're a business, and there must be account-ability. You *must* find a way to arrive on time." I tap my pen against the memo. "Please read, sign, and date where indicated. You've been a good employee for many years. This is your first warning. I expect it to be your last."

Selena stares at the paper, motionless. "What about the transfer?"

"If and when we find someone to cover your night shift, you're welcome to apply. Now, I have a meeting to get to . . ." I glance at the door, inviting her out, but instead she speaks low and firm.

"Then I'm afraid I'll have to leave."

"Leave?" That stops me.

"I've been offered a position at Peaceful Pastures. A day shift for better pay."

Peaceful Pastures opened its doors a year ago, a cheap replica of our high-end brand. Its motto is "Twice the fun at half the price." But it offers half our features too. For instance, it doesn't offer "forever care," which is an important part of our brand. For the price of our substantial down payment, our guests are guaranteed a lifetime of care. I'm sure Peaceful Pastures neglects to reveal that fact when marketing its cut-rate deal. We've lost four employees to those impostors. We can't afford to lose another. I can't help feeling betrayed, but I work hard to control my tongue. "Maybe we can figure something out."

"Can you let me know this week?"

"Yes." I wiggle my computer mouse and open the screen. Dozens of emails have piled up. "Anything else?"

"One thing. Loretta Thomas passed away last night."

"That's unfortunate." An email from my boss confirms our momentary meeting. I'd better hurry. I hate to be late. "Was she sick?"

"Bone cancer."

"Has the family been notified?"

"Yes."

"I'll send a note. Anything else?"

Selena stands and drops a pink slip of paper on my desk. "I found this."

I drag my gaze from the computer screen and pick up the Post-it Note. Loretta Thomas's name is scrawled across its face and beneath it, yesterday's date. "So?" I say, feigning disinterest.

"Mrs. Crawley had one like that, and Mr. Taylor too."

"So?" I repeat. "They were all very ill."

"The other day I overheard Mrs. Thomas saying something to her friend about a Goodnight Club . . ."

"A what?"

"A Goodnight Club. She also said something about a 'crossing.' And she seemed upset. Do you know anything about it?"

I level my gaze on hers. "Yes," I lie. "It's an exclusive club that gets together in the evenings to discuss an array of subjects." I've never heard of a Goodnight Club, but one of my jobs as VP of operations is to squash rumors in the ranks. "Any more concerns you'd like to discuss?"

"No," she replies, looking away. "I just thought I should let you know."

"I appreciate that. Now go home and get some rest."

I wait until she leaves the office before examining the note and filing it away with the others. It *is* strange. She's right. But I'll get to the bottom of this. I'm sure it's nothing sinister—just a disgruntled employee pulling a practical joke. Now if I can only figure out who it is.

Three

I step out my office door and almost trip over a uniformed caregiver crouching low to the ground. She looks up with a smile. "Good morning, Ruth," she says in her lilting voice.

"Good morning, Ember." I don't always recall the caregiver names, but Ember's is hard to forget. "How are you today?"

"I'm fine." The girl's skin is so pale it's almost translucent, her short-cropped hair nearly white as snow. She looks like a child playing dress-up, but she's close to my daughter's age. You'd think she'd be too frail to be a caregiver, but I'm told she can lift twice her weight.

"This poor thing got caught in a web in the rafters." She nods at the bee buzzing inside the overturned water glass she holds in her willowy hands. Straightening, she turns toward me, and I still can't help but flinch at the sight of her disfigured face. From her right temple to her jaw, the skin sags and swirls like a lump of melted wax. Her right eye barely opens, but she's been spared her nose and lips. I was hesitant to take her on, but I made the right choice. Despite her ghastly defect, our guests have twice voted her employee of the month.

"Kill it," I say. "Quite a few guests are allergic to bees."

"Oh no. I promise I won't let it hurt anyone. I'll release it outside." She graces me with her sugar-sweet smile. Although she's just finished her night shift, she doesn't look the least bit tired. I bet she's a healthy eater. Vegan? Vegetarian? I glance at her wrist. No Fitbit in sight. Maybe yoga is her thing. A seed of an idea pops into my head.

"Can we meet this afternoon? Before your next shift?"

"Of course. I'll be at your office at six."

"Good. I'll see you then." Problem solved. Ember already works the night shift and seems to handle it very well. If I promote the girl to supervisor, she's sure to accept the role. Then I'll move Selena to a day position, and hopefully all will turn out well.

As I continue on to the executive offices, my stomach begins to churn. There's nothing that bothers me more than arriving late for a meeting, and I'm minutes past the designated time. But when I hurry into Bob's office, he seems completely unconcerned.

"Sorry I'm late," I say. "But Selena . . ."

"Selena?" His gaze remains fixed on his computer screen. "Which one is that?"

I think to explain, but then I don't. Bob's never been interested in the staff. He leaves their problems to me. I take a seat in one of the two leather guest chairs and turn when there's a rustling at the door. "Come in, Kai," Bob says, still focused on his screen. "We're just getting started."

Kai drops his rucksack with a thump and slides into his seat. He crosses his legs and stretches his arms wide, releasing a musky scent. He bikes to work dressed in tailored shirts, tattered jeans, and spotless Vans. A stubble beard blurs his jaw; he wears his coal-dark hair in a bun. The ride is long enough to get him sweaty, but he doesn't seem to care.

"Morning," he says with a smile.

"Good morning." I hold my nose—metaphorically, of course. I've left anonymous notes in the suggestion box, but he still swims in his musky cologne.

"I had the best weekend ever. Went skydiving with a bunch of guys from my church. How about you two? Do anything fun?"

Bob mumbles something, and I do the same. Kai should know by now we're not the chitchat types. We come to work to do our jobs. Why Bob ever hired him, I'll never understand. I was overseeing sales just fine. I examine my nails until Bob finishes up and turns to us with a sigh.

"There's no easy way to say this." He removes his glasses and rubs his eyes, a sign he's not a happy man. "Serenity Acres has been sold."

"What?" I nearly tumble from my chair.

"The deal is set to close at the end of the month."

"But how . . ." My head is swimming with questions, although the announcement comes as no real surprise. Our owners' estate was destroyed in the Montecito mudslide, and there've been rumors that money is tight.

"Who's buying us?" Kai asks, a touch of excitement in his voice.

"Lost Horizons."

He snaps to attention. "You kidding me?"

"No."

"Wow! That's fantastic." Kai turns to me like a little kid who got hold of an ice cream cone. "You know who they are, don't you?"

"Of course." Everyone knows of Lost Horizons. They're considered the very best of the best.

"They're totally legit," Kai says, almost drooling. "I did my master's thesis on those guys. They have the highest price point in the industry, and yet their growth rate is phenomenal."

"Which means our rates could rise," I say primly.

"They *will* rise," Bob says without a smile. He clearly isn't happy, but Kai continues to babble on.

"They're based in Aruba and have campuses in New York, Boston, London, and Rome. Sixteen in total. And their bonuses are the highest in the industry." Kai rubs his hands together. "On a personal level, this could be great for us."

Bob nods. "That may well be. But as for our guests, prices will go up after the sale. So, if you have any on the verge of signing, you may want to close them this month."

"Or hold them until after the sale," Kai says. "It'll look much better for us."

"That's a selfish way to approach this." Disdain bleeds from my tongue.

"Or it's practical," Kai responds.

"Do you care one iota for our guests?" I ask.

"Do you?" he counters.

Bob looks from Kai to me and back again. I know it frustrates him that the two of us bicker, but he hired Kai over my objections, so what does he expect? He gives his eyes another rub. "Kai's right in that our new parent company is all about profits. They bought us because they see us as an underperformer. They plan to implement a number of changes, which they expect to result in growth."

"How much growth?" I ask cautiously.

"Twenty percent increase in revenues in year one. Twenty-five in year two."

"Twenty percent?" I almost choke. "But that's impossible. I mean, maybe in New York or Miami, but you'll never see that here."

"They're not asking. They're telling."

"But with all the negative press from the fire and mudslide, our totals have been going down, not up."

Kai stretches his legs and taps the tips of his Vans against the bottom of Bob's desk. "I hate to disagree with you, Ruth, but I think a 20 percent growth rate is completely within our reach."

I glance sideways at the village idiot. "You do?"

"Yes, and I have the statistics to prove it."

I open my mouth to argue, but Bob stops me with a wave of his hand. "Enough. We can discuss the proposed changes at our weekly management meeting. In the meantime, I have one more announcement. It's completely confidential and is not to leave this room, understand?"

"Of course," we reply in unison.

He sighs and leans back in his chair. "As you know, my health hasn't been the greatest since my incident last summer."

Bob's "incident" resulted in triple-bypass surgery, and he was away from work for two months. During that time, I was promoted to acting director. I received a Silver Certificate Award for going above and beyond. It hangs front and center on my office wall.

"So with the change in ownership, I've decided this would be a good time for me to retire."

Retire? My heart begins to race. Here it is. The goal I've been working toward for the past eighteen years. I picture the changes I'll make as executive director. I'll have this place humming in no time at all. Kai quits his tapping and sits up straight.

"I'm sorry you'll be leaving," he says in one breath. "Has your replacement been identified?" he asks in the next.

"No. Not yet."

"Then I'd like to be considered for the position."

I squelch a laugh. *Kai? Are you kidding me?* I glance at Bob, but he doesn't crack a smile.

"I've informed Lost Horizons of my decision," he says. "They'll be interviewing a number of outside candidates, but they've indicated a preference for continuity in management, so both you and Ruth are under consideration." Bob gives me a knowing look, and I try hard not to grin. The new management may require open interviews, but we both know who will get the job. "Corporate will be scheduling appointments with you within the next couple of weeks."

"Great," Kai says. "How should we prepare?"

"They've already asked for my assessment and for a copy of your HR files. But as for the actual interview, I would think you'd want to address how you might achieve their sales goals."

"Smart," Kai says, jumping up. "I'll start on that right away."

Out in the hallway, Kai stops me. "You think Bob's getting pushed out?"

"Of course not." I hadn't even thought of that.

"I wonder . . . I mean, he *is* getting old."

"He is not. He's only sixty-three."

"Maybe not old . . . but you have to agree, his views are old school, and from what I know of Lost Horizons, they're looking for energy and fresh ideas."

My cheeks grow warm. "Bob *is* energetic."

"You think?"

"And he's always thinking outside of the box."

"If you say so. Anyway, I didn't mean to contradict you on the growth thing, but I do think we can hit 20 percent. In fact, I've developed a new metric for expanding profits. I'd be happy to share my findings with you."

"No, thank you." I take a tissue from my pocket and dab at my sweaty brow. My hot flashes occur at the most awkward of times. "I've been working in this field long enough to know what we can and cannot do."

He peers at me closely. "You feeling okay?"

"I'm fine. It's warm in here."

"I guess." Kai takes on a sly look. "You know . . . you kind of remind me of my mom."

"I am *not* your mom."

"Of course not. She's a lot younger. But she's bright like you and also technically challenged."

"I'm not *technologically* challenged."

"Don't get me wrong. My mom is really smart and good at her job. In fact, she's one of the top fund-raisers in town. But she's been resistant to using the advanced analytics offered by social media. I'm afraid it won't be long before she's passed up by her younger peers."

"What are you trying to say?"

"That you might want to join the twenty-first century. Get those skills up to par. Anyway, I better get going. I have a potential guest to corral." Tossing his rucksack over his shoulder, he just about skips his way down the hall.

I stare at his scrawny back, anger clogging my throat. Then I make a beeline for my office, picturing the look on Kai's skinny face when my promotion is announced. Along the way, I pass two young housekeepers, pushing their oversized carts. One of them is laughing loudly; the other's face is lit with a smile.

"Keep your voices down," I snap. "Some of our guests like to sleep in late."

Their faces fall. "Yes, ma'am." They wait until I pass and then giggle. "*Pendeja*," one of them whispers just loud enough for me to hear. My shoulders tighten with the insult, but I don't have the time to deal with it now. Anyway, I reason, who are they to judge? I may be on the strict side, but in no way am I a bitch.

Four

Saturday, May 11

At six on a Saturday evening, Nips overflows with a lively crowd. It's one of those far too trendy restaurants that has popped up in Santa Barbara's new Funk Zone. Once filled with junkyards and factories, the area's been transformed into artsy hip. Wine bars grace every corner; craft breweries are stuffed in between. Next thing you know, there'll be pot shops. There've been rumors going around.

The restaurant is housed in a former warehouse with metal sheeting covering the walls. I've asked to be seated away from the bar, but the racket still deafens my ears. Not my choice for a relaxing dinner, but as usual, my daughter holds the cards.

Alice is late, of course. She's always late. Maddeningly, forever late. I don't know why I find it surprising. Why I think she will ever change. Maybe because she's almost thirty-three? And that it's about time she grows up? Find a real job. A career. A man to settle down with. Or a woman. I really don't care. Settle down like any regular person who knows that dreams are just that. Dreams. Sure, some people get to achieve them, but how many? One percent? Maybe two? The rest of us need to work. Just work. That's the way life is.

I mean, if she was going to make it as a singer, wouldn't it have happened long before now? For God's sake, her best friend from high school is married with her second baby on the way. I should know, because her husband, Eric, has tried to exploit that unlikely connection. Pokes his head into my office uninvited like we're the best of friends. As if I don't know what he's up to. But Bob has no time for a lowly loan officer from a hapless community bank.

The waiter appears by my side, sets down a glass of ice tea, and smiles. "Can I get you anything else?" The pearl stud in his tongue coats his words in an annoying lisp.

"No, thank you." His blond hair is slicked away from his face, tied back with a silvery bow.

"You sure? The brussels sprout appetizer is our specialty."

"Baked?"

He pulls a pad of paper from his pocket and stares. "Tossed in hand-picked organic herbs and sautéed in cold-pressed olive oil."

"I think I'll pass." I'm already short six hundred steps today. No room for a fat-ridden snack.

"Okay. Will your guest be joining us soon?"

"I believe so." I peer in and around the throngs to see my daughter nudging her way through the entrance. "There she is."

"Nice. I'll come back in a few."

Alice snakes her way across the room, looking out of place in the sea of beachy clothes. She's pretty but pale and dressed in her signature black. Has she gained a little weight? And why the purple hair? What's wrong with her natural blonde? Maybe she's going gray and doesn't want anyone to know.

"Hi, Mom." She leans over and gives my cheek a peck before settling into her chair.

"It's good to see you," I say a little stiffly. Does she know she's ten minutes late? "Traffic bad?"

"Not really." Her hazel eyes sparkle. "I'm sorry I'm late, but I was in the parking lot talking to my agent." She claps her hands together.

"I got booked to play backup singer with this great band. A ten-week tour along the East Coast."

"What band?"

"Atlas Shrugged."

"Never heard of them."

"They play indie rock."

"Any good?"

Her eyes narrow, and her brow lowers. "Don't burst my bubble, please."

"I'm not bursting anyone's bubble. I wondered if they were any good."

"Would I be touring with them if they weren't?"

"I don't know. I mean, I suppose you need the money."

She shakes her head with an exaggerated sigh.

"Don't get upset."

"I'm not upset. I'd just like a little support."

I breathe deep. "I'm happy if you're happy."

"Well, I'm happy."

"Then let's leave it at that."

"Yes, let's." She buries her head deep in her menu. She's angry; I can tell. She's been angry for as long as I can remember. Well, that's not quite true. It started the year her father left. That's when she first grew distant and depressed. The waiter appears, and Alice orders a glass of house chardonnay.

"I'll have the same," I say.

The waiter eyes Alice with a smile. "What about entrees?"

"Can you give us a moment?" she replies.

"Of course."

"Thank you."

"Thank *you*."

Her gaze lingers on the slim man as he sashays away. "He's cute," she says.

"What do you think of his tongue stud?"

"I like it."

"You'd never get one, would you?"

She buries her head in her menu again. "You're being judgy, Mom."

"I'm not being judgy. I'm asking what you think."

"I think I'll have the pasta Alfredo."

"You sure?"

She rattles her menu. "Yes, I'm sure."

"I'm having the Caesar salad, no dressing."

"Of course you are." She sets down her menu with a snap. "How's the new Fitbit?"

I glance at the purple rubber wristband attached to the rectangular metallic face. "I like it. It buzzes more than the last one; minireminders to help me stay thin and trim."

"You've always been thin and trim."

"That doesn't mean I shouldn't be careful. As we girls age, our metabolisms slow. It's a fact. Sad but true."

"Don't go there, Mom."

"Go where?"

"Let's talk about work. How's work?"

"Work's fine." The waiter returns with our wine and flirts with Alice for a little too long. When he moves off, we clink our glasses together, and then I take a sip. Ugh. The wine is oxidized. Should I take a chance and send it back? I glance at Alice. She doesn't seem to notice. I'll drink water instead. "I've been so terribly busy," I say. "I can't remember the last time I took a day off."

"Why's that?"

"Oh, there's been a lot going on at the campus." I look both ways to make sure no one's listening and then lower my voice. "This is completely confidential, but my boss just announced his retirement. I'm in line to take his place."

"Really?" Alice sets down her glass. "You want that?"

"Why wouldn't I?"

"Wouldn't the executive director position consume your entire life?"

"What's wrong with that?"

"It wouldn't leave you time for anything else."

"What do I need time for?"

"To live your dreams?"

"This is my dream."

"Are you sure?"

"Yes."

Alice doesn't look convinced. "Whatever happened to that novel you were writing? And you used to love photography. Remember? You thought you might sell your prints. And what about . . ." Her voice fades, and she drains her wine.

I press the creases from my linen napkin. "Well, things change, don't they? Sometimes we have to grow up."

"Don't be mean, Mom."

"I'm not being mean."

"You sound mean."

"Well, I'm not."

"Can't you retire?"

"Retire?" I have a vision of sitting alone in the house watching TV. Nowhere to go. No one to see. "I'm only fifty-two. And I couldn't afford to retire even if I wanted to."

"But you've owned the house forever."

"I had to refinance when your father left and then again to help your brother."

"I suppose you could sell."

"And go where?"

She rolls her eyes in that way she has. "Well, then, I hope you get your wish."

"It's not a wish. It's my right. I've worked hard. I deserve it."

"Lots of people work hard."

"Meaning?"

"Meaning the most qualified person doesn't always get the job, especially when that person is a woman."

I take a deep breath. "You're such a pessimist. Why is that?"

She rolls her eyes again. "I don't know, Mom. Maybe I was born that way."

"But you were such a happy little girl."

"Well, things change, don't they?"

The waiter appears and takes our order. Alice requests a second glass of wine.

"Is that a good idea?" I ask once he's gone.

Another eye roll. "I'm an adult, Mom. Can we leave it at that?"

"Remember what happened to my parents."

"I'm not an alcoholic."

"Well, you shouldn't drink and drive."

Alice drops her head in her hands. "I thought I could do this."

"Do what?"

"*This!*" She spreads her arms wide, and the couple at the next table glance our way. They're young and slim, dressed in expensive hippie casual. I frown at them, and they frown back. I then silently take in the crowd until our meals arrive. Alice dives into hers. I only pick at mine. She's cleared most of her plate before I've made a dent.

"Well . . . I should get going." She sets her napkin on the table. "It'll take me hours to drive back to Hollywood on a Saturday night."

A strand of hurt winds through my heart. "I thought you were spending the weekend with me."

"I was planning to, but then this gig turned up. I have a million things to do. I leave Monday for New York."

"Monday?" I set down my fork. "You're leaving this week?"

"Have to. The band's vocalist overdosed and got sent to rehab."

"But you don't know anything about this band, do you?"

"I know their music."

"But the boys . . . the men in the band? Have you checked their backgrounds? Do you know who they are?"

"I'm a grown woman, Mom. I can take care of myself."

"Remember what happened in Florida?"

Alice slumps like I've sucked the air from her lungs. "Of course I do," she says in a tiny voice. "I'll never forget, and neither will you." She finishes off her wine and sets her glass down with a clank. "Before I leave, I have something to tell you."

My breathing quickens. Pregnancy? Cancer? Money?

"I didn't want you to hear it from anyone else."

My thoughts rattle back and forth.

"Gigi's pregnant again."

"Your father's mistress?"

"She's not his mistress, Mom. She's his wife. They've been married for sixteen years."

I shrug. "So she's pregnant. Good for her. What do I care?"

"Oh, Mom. Don't be like that. I know you care. And I know it must hurt. But the twins are my sisters. And now I'll have another sibling too."

"Half sisters."

"What?"

"The twins aren't your real sisters. They're your half sisters."

Alice opens her mouth and then shuts it. And then swallows and opens it again. "You can be so cold."

"I'm not cold. It's the truth. Anyway, enough of that. Are you sure you want to go to New York? I thought we might spend some time together. Take a trip to Hawaii next month. I'd pay your way, of course."

"I can't do that, Mom. This is my big chance. Atlas Shrugged has just signed with Warner's. They're opening for some really good bands. They're the real thing, Mom."

"You've said that before."

"It's true this time." She dabs her lips with her napkin. "Why not invite Adam? I bet he'd like to go."

I dig a crouton from deep in my salad and take a bite. It's heavy on the garlic, short on the crunch. "Why would I do that?"

"It might help mend your relationship."

I pick up my wine and gulp it down. "I'm not sure it needs mending."

"Of course it does. You didn't even attend his wedding."

"That was Adam's fault, not mine. He chose your father over me."

"Adam *didn't* choose Dad over you. He invited him to the wedding."

"Along with his mistress."

"His wife, Mom."

"Whatever."

A shadow passes over Alice's face. "I feel sorry for you. I really do."

My Fitbit buzzes with a reminder to get moving. "No need for that."

She glances at her cell and gets to her feet. "I'll call you when I get to New York."

"Have a nice flight."

"Aren't you going to hug me goodbye?"

"I have to pay the bill."

She stares at me with sadness in her eyes. "I wish you'd stop."

"Stop what?"

"You know what I'm talking about." She comes around the table and hugs my stiff shoulders. "I love you," she says.

"I love you too."

Alice hesitates before turning and disappearing into the crowd. I take another bite of salad and then set down my fork. My arms feel heavy. I'm exhausted.

Lately I've been waking before dawn with a dream in my head and fear clogging my throat. The dream starts out peacefully enough. I've morphed into a grand old oak tree with birds singing in my branches

31

and squirrels scampering below. Then the sky darkens and thunder rumbles, and I begin to grow backward. First my leaves shrink into my branches. Then my branches shrivel into my trunk. My trunk grows smaller and smaller. Soon there's nothing left of me but a hollowed-out acorn. The sky turns black after that.

The bill arrives, and I scour the numbers, feeling a grateful tingle of relief. "There's a mistake here," I say to the waiter, tapping the bill with my credit card. "And that wine was horribly oxidized. You shouldn't charge me a cent for that."

Five

I can't seem to memorize the Lost Horizons mission statement. It's stupid. I know. I've always had the best of memories. Could recite entire poems by rote. But now I'm unable to recall a simple string of twenty-five words. Seems like it should be easy. Only one line—though a long one. I'll give myself that.

> *The mission of Lost Horizons is to offer distinctive, service-enriched housing and health care while contributing to a lifestyle that promotes quality, independence, and prosperity.*

I keep stumbling over *service-enriched* and *prosperity*. I have to remember those key words. The management team arrives tomorrow, and my interview is scheduled for nine. What if they ask me to recite the statement? It's something they might do. A test of sorts, and what if I fail? That could be the end of my dream.

Stop it. Think positive! Don't be so hard on yourself. I finger my Fitbit nervously. I'm the *perfect* age to be promoted to executive director, and of course I'm as sharp as they come. I shuffle through my papers and glance at the clock. It's after seven, and I'm still at the office. I've missed my evening walk. That means I'll be short a thousand steps today unless I head off into the dark.

I give the mission statement one last crack, and then I've had enough. I sort through a pile of mail and find an envelope addressed to Kai. For the briefest of moments I consider shredding it, but of course I'd never stoop that low. Instead, I gather my things and switch off the lights and head to the small office down the way. He's not there, of course. Never works past five. That would break his millennial code. I drop the letter in his in-box and am about to leave when I spot an interesting booklet on his desk. *SALES ANALYTICS—SERENITY ACRES.* I look over my shoulder before opening what appears to be a PowerPoint presentation for the Lost Horizons team. PowerPoint? If he's planning on presenting it at the interview, he's dumber than I thought.

I flip to the first page and read the chapter headings: "Sales Growth," "Profit Enhancement," and "Expense Reduction." All three of those make sense. But they're followed by "Efficiency Ratio." What's that? Then, "Delinquent Accounts," "Breach of Contract," and "Humane Eviction." *Eviction?* We don't *ever* evict our guests. I quickly skim through the document pages, pausing on the one titled "Breach of Contract," where Kai has listed ten "legal" ways to push our destitutes out the door.

Destitute is our internal term for a guest who no longer has the means to pay. We have over two dozen destitutes, many of whom are so old they've outlived their savings. But we also have had incidences of inheritances wiped out by bad investments, unethical guardians, and, more recently, natural disasters. According to Kai's questionable numbers, the destitutes are eating into our profits at a rate of $4 million per year.

"Spying?"

I spin around to find Kai leaning against the doorjamb dressed in fluorescent running gear. His cheeks are pink, his forehead sweaty, his bun in disarray.

"Why, no," I say, dropping the booklet. "I was . . . delivering your mail."

"Right." He saunters to his desk and opens his drawer. "Sorry to interrupt you. I went for a run. Left my keys behind."

"You didn't interrupt me . . ."

"No?"

"I . . . like I said . . . I found a letter addressed to you and thought I'd hand deliver."

"Nice of you." He taps the booklet. "So what do you think of my PowerPoint?"

"I . . . I don't know." His cologne is more powerful than ever. I try not to breathe through my nose.

"Really? You're never at a loss for words. In fact, you're usually happy to give your opinion. So feel free to do so here."

"Well . . ." I know I shouldn't say anything, but I can't help myself. "I did take a glance at the document. I wasn't snooping, just interested. I suppose I'm concerned about your use of the word *eviction*. I assume you're aware of our forever-care policy. We have yet to evict a guest."

"*Yet* being the operative word."

"What do you mean by that?"

He drops onto his chair and wipes his forehead with the back of his hand. "You must know the destitutes are dragging down our profits. We're losing millions on them every year."

A jolt of indignation stiffens my spine. "Technically, that may be true, but we have signed contracts with each and every one of them that guarantees we will care for them, even if their financial resources run out."

A smug look crosses Kai's face. "You might be surprised."

"What do you mean?"

"I mean I've had my uncle take a look at our paperwork. He's a lawyer who specializes in contract law. He thinks there's a loophole that would free us from our obligations to those people."

I begin to sputter. "First off, *those* people are our guests. Secondly, you had no right to show our contract to an outsider. It's against the rules."

"It was a blank contract," he says dryly. "No confidential information was revealed."

"Still . . ."

"Still, you do understand that our nonpaying *guests* are eating away at our profits, which is contrary to the Lost Horizons mission to maximize shareholder wealth?"

I throw back my shoulders. "Actually, their mission is to offer distinctive service and housing . . ." I pause, unable to grasp the next words.

Kai offers me a thin-lipped smile. "I believe the correct order is 'distinctive, service-enriched housing.' You might want to get that right. Anyway, I'm sure you know the difference between an outward-facing mission statement and the goal of a publicly held corporation. Management will be looking for ways to maximize profitability. You shouldn't forget that fact. Especially if you want to do well in your interview tomorrow. I'd be happy to give you a copy of my presentation. It might help you score some points."

I eye him with suspicion. "Why would you do that?"

"Why wouldn't I? I'm more than willing to share my ideas."

"Are you?"

"Yes."

"Well, no, thank you. I have my own ideas. Have a good night."

"You too. And good luck in your interview tomorrow. May the best man win."

"Or woman."

"That goes without saying. And don't worry. I won't tell Bob about your snooping. He'd be more than a little pissed."

I scurry down the hallway, stomach churning. I'm not worried about Bob. Not the tiniest bit. I'm 100 percent certain he'd take my side over Kai's. I was trying to be helpful. Deliver a letter. That's it. So what if I paused at Kai's messy desk. This is a place of business. Not a private home. Anyway, Kai's attitude is completely unbearable. He's an arrogant jerk. He belongs at a cutthroat Wall Street firm, not a life-care community. I wonder if there's a way to bring up his pitiless attitude in tomorrow's interview. But I don't want to sound like a tattletale. I'll have to think hard on that.

I decide to take the long route to my car to make up for my missing steps. But when I hurry through the assisted-living wing, an odd sight slows me down. The door is open to Ms. Kingsley's residence, which is strange since it's after six. At 104, she's our oldest resident and typically in bed by five. She's a founding member of our Pioneer Squad, a dwindling group of guests who have lived at Serenity Acres since the day the campus opened its doors. She occupies one of our larger units, a two-bedroom suite furnished with treasures from her travels around the world. I hear what sounds like crying, so I poke my head inside.

"What's happening?" I ask, trying to make sense of the scene.

Ms. Kingsley is seated in a wheelchair, wearing a pink satin nightgown with matching slippers. White hair billows around her skeletal face; tears run from her milky-blue eyes.

"They're moving me," she wails. "They're taking all my pretty things."

Piles of boxes are stacked every which way. Paintings have been removed from the walls.

"Who's moving you?" I ask.

"He is." She waves her hands, and Nurse Milo steps from the shadows, easing something into his pocket.

"It's moving day," he says in his heavy accent, "and Ms. Kingsley's not happy about that."

"Why should I be happy?" she asks, wringing her gnarled hands. "This is my home."

"Don't worry." Nurse Milo pats her on the shoulder. "You'll love your new room. I promise."

"*Don't touch me!*" she howls.

Nurse Milo has been with us for two years. He's a short, stocky man with peppered hair that's shorn close to his square head. He emigrated from the Ukraine over a decade ago and has worked in health care ever since. There's always a smile pasted on his middle-aged face, but there's something about him I don't like. Maybe it's the dark eyes that twitch but don't blink. Or the frosty hands that never warm. Or the scent of stale cigarettes that follows him wherever he goes. If it wasn't so hard to find eldercare nurses, I'd have let him go by now.

"Where are you moving her to?" I demand. "And why this late in the day? You know it's against the rules any time after three."

Nurse Milo fixes his gaze on the ceiling as if the answer might be written up there. "She's being moved to casita 510 in the new wing. Why now, I don't know. I'm just following orders. I was asked to keep her calm." He drops his voice. "I might need to sedate her. She's not taking this very well."

"The new wing? Did the family request a move?" Construction on the new wing was completed last month. Twenty ultramini apartments for our more frugal guests. The bathrooms are large enough to fit oversized wheelchairs, but the studios barely hold a single bed.

Nurse Milo shrugs. "Does she have family?"

I think for a moment and then shake my head. Ms. Kingsley never married, and her siblings have long since passed. She was a famous travel writer in her youth. Made enough money to live well for years.

But last year her trust fund ran dry, and she joined the ranks of our destitute guests. I have a sudden, concerning thought. Kai wouldn't dare. Or would he?

Two handymen enter the room and begin to pile boxes on their hand trucks. "I don't want to move!" Ms. Kingsley wails. Her eyes go wide with fear, and she grapples for my hand. "It's because of the money, right? But they promised me, at the very beginning. They promised to take care of me no matter what state my finances were in. Was that a lie? Was it? *Was it?* Are you going back on your word?"

She's right, of course. I'm sure whoever signed her up did promise her, because I, too, have made that promise to every guest I've ever enrolled. It's what I was told. It's what I believed. "Wait a moment," I say to the handymen. "Do you know who ordered this?"

The fatter of the two men shrugs. "That guy should know." He nods at Nurse Milo. "He's the one that sent for us."

My gaze fixes on Nurse Milo. "Who gave you the order?"

His eyes shift back and forth, never settling on one spot. "I think it came from sales."

"It came from Kai?"

"I think so."

"But he has no right," I sputter.

The fat man leans against the wall. "Are we moving this lady or not? I'm already working overtime."

I fold my arms. "I believe it's best if we hold off for now. Let me get to the bottom of this."

"Okay," he replies. "But cleaning is scheduled for first thing tomorrow, and we got orders to paint the place in the afternoon. A new guest is scheduled to move in this weekend."

"It's someone important," the second moving man adds. "A former governor's wife."

My body temperature begins to rise. "Shirley Bentley?" I ask.

"Yeah. That's the name."

I take a step back. I'm so angry I can barely breathe. I know all about Shirley Bentley. Met with her demanding son last week. He insisted on pushing his weight around. Wanted his mother placed at once. But the woman didn't qualify for residency here. She failed our basic health test.

"The move will have to wait," I say. "I'll speak to our executive director in the morning. He'll instruct you on what to do."

The fat man pulls a work order from his pocket. "If you're meaning Bob Knight, he signed off on the bottom of our paperwork right next to that marketing guy."

"Next to Kai?"

"Yeah."

"Why didn't you show me this before?"

"Guess I forgot."

A curse is close to spilling from my mouth, but then I remember our management training. Never let the staff see that there's disagreement among the upper ranks.

"All right," I say, biting my tongue. "Keep going." I crouch next to Ms. Kingsley, her breath blowing stale and warm. "Don't worry. You're going to be fine. We'll fix up your place extra nice. And Nurse Milo will be giving you a special shot that'll help you sleep through the night. In the morning, your things will all be in place, and I promise you'll be pleased."

I wait until the shot is administered and then march from the apartment to my office, where I send a scathing email to Bob.

Six

Jane and Franklin Carver may seem like an odd couple, but from what I've learned about Montecito, they're actually part of the norm. She's middle-aged, maybe forty. Or fifty with some work. And he celebrated his ninety-first birthday last week. A May-December relationship coming to its predictable end. The two of them sit across from me now. I have their paperwork in front of me. I'm afraid they won't like the outcome.

Franklin, frail as a starving bird, has a mind that seems to be riddled with holes. He hasn't answered a single one of my questions. Didn't respond when I introduced myself. Now he sits with eyes closed and head cocked, spittle wetting his pointy chin. I do hope he's wearing a diaper, or I'll have to reupholster another chair.

"Anyway," Jane says, crossing her sleek legs. "We need help." She's dressed in a peach-colored frock with matching heels that blend well with my office walls. A tiny white hat is perched on her head, her dark hair pulled tight in a bun. She makes me feel old and frumpy, although I'm dressed in my nicest black suit.

"Poor Franklin was fine until the mudslide." Jane fingers the string of luminous pearls that drape from her ultrasmooth neck. "His neurologist says it's catastrophic for an Alzheimer's patient to lose his longtime home." She pats Franklin's gnarled hand and smiles. "Poor old thing. I've tried round-the-clock care, but it's *so* unreliable. I can't tell you how many times I've had to cancel an outing. I'm at the end of my rope."

"I understand," I say. "I really do. And I wish we could be of help. Unfortunately, Franklin won't fit into our Champion's Club."

"I'm not asking for him to join a club," she says, her smile starting to fade.

I glance at Franklin and lower my voice. "*Champion* is our euphemism for dementia. All dementia patients live in our champion's wing."

"Oh." She straightens and blinks her eyes.

"Anyway, Franklin didn't pass our cognitive tests, but I'd be happy to give you a referral."

Jane's smile snaps off like a blown kitchen light. "What do you mean 'didn't pass'?"

"He didn't pass the entrance exam."

"Entrance exam? What're you talking about? He's not applying to college. He needs a place to live."

She obviously didn't read our brochure, so I do my best to explain. "You must understand that Serenity Acres is not just a retirement home; it's a life-care community. Once an applicant has been accepted as a guest, we support them to the very end." I pause here, thinking of Kai's words. Is our commitment to forever care about to be abandoned? But in a heartbeat, I continue on, professional that I am. "As such, at the time of entry, an applicant must pass our physical and cognitive exams." I hold up Franklin's assessment. "Unfortunately, Mr. Carver failed in every category."

"I don't understand . . ."

"We simply can't accept him."

"But . . ."

"The rules are clearly outlined in our brochure." I try to hand her a copy, but she waves it away.

"I'd be happy to pay you immediately," she says, whipping a checkbook from her purse. "That's one million, correct?"

My face grows warm. "I'm sorry, but . . ."

"And I can pay the first year's dues as well." She taps her checkbook with her pen. "And I'll add a tip. Just tell me how much."

Jane's not the first to try to bribe me, and I doubt she'll be the last. I slide a business card her way. "I suggest you call Bright Memories. They support all stages of cognitive decline."

She sniffs. "Bright Memories? Where are they located?"

"In Goleta."

"Goleta?" She shakes her head. "No. We're not going there." She leans forward, her puffy lips growing thin. "The thing is, I ran across Kai last weekend at the club."

"The club?"

"The Montecito Golf Club. I don't imagine you've ever been there, but you must know of it."

"Of course I do." I don't like her tone.

"Well, Kai's family are founding members. Franklin used to play a round of golf with his grandfather every day."

"That's nice, but . . ."

"And one of Franklin's grandchildren attends church with Kai. In college they traveled to Haiti together to volunteer on a Habitat for Humanity home. The two of them are quite close."

Kai did something for a person in need? I find that hard to believe. "I appreciate the connection," I say, "but it doesn't change a thing."

Her eyes narrow. "Are you from Santa Barbara?"

I nod. "I've been here for over thirty years." Franklin slumps to one side and almost topples off the chair. Jane grabs on to his sleeve.

"But where were you born?"

"Fresno."

"Fresno?" She leans back in her chair, a smirk tweaking her ageless face. "Then you don't understand how it works here. We locals take care of our own."

"I *do* understand. Unfortunately, rules are rules. There's nothing I can do."

Jane tugs her cell phone from her purse. "Kai told me to call him if I had a problem. I'm sure he'll work this out. He's the vice president of sales, after all. And you? What do you do?"

"I'm the VP of operations," I say, wishing I could toss her out.

"Well, let's give him a call."

Clattering down the tiled hallway, I pass our Texas belle, Kate Harrington, who smiles and calls out hello. I do my best to return the greeting, but the words get stuck in my throat. I'm so angry, my vision is blurry. My heart thumps hard in my chest. Hell hath no fury like a woman scorned. I barge into Bob's office unannounced.

"I've got to speak with you, *now!*"

Bob startles like a frightened cat and springs from his chair. "I take it you've heard?"

That stops me. "Heard what?"

"Nothing." He takes a deep breath and settles back down. "Feel free to take a seat."

I plop onto the guest chair and lean forward, ready to launch an attack. I sum up the meeting with the Carvers. Recount how Kai tried to overrule my decision in front of a prospective guest. Remind Bob that *I'm* the VP of operations and won't tolerate the dismissive behavior of an unethical millennial jerk.

Bob presses his fingers together, nodding his head nonstop. "Slow down," he says. "I'm having a hard time following your words."

I barely pause to hear him, then rush forward. "And I *will not* have Kai lording his Montecito connections over me. Who does he think he is? And by the way, you never responded to my emails about Eleanor Kingsley. Why did you allow Kai to downsize her apartment?"

"The decision wasn't up to me."

"What do you mean? You run this place."

"I ran this place. Now I'm a lame duck."

"So who . . . ?"

"The new management, of course." Bob removes his glasses and rubs his tired-looking eyes. "As for your emails, I recommend you be careful about what you put in writing."

"Why's that?"

"They're watching."

"What do you mean?"

Bob sighs and pushes his glasses back in place. "Just be careful. And give the transition time before you pass judgment."

"But Ms. Kingsley . . ."

Bob holds up his hand. "We were asked by corporate to accommodate a new guest, and we complied."

"But in no way did she qualify."

"Doesn't matter. They overruled our decision."

"Are you saying our current processes and procedures have been tossed into the trash?"

Bob gets up and grabs a bottle of water from the corner closet. "Have a drink and try to calm down."

"Calm down?" I push the bottle away. "How can I? I've worked here eighteen years, and I've never been treated with such disrespect."

"Please?"

"And that woman, Jane? She only married the old guy for his money, and now she wants to move on."

"You don't know these people or their circumstances."

"I know their type."

Bob folds his arms and leans back in his chair, a frown further aging his face. "What's happened to you, Ruth? Where's your sense of compassion?"

My Fitbit buzzes, and I give it a tap. "I reserve it for those in need."

"There was a time when you seemed to truly care about our families. Sympathized with the difficult decisions they faced."

"I still care."

"You're not acting like you do."

I open my mouth to argue, but I'm stopped by the look on Bob's face. "What's wrong?" I ask.

His weary gaze meets mine. "I was going to tell you later today."

"Tell me what?"

"It was a difficult decision."

I stare at Bob, comprehension dawning. "Don't tell me . . ."

He nods.

I dig my fingernails into my palms. "Who'd they hire?"

"I'm sorry. I really am. I told the new management they were making a mistake. But it's all about sales with this new regime. That's why I'm getting out."

"But who . . . ?"

Bob kneads his hands together. "Kai will be taking over as executive director."

"Kai?" I gasp. "You've got to be kidding."

"I'm afraid not. But please know this isn't about you . . ."

I slap my hand hard on his desk. "*Of course* it's about me."

"I mean . . ." Bob shifts uneasily in his chair. "They were impressed by you. Very impressed. But they were more impressed by Kai's analytics. They're going to use his profit model throughout the organization. They think he's the man for the job."

I stumble to my feet. "The *man*? Are you kidding me? Is that what's going on here?"

"Absolutely not."

"Or is it my age?"

"Ruth . . ."

"Or both? Because my years of experience run rings around Kai's sloppy attitude and tenth-rate MBA."

Bob rubs his temples like they're hurting. "Please, sit down," he says in a dull voice.

"Why should I?"

"Because I don't want you to do something you'll regret. Give me a chance to explain."

I fight my urge to run from the room and perch on the edge of my chair. "Explain away."

"Can I be honest here?"

"Please do."

"The job was yours to lose."

A blow to my heart. "What do you mean?"

"I mean, I gave you the highest possible recommendation. But you refused to tell the new management what they wanted to hear."

"Are you talking about their ridiculous goals?"

"Exactly."

"But they *are* ridiculous."

"Sure they are. But you shouldn't have thrown that in their faces."

"So I should've lied?"

"It's called *playing the game.*"

"So Kai got the job because he's better at *the game*?"

"Kai got the job because he developed what management believes is a viable plan. Whether or not it will work, only time will tell."

"A mean, tightfisted, and possibly illegal plan. Do you know he wants to break our guest contracts? Toss our helpless destitutes out the door?"

"I do."

"And you don't care?"

"Of course I care. But I have no power."

"That's bullshit."

Bob runs his hands through his hair. "Come on, Ruth. Don't be naïve. We've been bought by a major conglomerate. There are bound to be changes."

"But Kai's an idiot. He's totally incompetent."

"Possibly. But he's also your new boss."

I try not to gag. "As of when?"

"Monday."

"But what about you?"

"Today's my last day."

"You were supposed to stay through the end of the month."

"Plans change."

"Well, I'll . . . I'll resign before I work for Kai."

"Can you afford not to work?"

That stops me. I think about my mortgage. About health insurance. About my car. About the credit cards I ran up to pay for Adam's rehab. "I can get a job elsewhere," I say. "Peaceful Pastures is hiring."

Bob shakes his head. "You'd hate it there. They wouldn't live up to your standards."

My anger drains like water from an unplugged sink. It's replaced by a panicky sadness. "But Bob," I say, my heart thrumming. "The ED position means everything to me. I've worked hard to achieve that goal. I've worked weekends, overtime. Set aside my personal life."

"Believe me, I know that."

"And then some arrogant kid walks in with a couple of untested ideas and he gets the job? It's not fair. It's not . . ." *My God!* I have never cried at work before, and now tears are spilling down my cheeks. I hastily wipe them away.

Bob gets up and comes around the desk and gives my shoulder an awkward rub. "I like you, Ruth. I always have. I've enjoyed working with you over the years. You're smart. You're mature. You're a hard worker. You must know if it was up to me, you would've been offered the job. Unfortunately, there's a new sheriff in town, and they have their own ideas. The thing is, if you're right about Kai, he won't last six months, and the opportunity will circle back around to you."

"Impossible," I say, straightening my shoulders and willing away my tears. "There's no way in hell I'll work for him."

"Think about it over the weekend. I don't want you to make a decision that you'll come to regret."

"You bet I'll think about it." I get up and march out of his office with no idea where I'll go. If I head toward my office, I might run into Kai, and there's no way I can face him right now. I don't want him to know I give a damn about the position. That would be the final blow.

Laughter spills down the hallway, and I spot Selena and Nurse Milo strolling in my direction. I look around and then stumble through a nearby door and make my way to the paved path that skirts the golf course. When I reach the path's end, I pass a cluster of maintenance buildings and keep going until I reach the entrance to the memorial garden. It's bounded by a soaring Eugenia hedge that creates a private walled space. It's set a little too far from the residences, so it's empty more often than not.

I enter the garden and take a seat on the cement bench that fronts the miniature koi pond. On the far side of the pond towers a granite slab etched with several hundred names. As I gaze at the slick black surface, I'm filled with an overwhelming sense of doom. Does anyone remember those guests? Is anyone sad they're gone? And what about me? Who will give a damn when I'm stuck six feet under? Maybe Alice and possibly Adam. Carlyn? Who else? I don't really know. *My God.* I used to have lots of friends. When did my life become so small? I drop my head in my hands and weep until a kindly voice interrupts.

"This is a good place to come when you're sad."

I look up to find Ember hovering above me, a smile lighting her damaged face. I swipe at my tears. "I'm fine," I croak.

"Of course you are." I wish her away, but she settles beside me, a hint of lemon scenting the air. "I love watching the koi," she says. "They're so incredibly soothing. They never argue or fight. Just move through the water like dancers. We can learn a lot from them, don't you think?"

I don't know how to respond, so I rub my Fitbit between my fingers until I think of something to say. "Do you come here often?" I ask.

"Nearly every day."

"For the quiet?"

"I suppose." My heart clenches when a single tear slides down the healthy side of her face. "I'm sorry," I say. "I didn't mean to pry."

"No . . . that's okay. I come here to pray for the ones that I've lost."

"Oh." I feel sorry for her, but I don't inquire any further. I am her supervisor, after all. Several moments pass, and then Ember reaches out. "Do you mind if I take your hand?" She doesn't wait for an answer but settles her cool hand on mine. I'm about to pull away when I feel a strange sensation, like the beating of a hummingbird's heart. The humming moves along my hand and up my arm and deep into my chest. My shoulders relax. My eyes close. Then I awaken with a start.

"What is that?" I ask, shaking her off. "What are you doing to me?"

Ember's shoulders have slumped, and she's turned as pale as a ghost. "I'm healing your hurt," she says in a whisper. "It's very deep."

I get to my feet. "I don't know what you're talking about."

She eyes me sadly. "I think you do."

I check the time on my Fitbit. "You better hurry, or you'll be late for your shift."

She nods. "Yes. Of course. I'll be leaving in a moment."

I turn on my heel and exit the garden and head straight for my office. There I check my Fitbit once again. Quarter past six. It should be safe to move around. Kai is long gone, I hope.

Seven

I return home just as the evening shadows are deepening to gray. Change out of my suit and into a baggy shirt and my most forgiving shorts. Measure six ounces of Pinot and settle onto one of the two old chairs that inhabit my back porch. They're all that's left of an outdoor dining set Doug and I purchased when we first moved into our home.

The yard is hemmed in by a rotten wooden fence propped up by bug-infested trees. The once green lawn has given way to dirt; the untended roses are yellowed and slumped. The cement fountain is cracked at the base and filled with dirt and weeds. There's an ancient gate that separates my home from Zach's, installed when our kids were young. It's hard to believe there was a time when the lawn had been lush and crowded with children, pets, and toys. I wonder if the sad decline of my backyard mirrors the direction my life will take.

Stop being overdramatic, I order. *No more wine for you.* I try focusing my thoughts on the mellow guitar notes floating in on a gentle breeze. Zach likes to strum on his back porch in the evenings; he's actually rather good. Writes his own music—sad and mournful tunes that revolve around heartbreak and loss. Before his life imploded, he played bass in a band made up of first responders. I wonder if his music brings him any comfort or if it's a reminder of all that he's lost.

I break my rule and have a second glass of wine. And then break it again and have a third. The evening sky darkens to purple; a trace of pink outlines a cloud. An owl hoots, raccoons chitter, bats dart to and fro.

The wine doesn't make things better—for me, it never has. Instead, it carries me back to a time I spend most days trying to forget. I flash on how at the age of ten, I broke my arm and kept it a secret for three long days. I suffered alone in misery until my anguish overcame my reserve.

I've often thought about that little girl in my ensuing forty-two years. Why would a child fold into herself? Hide like an animal nursing its wounds? Was it the squabbling between my drunken parents or the need to control my space? Even the doctor couldn't get me to talk. I begged to be left alone.

In college I met with a therapist to try to make sense of my peculiar past. My parents were dead by then; the years of alcoholism had taken their toll. But as we circled closer to the truth, waves of panic swallowed me whole. I couldn't admit my parents had never loved me. My secret brought too much shame. So I dumped the shrink and turned to running. The endorphins helped me forget. When an injury ended my jogging days, I took up speed walking instead.

My Fitbit quivers, reminding me I have many more steps to go. I set down my empty glass and head down the stairs and walk in circles around the yard. *One, two, three, four . . .*

There's a knock at the adjoining gate; the rusty hinges squeal. "Can I come over for a few?" Zach calls from the shadows.

He's the last thing I need at the moment, but it would be mean of me to say no. "Sure. Come in." I sprint up the steps and slide the wine glass behind a withered potted plant.

Years ago, our families spent evenings together hanging in our backyard. Our kids would career about like drunk kittens while we adults planned our future lives. We'd chat of dream vacations, preferred school districts, outrageous home improvement projects. Laugh over our favorite sitcoms. Cry over a sad book. We were young and innocent and full of hope, believing our lives would never change.

Zach lumbers up the steps and settles beside me, giving his bad knee an extrahard rub. He first hurt it the night Tina died. Got drunk and drove his car into a tree. He smells of soap, so he's freshly showered, although he still reeks of despair. My darkness grows a little darker. My shoulders sag with his weight. "Know what today is?" he asks.

"Friday?" A warm breeze rustles the leaves, and a burst of jasmine scents the air. Zach is quiet, and then he says the words I never want to hear.

"It's the anniversary."

"Oh. Yes. Sorry." Somehow that skipped my mind. "You doing okay?"

"Best I can." He runs his hands through his shaggy, gray hair. "I wish things could've turned out different."

"Don't we all."

"I mean, if only we hadn't . . ."

I give my Fitbit a quick rub. Do we have to do this again? "It was an accident, Zach. A terrible accident. Let's leave it at that."

"An accident based on stupidity."

"Don't go there, Zach."

"I don't have a choice."

"Yes, you do."

He rocks back and forth, his hands clenched tight. Then he mumbles something I can't hear.

"What?"

"Nothing."

"You sure?"

"I don't know what I'm sure of. I feel like I need to talk to someone. Anyone."

"Then talk to me."

"I mean, I want to *tell* someone."

Panic clutches my throat. "You can't do that, Zach. I mean, why would you after all these years?"

He works his eyes with his fisted hands. "Guilt is an awful thing. It eats at me every day. And I can't be the only one having that problem. You must feel the weight of it too."

I try to speak forcefully. "What's done is done. We made a horrible mistake. Why relive it now?"

"It might help me," he says with a shaky breath. "And it might help you too."

"I don't need any help," I say firmly. "I'm fine the way I am."

He stops his rocking and gazes at me. "You have any friends?"

"Of course."

"Well, I never see anyone hanging around anymore. Not Carlyn or your kids."

"My children lead busy lives, and Carlyn . . . well, you know what's going on there." I get to my feet, feeling shaky. "It's late, Zach. I've had a long day."

Zach stands and turns to me. It's grown so dark I can barely make out the ruins of his face. "Truth is," he says, "I think you're as messed up as I am. Only you've dealt with things in a different way. I drank myself into oblivion, and you've pushed everyone out of your life."

"What are you? My therapist?"

"Our secret has hurt us, Ruth. And I know it's messed with Adam's head. He deserves to know the truth."

"Our secret has nothing to do with Adam. His problems started with Doug's affair."

"You're sure about that?"

"Absolutely."

"Then you won't mind if I tell him."

You can't! Adam and I may not be speaking, but this revelation would only make things worse. Adam would tell Alice, and Alice would hate me. Then they'd tell their father, and he'd think he'd been absolved.

No. That can't happen. I need to do something, and I need to do it quick. I comb my mind for a solution, but my thoughts are running slow. Then a trace of an idea begins to take shape. "I think you have too much time on your hands," I say in an almost calm voice.

"That's an understatement."

"You spend every waking moment focused on your past."

"I like it there."

"But it'll kill you sooner or later."

"Maybe that's the point."

"Come on, Zach. You're only sixty. There's got to be something you still want in life."

"Yeah," he says in a dull voice. "I want to go back and start my life over. I want to erase our mistake."

I almost scream in frustration. "You know we can't do that."

"Then for God's sake, get that woman out of my head."

"What woman?"

"Or give me a dose of dementia. Or Alzheimer's. A nice little brain disease."

"Zach . . ."

"Or a bullet to the head."

"*Zach!*"

"All right then." He turns away and kneads his hands and stares out into the night. "Why don't you tell me how I'm supposed to move forward? How I'm supposed to get on with my life."

I carefully tender my idea. "What about a job?" I ask. "That would keep you busy. Help you move on to something else."

Zach mumbles a few words, and then he's quiet for the longest time. "Maybe you're right," he finally says. "But how's that going to happen? I haven't held a real job in years."

"There's an opening for a security guard at Serenity Acres. It's the evening shift, but the schedule's not bad. You work four tens a week."

"They'd hire *me* with my pitiful work record?"

"*I'd* hire you, yes. And besides. It's not so pitiful. You used to be a detective."

"A lifetime ago."

"Still . . ."

"What about my bum knee?"

"Can you outrun an eighty-year-old?"

"I guess."

"Then you'll pass the test with flying colors."

"You set a low bar."

"It's not easy to find employees in this town. At least not with your experience."

"I don't know . . ."

"Come on, Zach. It's better than sitting at home picking apart the past. And if you stay long enough, your insurance will kick in, and you can do something about your knee."

"Maybe."

"Promise me you'll think about it."

"Yeah. Sure."

"I need to know by next week. Friday at the latest."

"All right."

When the gate clicks shut, I breathe a sigh of relief. Then I get up and begin another round of laps until my heartbeat slows to my steps.

II. SLOTH

The way of the sluggard is blocked with thorns, but the path of the upright is a highway.

—*Proverbs 15:19*

The Angel

I wake to the scent of smoke and ash. The nose-biting, teeth-crunching, lung-burning ash that sifts through the air when the wildfires burn. I check on the local news feed, but alas, it was but a dream.

My thoughts drift back to the Thomas Fire, which spewed incense for weeks on end. It burned through hundreds of thousands of acres on its march along the coast. When it reached the hillsides above Santa Barbara, the residents scattered like frenzied ants. They knew the devil had been set upon them; fear bloomed in the Promised Land.

On those marvelous winter evenings, I'd prepare a proper picnic and stroll to the far end of the wharf. I'd take a seat on my favorite bench and hold my crossing journal close. Would the flames engulf the city? Would the inhabitants be forced to move? Would they trade their lives for their secrets? Would those secrets be enshrined in my book? Just the thought brought on tremors of ecstasy in a way no lover ever could.

It's no coincidence I settled in a town named after one of my all-time favorite saints. The Holy Great Martyr Barbara died a virgin's sanctified death. She was a woman of unsurpassed beauty who refused the hand of every marriageable man. Insisted on saving herself for her maker, which provoked her pagan father's rage. For her love of Christ and the Trinity, her father thrashed her with his sword. He then starved and tortured the girl before tossing her to a savage crowd.

Her body wounded with bloodied hooks, she was led naked through the streets. When an angel attempted to cover her shame, her father beheaded his virgin child. The wrath of God was swift and immediate; the man was felled by a lightning bolt. Was he unaware of the Lord's penchant for vengeance or just a sinner filled with contempt?

I like to visit the statue of Saint Barbara displayed at the downtown historical museum. Examine her exquisite features and imagine the secrets she might have told. Was there a sin that was never uncovered, an illicit lover in her past? A penchant for greed or gluttony, self-adoration for her face? I've begged her to speak to me, share a confidence or two. I've promised to never tell; it would be forever locked away. For what is a truly great secret if not a window into a soul?

ZACH RICHARDS

One

Damn. I limp back to my house, left knee burning. *Damn, Damn. Damn.* Why'd I do it? Why poke at Ruth? Am I a jerk or something worse?

Something worse.

"Be quiet."

So what if Ruth forgot the anniversary? I wish I could too. But there's no reason for her to worry. I'm not going to talk. It's true that in a weak moment I spewed to Carlyn, but it didn't make me feel any better. Didn't erase Tina's voice from my head. I drop onto the living room couch feeling distant and depressed. Flick on the TV and flick it off. Eye the room with growing disgust. Cobwebs droop from the ceiling; spiders hang from their webs. I could get the broom and knock them off, but that would barely make a dent.

How about I start with the hordes of shipping boxes stacked against the pee-yellow walls. They're an indication of a little problem, but it's not like I'm mainlining crack. Fishing poles. Gardening tools. Gadgets. You name it. I'm a sucker for useless toys. Maybe get rid of the old magazines piled high on the corner desk. *Field & Stream. Outdoor Life.* An old *Playboy* or two. I'm not sure why I save the rags.

They're a haven for the throngs of silverfish that scurry from floor to drawer.

You don't like change.

"That's not true."

It sure is.

"Go away." Focus. Don't listen to her. Tomorrow's a brand new day. I'm going to change my life. Clean up this place. Scrub everything in sight.

Scrubbing won't make you feel better.

"Shut up."

There's only one thing that will.

I knock the side of my head with the flat of my hand, hoping Tina will go dormant again. My dead wife doesn't bug me as often these days. Only once or twice a week. It was worse when I was living in the bottle. Then she'd visit me every day. But when she does appear, her nagging voice drills holes in my pounding head.

Raking my hands through my thinning hair, I get up and head for the kitchen. There, I inhale my nightly can of beef chili lathered on a half dozen corn tortillas. I leave the unwashed dishes in the sink with the others and try to come up with another task.

You've delayed long enough, Tina says, this time in a kinder tone.

"You think?"

I pull up a chair, step up, and reach deep into the kitchen's topmost cupboard. Out pops the bottle of whiskey I hide from my sponsor and my better self. I fill a tumbler with the golden-brown liquid, then carry the drink through my house of horrors and ease open the hated door.

The streetlight bathes Hunter's room in watery-blue shadows; a slice of light falls across his miniature bed. The scent of mildew prickles my nose from the roof leak I never got fixed.

This room makes me sad.

"Me too."

I set my tumbler on the bookcase, a sour taste flooding my mouth. *Why?* I ask for the millionth time. *Why me?* I wasn't greedy. Wasn't evil. Didn't long for money, fame, or success. All I wanted was a simple life with my wife and my boy. A nice vacation every now and then. Enough money to put my kid through school. Maybe have a grandchild or two. But no such luck. God wouldn't have it. And why the hell not?

Think of the multitudes who do so much worse. The unpunished thieves, druggies, child molesters, and murderers. I punch my fist against the doorjamb and feel nothing. I punch until my knuckles bleed.

Time goes by. I must've slept. I'm not sure. But when I open my eyes, I'm curled up like a dog on the cold wooden floor. I crawl to the bookcase, flick on the night-light, and pull the photo album from the shelf. The album was Tina's idea. She thought Hunter should have a collection of photos that told the story of his life. There's our wedding photo at the courthouse. A picture of us dancing in front of our newly purchased home. Of Tina eight months pregnant. Of me holding our newborn son.

I was pretty back then, Tina says.

"You were beautiful," I reply.

I pause on a photo of Tina beaming at our fair-haired boy. He's surrounded by a half dozen laughing toddlers seated around a picnic table at the zoo. His shining eyes are fixed on a colorful cake covered in dinosaurs and topped with the number 2. I close my eyes like I'm watching a movie and smile at what happens next. He doesn't wait for his mom to cut the cake but snatches a hunk with his tiny hands.

He got in trouble for that.

"I remember."

My arms ache with a sudden memory of the warmth of Hunter's body pressed against mine. The way he would whisper *Papa* in my ear when he was tired and ready for bed. Hard to believe he'd have been twenty-three next month. He'll always be my little boy. For the millionth time, I wonder what kind of man he would've become. I picture him tall, handsome, and smart. A college graduate with plenty of friends. He'd have been a surfer. A kayaker. A fisherman for sure. He would've turned out to be an incredible person. And maybe I would've too.

It's sad.

"I know."

I trace my fingers along the angles of Tina's pretty face and try to recall how it felt to make love. She liked it long and slow, preferred the afternoons. Her body was smooth and tight. I catch a whiff of her long-ago scent. She was a sucker for the coconut body lotion she discovered on our Hawaiian honeymoon. I smile, and then the other vision slaps me hard. The melted skin, the broken bones, the stench of a fiery death. On the six-month anniversary of Hunter's death, Tina's car ran off the steepest cliff atop San Marcos Pass.

"Did you do it on purpose?" I ask yet again.

That's for me to know and you to worry about.

Which, of course, I do. After returning the album to the bookcase, I wobble to the kitchen and slide my handgun from the silverware drawer. I carry it into the master bathroom and stare deep into the oxidizing mirror. My eyes are puffy and rimmed in red. My once firm jaw has grown slack. I close my eyes, and for the twentieth time since my son died, press the muzzle between my teeth. The metal feels cool against my lips; its bitterness coats my tongue. I sink alone into my darkness and for the briefest of moments feel eternal numbness coat my throat.

No chance, buster, Tina says. *No leaving until you tell the truth.*

I yank the gun from my mouth. "Damn."

Staggering back to Hunter's room, I set the gun next to my near-empty glass. Light a candle and position it next to a photo of Tina holding our newborn son. Then I ease to the ground and sit cross-legged, the pain in my knee roaring up my spine. I slug down the last of my drink and fix my gaze on my family. Tina's right, of course. I don't deserve an easy way out. Not until I undo my wrong.

Two

The olive-and-black uniform fits a little snug, but it's really not that bad. I could've asked Ruth for a larger size, but I do have my pride. Truth is, it feels good to wear a uniform again. Not like I have any power. I'm lower than a police volunteer. But I feel a tingle when I slip on my work clothes. Like maybe there's some life in me yet.

"Evening, Zach."

"Evening, ladies." I like working at Serenity Acres. Total surprise to me. Thought I'd hate hanging around old people, but they seem to cheer me up.

"Come sit with us," Kate Harrington drawls. Only two weeks in, and my good feelings have a lot to do with this old bird. Not sure why she's taken a liking to me, but I'm totally okay with that.

"You know it's against the rules," I say, eyeing their bridge game. "Besides, I never learned how to play."

"Oh, I could teach you how to play." Mrs. Harrington bats her wide green eyes. "I'm happy to give you a private lesson on your off time. Pay me a visit at villa fifty-four."

"I doubt Gordon would appreciate that," one of her friends says.

"Oh, he wouldn't care."

The eight women gathered around the tables squawk like a flock of startled birds. But my eyes stay focused on Mrs. Harrington. There's something about the woman that demands attention. She's tall and slim, and her weathered face still shows signs of her former beauty. Aquiline nose and high cheekbones prop up her liver-blotched, sagging skin. Tonight she's dressed in a flowery pantsuit, her hair towering above her like a bright-red flame. She comes from oil money in Texas, but she's not some stuck-up bitch. She's nice to the staff, worshipped by the guests, and always surrounded by a cauldron of friends. I'm betting her entourage is nothing unusual. She's a gal who's spent her lifetime as the leader of the pack.

"I might take you up on that visit," I say with a wink. We share a laugh, knowing it'll never happen. Management frowns on any attempt by the riff to mix with the raff.

"Onward," I say. "Good night, ladies."

"Good night," they titter.

I head outside into the cool night air to make the first of my evening rounds. I'm required to do this at least two times each shift, but I've been trying for three or four. I'm not fond of the interior of the buildings, where scented candles can't mask the old person funk. I prefer the outdoors, with its hints of sage and eucalyptus wafting from the nearby hills. Makes it seem like I'm out in the backwoods, when I'm only a few miles from downtown.

There's a half moon rising, and a soft breeze caresses my closely shaved chin and cheeks. The Big Dipper is shimmering through the folds of a silvery cumulus cloud. A dog barks. A coyote yips. A catfight explodes in the dark. Passing by the edge of the golf course, my light scatters a family of wild rabbits feeding on the freshly mown grass.

I continue on to the towering wall that rims the outer boundary of the campus. Razor-sharp stakes embedded atop foot-thick sandstone to keep the guests inside and the rabble out. Can't imagine what it must've cost to build such a barrier. A million dollars? Maybe two? Who has that kind of money? The upper 1 percenters, of course.

While passing by the campus memorial garden, a rhythmic chanting floats through the air. Strange, as the guests should be buttoned down at this time of night. Maybe some local kids sneaked in? Sharing a few beers or some pot? I did that a few times when I was a scruffy teen growing up in Missoula, Montana. Broke into empty vacation cabins with my high school bros in tow. Smoked packs of ciggies and drank whatever crap one of us could pinch. Caught the thrill of a little harmless trespassing to get our teenage fix. Then I'd been popped by the local sheriff—he sent me home with a stern warning. Said the next time he caught me acting like a delinquent, he'd hand me over to my dad. That was all it took to end my dabble in crime. It's not like my father was a violent man, but he wasn't above using his fists to rein in a wayward boy.

I step into the confines of the hedge-rimmed garden, and the scent of lemon fills the air. I sweep my light across the pool of darkness, and it lands on a head of closely cropped white hair. "Can I help you?" I ask, thinking it must be a guest resting on the bench. "Are you hurt?"

There's a rustling, and I spy a human-sized shadow slipping behind the far side of the hedge. "*Stop*," I order. I instinctively reach for the nonexistent gun that once sat on my hip. Then I rake my flashlight across the gnarled bushes before refocusing it on the guest. She turns to me, and I'm surprised when my light illuminates the smooth face of a teenage girl.

"Who are you, and why are you here?" I demand. There's another rustle in the far corner, followed by the sound of footsteps. "Who's with you?"

The girl offers up a sweet smile. "It's just me and a skittish cat. I think you've scared him away."

If that shadow was spawned by a cat, then surely I must be a dog. "You're trespassing," I say in my firmest voice. "I could turn you in to the police."

"You have it wrong," she replies. "I'm the night supervisor in assisted living. I'm taking my evening break."

"You're a supervisor?" I'm more than a little surprised.

"Yes. My name's Ember."

"Oh. Then . . . sorry. That was stupid of me." I'm relieved and not a little embarrassed.

"What's your name?" she asks.

"Zach. Zach Richards. I'm new here. I don't know everyone yet."

"Nice to meet you, Zach." The slip of a girl gets to her feet and seemingly floats toward me like a ghost. Shining my light full on her face, I catch sight of her melted skin. I grunt and stumble back, my mind flashing on the memory of Tina's charred corpse. The flashlight slips from my fingers and hits the ground with a solid clunk. The light snaps off, and for a moment, the only sound is my guttural breathing. I crouch and scuttle my hands across the gravel, my heart ricocheting in my chest.

"Let me help you," Ember says. "My eyes are used to the dark." She sinks next to me, and I feel crazed. I might puke my guts. The girl fumbles around for a moment, and then her cool fingers close on mine. She slips the flashlight into my hands. "Seems like it's broken. Do you know your way back to the office? If not, I'll be happy to walk you there."

"No." I jump to my feet. "I mean, no, thank you. I know my way." I nearly trip over myself backing out of the garden before I turn and begin to jog. Ember calls out, but I only hurry faster, my knee screaming that I should stop.

Memories? Tina asks.

"Go away."

You shouldn't have spied on me at the coroner's.

"Leave me alone!" I hurry back to security and stumble into the light, where it takes several moments for my heartbeat to slow. It will take longer than that to get the memory of my wife's scorched body out of my freaking head.

Three

"Who is she?" I ask Ruth the next day in her office when I arrive a little early to work. My night shift runs from seven to five, four rotating days a week. I thought we'd spend more time together, but Ruth is typically gone by the time I start.

"Who?" she asks distractedly, not looking up from some report.

I study Ruth for a moment, thinking how much she's changed from the girl I met years ago. She'd been a free spirit back then—a hippie with waist-length wavy brown hair laced with streaks of gold. She'd rarely worn makeup, and her body had been curvy; she'd been sexy in an uncaring way.

And that's what got you into trouble, Tina says.

That and a few too many beers.

Now her hair hangs straight, blunt cut above the shoulders; her makeup is carefully applied. Her body has been thinned from years of power walking; from the back, she looks like a boy. Expensive black suit, collared neck. Perfectly manicured hands. Coldly professional, an ice maiden, tied up in a flawless bow.

"The girl? The one with the burned face."

Ruth glances up with an irritated look. "You mean woman. Ember's one of our night supervisors."

"I know that, but what's her story? What happened to her?"

"I don't know." She stares at me with dazed eyes. "Can I ask you something?"

"Sure."

"You promise to tell the truth?"

"Of course."

"You've been here a few weeks. Have you heard complaints from the staff?"

"What kind of complaints?"

"About me." She fingers her Fitbit.

"What would I hear about you?"

"Something bad?"

"Like . . . ?"

"Like I'm overly critical or harsh?"

I shrug. "Nope. Not a thing." I may have heard a little grumbling, but I don't plan to be Ruth's campus spy.

"Anyone say that I'm cold and aloof?"

Tell her the truth. The staff thinks she's a bitch.

I shake my head. "Nothing," I say. "I haven't heard anything at all."

"Exactly. This is ridiculous. I won't have it. It's nothing but a pack of lies. On what planet is staff allowed to rate their supervisor?"

"They rated you?"

She nods. "On something called a *360*. Corporate mumbo jumbo at its best." She holds up her report. "There's also a comment that says I'm not a team player. That I don't support senior management. Me. *Me!*" She slaps the pages against her desk and glares at me like I wrote the thing. "You have to understand," she continues. "In the eighteen years I've worked here, I've only had exemplary reviews. And then that joke of an executive director takes over, and suddenly *I'm* the problem employee?"

"You're talking about Kai?"

"Who else would I be talking about?"

See? Tina interjects. *She's a bitch.*

My plastic earpiece crackles. *"Richards to the Highlife. Code orange. "*

"There's a code orange," I repeat. There's a color for every event in this place. I had to memorize them my first day. Code brown, a theft. Code blue, an escapee. Code black, a death. Code orange could mean lots of things, but usually it refers to a disruptive employee, visitor, or guest.

Ruth glances at her phone. "I see it here. I get the alarms on my cell. I only respond to code blue."

"Why code blue?"

"A wandering guest can become a public relations nightmare. They often make front page news. It's my job to tamp that down."

"Well, I haven't dealt with a code orange before. Want to come along?"

Ruth hesitates and then shakes her head. "No. I'm tired. I'm going home." She gets up and gathers her things and pushes past me, face flushed. I eye the report on her desk.

360 EVALUATION—RUTH MOSBY—CONFIDENTIAL

I glance behind me and then flip it open to the first page, which lists a summary of Ruth's skill set. No wonder she's in a foul mood. *Unsatisfactory* is stamped in red. My earpiece crackles again.

"Richards! Code orange!"

I hurry from the office to the Highlife, the most casual of the campus's three dining options. It looks like a fine restaurant, except at mealtime, when a slew of metal walkers crowd the room. There's a slow stampede when the doors open at four, but it usually clears out by seven. After that, it turns into a staff hangout. I've stopped in once or twice.

I arrive to find an enormous man dressed in a pinstripe suit yelling at the top of his lungs. He towers over the campus pastor, who stands with her arms folded, nodding her head. In a nearby booth cowers a crying caretaker, her hands clutching her face. The dining room is almost empty, a few guests scattered here and there. Most of them aren't paying attention—must be part of the dementia crowd.

"You must calm down," the pastor says. I haven't been introduced to Pastor Sam, but I've come across her a few times. She lives somewhere on the compound. She's always out and about.

"Hell if I'll do that!" The behemoth is dressed like a polished businessman, which doesn't match the cusswords spewing from his mouth. I straighten my shoulders in an attempt to look taller. "What's the problem?" I ask in a stern voice.

Pastor Sam turns her calm gaze on me. She's close to my age, maybe a little older, and dresses in black pantsuits and matching clogs. She has a wiry body and cropped hair that's as gray as her makeup-less face. Not a hint of lipstick or a dash of eye shadow to brighten her sallow skin. The only touch of color is a thick gold cross encrusted with eye-popping jewels that dangles from her skinny neck.

"I'd like to introduce you to Dario Panini," she says, caressing her cross with her fingers. "He's upset about the passing of his mother, Mary."

"You're damn right I'm upset about my mother," Panini says. "What the hell happened? She was fine when I spoke to her last week."

"Dario's mother passed away last night," the pastor adds.

"Ma didn't *pass away*," Panini says. "She was killed."

I'm not exactly sure what my role is here, so I let the detective in me take over. "Settle down," I say sternly. I nod at the caretaker. "Is she hurt?"

"She'll be fine," the pastor says. "He scared her; that's all."

"He slapped me," the caretaker sobs. "I think he broke my nose."

"You hit her?" I reach for my nonexistent handcuffs.

"He didn't mean it," Pastor Sam says calmly, "did you, Dario?"

"If he hit her, we should call the police."

The pastor gives me an inquisitive look. "You're new here, aren't you?"

"Yes, ma'am."

"What's your name?"

"Zach Richards."

"Well, Zach, you'll learn we prefer not to involve outsiders. In fact, your role as a security guard is to help us take care of our own."

I want to argue that an assault should be reported, but then Tina jumps into my head.

Don't blow this job, she says. *Keep quiet and follow their rules.*

Pastor Sam turns to Panini. "It would be best if we discussed your concerns in private. Zach will accompany you to our chapel. I want to have a few words with our caretaker, and then I'll meet you there."

"I don't want to *air my concerns* in private," Panini yells. "Everyone here should know what you're up to. You're murderers, and I have proof."

The pastor reaches out and rests her hand on Panini's massive arm, looking like a David to his Goliath. "It'll be okay," she says in a soothing voice. "I promise you. We'll have a nice chat and work this out. Now please follow Zach to the chapel. It's not far from here."

Panini looks like he might argue, and then his body slumps. "All right."

It's like he's been hypnotized, Tina says.

I know. What's up with that?

Four

Serenity Chapel is housed in a sandstone building near the golf course's seventh hole. Big and dark, it's full of strange echoes, the ceiling swallowed in a dusty gloom. It reminds me of the church my mom dragged me to when I was just a kid. She always told me God was waiting in the rafters to punish me for my sins. That was the beginning of what my dad called her *crazies*. She was committed by the time I was ten. I can't help but think of Mom's mental illness when Tina rummages around in my head.

The setting sun streams through the stained-glass windows, casting a hellish glow across Panini's face. He doesn't speak. Doesn't blink. It's like I'm not even there. He stares at the oversized altar, his large hands gripped tight into fists.

"You have a mom?" he asks after a while.

"She passed away years ago."

"Dad?"

"He's been gone a long time too."

"Siblings?"

"Nope."

"Lucky you."

"Lucky?"

He turns to me, and in the streaming light I see there's something odd about his eyes. One's blue, the other green, and they're set so far apart you can't tell where he's looking. He chews on a ragged fingernail while he continues to gripe. "It's been a bitch," he says, "flying cross-country every month. I mean, hell, I've dropped so much money on this place, you'd think Ma would've been taken care of. But Serenity-goddamn-Acres is as bad as any Medicaid dump." He shakes his head and begins to pace.

"Ma only moved out here 'cause of my pain-in-the-ass sister, Annette. She was living with her jerk boyfriend in Montecito when that mudslide hit. Hell if those chickenshits didn't up and move to Costa Rica." He stops his pacing and tugs at his hair. "Can you believe that? My sis got scared and took off, leaving her poor old ma behind. What kind of person does that?" He glares at me like I'm supposed to have an answer.

"I don't know . . ."

"Well, I do. It's called a *selfish bitch*."

I glance at the altar and think he shouldn't be using foul language. But I doubt it's my place to intervene.

"It was Annette's way of screwing me over," he continues. "Knew I'd have to drop everything and fly out every couple of weeks to keep my eye on Ma."

He stops talking, and I speak up when the silence becomes deafening. "So why didn't you move your mother back home?"

Curling his hands into fists, Panini leans my way. "I tried to, but you guys refused to cough up her deposit."

"Oh. Sorry."

Ask him if he's in the habit of slapping women, Tina orders.

"Not now."

Ask him, she insists.

"No!"

"You talking to me?" Panini asks, his blue eye wandering.

"Sorry. Got a dispatch." I tap my earpiece. "And sorry about the deposit."

"Well, you should be." He works his monster-sized hands together. "Got a question for you. Ever hear of something called the Goodnight Club?"

"The Goodnight Club?" I shake my head, my detective ears perking up. "No. Why?"

"A couple of months ago, Ma told me she joined something called the Goodnight Club. It's not some regular club. It's a bunch of old people that don't want to hang on this earth no more, and there's some guy that helps them out."

"He does what?"

"Someone helps them," he says angrily. "Gives them some juice. Sends them on their way. You know what I mean."

"Assisted suicide?"

"Assisted nothing. It's murder in my book. Thing is, Ma wasn't ready to go. Told me so herself. You gotta agree on a date or something, and Ma said she hadn't done no such thing. She just liked hanging out with some of the oldies that had her twisted frame of mind. Anyway, you wear a uniform. Why don't *you* investigate?"

"Excuse me," Pastor Sam steps up beside me, and I jump like I've done something wrong.

"Mr. Panini was just telling me . . ."

"I heard what he said. I'll take care of things from here." She stares at me until I turn and shuffle off. "Now why don't we take a seat?" she says.

I head to the back of the chapel, where I can't help but pause and listen in. Panini slumps into the front pew and drops his head in his hands. His back is twitching, like he's crying. Or at the very least, he's choking back tears. "I'm so sorry for your loss," the pastor says, placing a hand on his shoulder. "Your mother was a wonderful woman."

He lifts his head. "You knew her?"

"Of course I did. She was quite engaging. Had made many friends at the campus."

"Yeah. That's my ma. The life of the party." His voice turns mean. "But that doesn't change a thing. I'm gonna go to the police."

"Now why would you do that?"

"I wanna autopsy. I wanna know why Ma died."

"I understand, Dario. And I feel your pain. But your mother was eighty-seven. Isn't it likely she died from natural causes?"

"That's what you want me to think. But she told me that some guy at the Goodnight Club was gonna help her kick off. I thought she'd gone daft with dementia. But maybe I should've listened better, 'cause I know as God is my witness she couldn't have been ready. My little girl's getting married next month, and Ma planned to be there. So I want you to get to the bottom of this. I wanna know if she got herself killed." At this he begins to sob in an awkward way, more barking seal than man.

"I'll tell you what," the pastor says. "I'll arrange to have a grief counselor meet with you tomorrow. And with any others in your family that might need a little support."

"There's only me," he snuffles. "My sister lives out of the country and doesn't give a shit."

"All right. Then the counselor will meet with you."

He stops his crying. "That doesn't change anything. I want an autopsy. I demand it."

Pastor Sam gets to her feet, arms folded. "All right, Dario. If you want an autopsy, we'll order one. But if we bring in the coroner, the police will get involved, and that could get messy. I don't think our caretaker will press charges, but we'll have to let the police know you hit her. It's possible they could charge you with aggravated assault."

"Assault?" Panini stands, looming over the pastor like a cartoon character. "I didn't assault her. She was talking nonsense, so I gave her a tap on the cheek."

"You hit her, Dario. You may have broken her nose." She pats his arm like he's a child. "So maybe we shouldn't order that autopsy. What do you think?"

He hesitates. "I . . . I can't afford for this to get messy. I can't have the police rummaging through my life. Got loads of work to get back to in Jersey. I don't want any bad press."

"Then you agree there's no reason to involve the police in your mother's death."

He nods. "Yeah. I agree."

"Good."

There's a tap on my shoulder, and I just about bang through the roof. I spin around and come face to face with our baby-faced executive director. "Is there a problem here?" he asks.

Five

I feel an immediate flush of guilt, like I've been caught sleeping on the job. I glance at the altar, then hurry outside, Kai following close behind. When I get to the chapel herb garden, I pause and turn. "There was a problem with a visitor," I say, giving Kai a discreet once-over. He's dressed in faded blue jeans and a striped button-down, his dark hair slicked back into a ponytail. He reeks of musky cologne, or maybe the odor comes from the crap in his hair. He seems to use a lot.

"Define *problem*," Kai says, his gray eyes fixed on mine. I wave my hand toward the chapel entrance.

"Code orange. Unhappy family member. Pastor Sam seems to be handling it fine."

"I'd expect no less. And you are?"

I point to my name tag. "Zach Richards. Started working here last month." I hold out my hand, and Kai makes a face like I've offered him a snake. I let my hand drop to my side, thinking handshakes must not be his thing. Kai glances past me into the chapel.

"Were you eavesdropping?" he asks.

"No."

"Pastor Sam would be pissed if you were."

"Well, I wasn't," I reply firmly. "I was trying to be of help." I tap my earpiece. "Better get back to my rounds."

"That can wait. I was looking for someone in maintenance, but I guess you'll have to do. Follow me." He starts down a well-worn path between the trees.

Go on, Tina says. *Follow the kid.*

"He's a jerk."

And you're not?

I rap on my head and then follow Kai to the administrative building and into a small windowless office crammed full of cardboard boxes.

"Maintenance was supposed to move my stuff today," he says, "but a couple of their guys called in sick." He rolls his eyes. "I'm sure it has nothing to do with tonight's All-Star Game." He waves his hand at the pile of boxes. "Mind helping me with a few of these?"

Yeah, I mind, thinking of my knee.

Careful, Tina warns.

I shrug. "Where to?"

"My new office in the next building over. It's not far." He picks up a half-empty box.

"Got a hand truck?" I ask.

"No. But these aren't too heavy."

I sigh and pick up a box loaded with books and hobble out the door.

Kai's new digs are a major upgrade from his former office. A three-room suite, freshly painted with a private bathroom and a bar. A flat-screen TV hangs on one wall; modern artwork fills the others. Colorful furniture that cries expensive. The kid can't help but gloat once we've finished moving his boxes, a sheen of sweat coating his face. "Pretty damn sweet," he says, his arms spread wide. "Don't you think?"

I nod. "Yeah. Not bad."

Kai opens one of the boxes and pulls out a jug of Patrón. "Have a drink with me?" he asks. "A little moving day celebration?"

"No, thanks."

"You sure? It's a limited edition. Goes down extra smooth." He holds up his half-full tumbler, and I can't say I'm not tempted.

Don't you dare, Tina whispers.

"It's against the rules," I say.

"This is a special day. I'll give you a onetime exemption."

I shake my head. "Got a long night ahead. That stuff'll put me to sleep."

"Too bad."

I lean against the wall, my knee twinging with a surging current. I'm ready to be released from my domestic duties, but the kid seems to have other ideas. He wanders from box to box, sipping on his evening cocktail. "You always been a security guard?" he asks.

I shake my head. "I was a police detective at one time."

Kai sets down his empty glass and looks at me with interest. "Really? Then you'll know what this is." He reaches into his back pocket and whips out a knife. I take a step back, chilled. I know exactly what it is and have the scar on my chest to prove it.

"Why're you carrying a karambit?" I ask, my gaze fixed on the wickedly curved blade.

He makes a few amateur moves, slicing the knife through the air. "A friend got me into the Apollo Reed videos. We're flying to Vegas next week to take one of his workshops."

Apollo Reed is a legend in his own mind, teaching a nation full of whacked-out preppers how to maim and kill under the guise of self-protection. "You a survivalist?" I ask.

"No, I just think the concept is cool."

The perp who cut me was a survivalist, and a nutcase on top of that. The guy came out of nowhere and sliced me across the chest. "Well, I wouldn't wave that thing around until you know what you're doing."

Kai pockets the blade with a sullen look. "I told you I've been watching the videos."

"Any idiot can do that," I mumble.

"What?"

I tap my headpiece. "Sorry. Another dispatch."

He stares at me for a moment, like he's trying to make sense of who I am. "Anyway," he says, "I've gotta get moving. I have a Kali class tonight."

"*You're* studying Filipino martial arts?"

"You know about that stuff?"

"Weapon-based training? Yeah. I do."

Years ago.

"Shush."

Kai chuckles. "Well, my class is the vegan version. More like tai chi." He tugs his cell phone from his pocket and makes a face. "Can I get you to empty a few of these boxes?" he asks. "You don't need to arrange them or anything. Just stick the books on the shelves and leave the supplies on the desk. My new receptionist starts tomorrow. Her name's Uma. Like Uma Thurman. Only younger and hotter and smarter. She just graduated magna cum laude from UCSB."

"And she wants to work here?"

He nods. "Lots of graduates want to stay in town, and there's not so many jobs. I'm planning to take full advantage of that. We've got enough old people wandering around this place. We need some energy, some excitement, some . . . well, some basic drive."

Tina barges in. *He's dissing you,* she says.

"No, he's not."

What a prick.

"Shush."

Kai grabs his rucksack and heads for the door. "Get everything ready for Uma to organize. Don't want her to have a workers' comp claim on her first day. Got it?"

"Got it."

"Good." He hurries out the door.

I settle on a shiny purple sofa and give my knee a good rub. The sofa is one of those modern things that may look good in some froufrou showroom but is about as comfortable as a straight-backed chair. I can't help but feel all pissy inside. It's one thing to play maintenance man and move the jerk's boxes, but hell if I'm going to sort his pencils and pens. That's a job for Uma and her kick-ass degree. I decide to do the minimum and dump a load of supplies onto his desk. A manila folder tumbles out, spilling its contents across the floor. "*Shit*," I swear, easing down on my knees.

I pick up a bill with *Past Due* stamped across its face. Student loan. A big one. Looks like Kai hasn't made a payment in months. There's also a Nordstrom bill with a $10,000 balance. A MasterCard over its limit. I shake my head and whistle. Hell if our new boss isn't a spendthrift. He comes off like some Montecito trust funder, but that must be part of his shtick.

"Can I help you with something?"

Pastor Sam stands in the doorway, looking anything but pleased. I get to my feet with a grunt. "Kai asked me to empty his boxes."

"Did he?" She crosses the room and plucks the folder from my hand and pages through its contents. "Did he ask you to go through his personal things?"

"No."

"I didn't think so." She stares at me, and I get a creepy sensation the woman can read my mind.

"I better get going," I say, taking a few steps toward the door. "Gotta make my rounds."

"Wait." She fingers her jeweled cross. "Is Kai gone for the day?"

"Yep."

"Too bad. I wanted to speak to him about Dario Panini. Unless you did."

"Why would I?"

"Weren't you listening in on our conversation?"

"I wanted to make sure you were safe."

"Safe?"

"Yes."

She hesitates and then cracks a thin-lipped smile. "I should formally introduce myself." She extends a hand. "I'm Pastor Sam."

I take her hand in mine. It's strong and cool to the touch. "Zach Richards." She nods and releases her grip. "Well, Zach Richards. I owe you an apology. I'm afraid I've been quite rude."

"Not at all."

"It's just that Mr. Panini had me running scared."

"I wouldn't have guessed."

"There's some family history that I'm not at leave to discuss. Let's just say he should be considered a dangerous man. He's also quite litigious. I believe he was trying to set us up with that nonsense about his mom."

"Then you might want to turn him in for hitting the caretaker."

She sighs and leans against the desk. "I believe I've handled the situation correctly, but you never know. That's why I'm here. I wanted to update Kai. It'll be up to him to decide if we should press charges. I think I'll leave him a note."

"Okay. I better get back to my rounds."

She smiles at me, quite kindly this time. "I'm looking forward to working with you."

"Thanks." For some reason, her words make me happy.

That's because you're a needy man, Tina says as I head off into the night.

"No, I'm not."

Wanna bet?

"Nope." Not when I'm sure to lose.

Six

It's midsummer, and the night is muggy hot. The tropical storm brewing off Baja has sent high waves and humidity all along the Pacific coast. I'm making my second loop around the perimeter of the campus when I hear voices drifting from the memorial garden.

"Hello?" I call out, hoping against hope I don't run across Ember.

It's mean the way you avoid her, Tina says.

"I'm not trying to be mean."

Well, you are.

"Go away."

Would you avoid me if I hadn't died?

I slap my forehead like I'm gunning for a gnat.

There's no moonlight to pave my way, but when my flashlight brightens the inside of the enclosure, I see only hedges standing tall and firm. I step behind the memorial stone, and a shadowy cave catches my eye. I kneel to find a tunnel in the hedge, large enough for a human to slip through. A piece of black cloth is caught in a branch. I press it between my fingers and catch a whiff of something old and musty. Could a guest have crawled through here? Doubtful. So who else could it be?

After stuffing the cloth in my pocket, I get to my feet, and a bolt of pain shoots through my leg. Stumbling backward, I sink onto the cement bench, where I rest for a while before lugging myself up and out of the enclosure in search of aspirin and coffee. I take a shortcut through the outlying villas, where the wealthiest guests reside in three dozen single-story duplexes. I've heard these guests spend millions outfitting their pads, and most of their storybook gardens are overseen by private staff.

I hear a rustling coming from a nearby garden, so I limp up the stamped cement sidewalk and shine my light behind a vine-covered hedge.

"Who's there?" a voice calls out.

I flash my light across the darkened veranda; it lands on a tower of flaming-red hair.

"Security, ma'am."

"Zach? Is that you?" Draped in a yellow-and-black leopard-print robe, Mrs. Harrington rests on a lounge chair. The tip of a cigarette glows between her fingers; a drink tinkles in her hand. There's a single wavering candle on the glass side table, giving off a sweetish wisteria scent.

"Sorry to bother you, Mrs. Harrington. Conducting a security check."

"Why be so formal? Please call me Kate."

"All right, Kate."

"Now turn off that light before you blind me and come take a seat."

I've broken enough rules since I've been here without adding fraternizing to the list. "I can't do that," I say, snapping off the flashlight. "I have my rounds to finish up." My voice sounds harsh to my ears. I try to tone it down. "Besides, it's past two in the morning. You should get your beauty sleep."

"Beauty sleep?" she laughs. "I like that." She pats the chair beside her. "Won't you entertain me for a few moments? Please? Do something nice for a lonely old gal? Share a glass of whiskey with a former Texas belle."

"I shouldn't. It's against the rules."

"Rules? Life is way too short to play by the rules. Besides, I pay a fortune for this place to make me happy. And at the moment, it would make me happy to chat with you. If nothing else, your kindness will help an old lady through another long and lonely night."

Poor thing, Tina says. *You should stay.*

"And lose my job?"

At this time of night, who's to know?

"Talk to yourself much?" Kate asks.

I tap my earpiece and glance at the French doors. "What about your husband? He won't mind?"

"Gordon?" She sighs. "Poor man doesn't know day from night."

"Dementia?"

"Compounded by a stroke."

"Why isn't he living in the champion's unit?"

"I prefer he stays with me."

"That's a lot of work for one person."

"I'm not alone. I have a steady stream of caretakers that watch him around the clock."

"Serenity Acres employees?"

She shakes her head. "I use an outside service."

"And management allows that?"

"As long as I pay the bills."

"That must cost you an arm and a leg."

"Thirty thousand a month, give or take, but what else can I do? I refuse to stick my husband in a dementia home or a snif."

"A snif?"

"A skilled nursing facility. Terribly dreary places. No. I'd never do that. I know I'm an old lady, and you might find this hard to believe, but Gordon was the love of my life."

"Was?"

She finishes off her drink. "The man in there isn't my Gordon. *My* Gordon is long gone. Still, I feel responsible for his remaining shell. I'll take care of him until it's too much."

"Too much for you or too much for him?"

She hesitates. "Both, I guess. Now, have that drink with me, please? Just one? Entertain me for a little bit? I promise no more depressing talk. I want to forget all that."

I glance at the woman and consider and then proceed to shrug off the rules. "All right," I say. "But you can't tell anyone, and that includes your gal pals."

"I pinky promise," she says, laughing. "This rendezvous will be our little secret. Now let me pour you that drink." She whips out a bottle of Maker's Mark from beneath her chair and pours it into a waiting glass. It's like she knew I'd pass by this evening. A nursery rhyme pops into my head. "*Will you walk into my parlor,*" says the spider to the fly.

I think to tell her I don't drink, but then I stop, because the truth is, I do. And who's it going to hurt? If nothing else, it might take the edge off my aching knee.

It gets to be a thing with Kate and me. Between rounds, usually at one or two in the morning, I'll take a break and sit with her out on her covered veranda. She has a western-facing view, so on clear nights, we can watch the moon settle into the darkness. My whiskey always waits for me, poured as I like it. Two inches, neat. Never more, never less.

What I'm doing is against the rules, but hell, I enjoy the old lady, and she enjoys me. We sit in the darkness of her veranda, lit up by a scented candle or two. She has those twinkly lights strung in and around the hedges. Some nights we'll share a cigarette. On occasion she breaks out her medicinal pot. And something about the time of night and the shadows lead us to tell our truths. It's like we're not really talking to each other but carrying on a conversation with ourselves. It's a kind of therapy, I suppose.

After a few nights of chatting, I tell her about Hunter. From the catch in her voice, I know that she knows how much it hurts. I also spew about my years of hard drinking and my tendency to hoard. Eventually I mention Tina. Kate wants to meet her, but that's not up to me. Tina doesn't show up on demand, and she's not sure we can trust my new friend.

Tonight, Kate has had a couple extra drinks and exudes a quiet sadness. After a while she opens up.

"Gordon had an incident this morning."

"An incident?"

"He dislodged his feeding tube."

"He can't eat on his own?"

"No. His throat muscles have stopped functioning correctly, so bits of food and drink can slip into his lungs. It's called *dysphagia*, a common but horrific symptom of advanced dementia that results in ongoing bouts of pneumonia."

"That sounds awful."

"It is. And it's made worse by the feeding tube stuck in his side. That thing may keep him alive, but his quality of life is at an all-time low."

"So why use it?"

She makes a face, eyes flashing. "I wouldn't if it were up to me, but his absentee sons insisted. In fact, they went to court to force the procedure. He hates the feeding tube. I know it. I have to keep his hands tethered so he won't yank it out. It's a form of torture—a horrible thing to watch."

I shiver at the thought of strangling to death with my hands tied by my side. "Would he have wanted the tube?"

"Not in a million years. It's cruel and dehumanizing. We treat animals better than we treat humans. It's immoral as far as I'm concerned."

"So you're a proponent of euthanasia?"

She takes a sip of her drink, the ice tinkling like wind chimes. "Can you imagine the cruelty of seeing a loved one slowly choke to death? Because that's what's happening to my Gordon."

"I can't imagine," I say. I picture Tina for a moment. Her burned body at the morgue. How I'd damned God for not letting her live and then thanked him for not letting her suffer. "So who are these sons?" I ask. "They ever visit?"

"My stepsons? No. Never." Her tone sounds harsh, but I catch her swiping at a tear. "Anyway," she says, "enough of that. Would you mind helping me with an errand?"

"As long as it's not illegal."

"It's not." She whips a thick envelope from her pocket and hands it to me. "There's $6,000 in here, cash. I'd like you to deliver it to Selena Ornelas. She's not to know it came from me."

"Who's Selena?"

"A senior caretaker in assisted living. She's quite good at her job."

"So, this is some kind of tip?"

"Let's call it a donation to a private cause. Her oldest daughter needs braces, but her husband's been deported, so she's struggling to care for three little ones all on her own."

"Bummer."

"Yes. Bummer is right. Anyway, I want you to give her the money and tell her what it's for. Under no circumstances should you disclose who is behind the gift. Not to her, nor to anyone else."

"But why . . . ?"

"Let's just say it's a way to relieve my conscience for an incident in my past."

I can't help but laugh. "What? You were mean to one of your sorority sisters?"

"That and more. Besides, I've lived a fortunate life, and I like to give back to those I consider deserving, but I prefer it to be a private act. I don't want or need to be thanked. Or have my photo splashed across the press, or God forbid someone presents me with a frivolous award at some over-the-top fund-raiser. I have money, and I'll spend it as I wish, my greedy stepsons be damned. So, will you help me?"

"Sure." What can it hurt?

"Good. Now, tell me about your day. Anything interesting happen?"

I open my mouth to respond but pause when my earpiece crackles. *"Richards to the security office. Code blue!"*

"Gotta go," I say, finishing off my drink. "There's a code blue."

"Code blue?" She laughs. "Better hurry. One of us chickens must've flown the coop."

Seven

At three a.m. the security office is a whirr of activity with our supervisor, Finn, yelling on the phone. Three young guards are standing nearby. They're inseparable and not especially friendly, so weeks ago I nicknamed them Manny, Moe, and Mac. They jump like startled puppies when Finn bangs down his phone. "Hell if we haven't lost one," he says. Our square-jawed boss with the iron handshake looks like he's getting ready to kill. "That doesn't happen under my watch." He almost spits the words.

Finn is new here, and his reputation preceded him. A decorated marine turned professional soldier for hire, he spent twenty years in and around Iraq before landing a cushy job overseeing Lost Horizon's security. He arrived on our campus at the beginning of August to implement beefed-up security plans.

"What kind of shithole place is this?" he demands, staring straight at me. The man lacks a single eyelash. I picture him plucking them one by one. "Are you awake?" he barks when I don't answer.

"Sure, but . . ."

"But what?"

I shrug. "I don't know."

He places his hands on his hips and swivels. "That's the goddamned problem here. No one knows nothing 'bout nothing. Bunch of idiots running the farm." He fixes his laser sights on me. "What's your name again?"

"Zach."

"Last name."

"Richards."

"Well, Richards the Ungreat, you were supposed to be on perimeter duty."

Perimeter? Should I tell him this ain't Iraq?

"See anything strange out there?"

Out in the wilds of Santa Barbara? "Nope. Not a thing."

"What? Sleeping on the job?"

I open my mouth to argue and then think back on the whiskey neat. If I'm not careful, he'll order a drug test, and that'll be the end of me.

"Shit," he says for the umpteenth time, shaking his head in disgust. He points to each and every one of us. "Your slack behavior will change, starting *right now*." He shouts these last two words, his ruddy face gone beet red. "Understand?"

We all nod our heads in agreement, no one daring to say a word.

"Good. Then I don't have to explain why I need our little problem to be solved, faster than quick." He turns to his computer and brings up a headshot of an elderly guest. "A Simon Appleton has gone missing. He's eighty-five, diabetic, and housed in independent living. A rich bugger, made his money in pharmaceuticals. Anyone know the man?"

"I've seen him around," Moe answers. "He's mobile and doesn't use a walker. Could be a mile away by now."

"Why the hell don't we lock them in?" Finn asks, as if we're personally responsible for management's decisions.

Moe sticks his neck out again. "There aren't any restrictions in independent living, so the guests can come and go as they please."

"Maybe we need to change that."

Moe shrugs. "Maybe."

Finn runs his hands through his crew cut like he might rip out the nubs. "You idiots head out on foot," he says, signaling to the security triplets. "You," he points at me. "With that gimp leg of yours, you'll have to drive." He tosses me a set of keys, which I promptly proceed to drop.

"I'll come with you." Ruth stands at the doorway, dressed in black sweats and running shoes. She looks pale and thin, charcoal shadows ringing her eyes.

"What're you doing here?" Finn asks with a frown.

"I always get called when there's a code blue. I'm the supervisor in charge."

"Not anymore, you aren't."

Ruth's bristles with anger, her cheeks flushing red. "As the VP of operations, I've always managed the code blues."

Finn turns to his computer. "I suggest you check in with your boss. You'll see those duties have been reassigned to security. I'm in charge now." He sits and fumbles with the mouse. "But since you're here, you're welcome to help out. You can play shotgun to Richards the Ungreat."

"Who?"

I grab Ruth's arm and lead her from the room before she can say another word. Once outside, she yanks away. "I'm going back in there," she says. "He can't speak to me like that."

I shake my head. "Maybe you should check with Kai first. I mean, why would Finn make it up?"

She exhales. "I suppose this *is* something Kai would do. I'll ask him tomorrow." She glances at her Fitbit. "I mean I'll ask him today. My review's in a few hours."

"Your review? That 360 thing? Didn't you get it weeks ago?"

"Yeah. But he's been too busy to discuss."

"You better control yourself."

"I will. Now let's go."

We head across the shadow-lined parking lot and climb into the security van. "Which way?" I ask when we reach the gates.

"Turn right. They usually head toward town."

"Do escapes happen often?"

Ruth shakes her head. "Not since we started tagging the champions. It's the in-betweens that usually slip through."

"In-betweens?"

"Guests who are in transition from mentally stable to cognitively dull. That's usually when we lose one. And that typically gets blamed on me."

"I thought Finn said he was responsible."

"I doubt they'll point the finger at him."

"True." I focus on the task at hand. I'm driving ten miles per hour in the thirty, peering deep into the shadows.

Ruth leans forward. "Over there," she says. "In that field. I saw something move between the trees."

I slow the van to a crawl.

"Yes. There he is. Right there."

I park, and we hurry out into the moist predawn air, my flashlight bobbing across the field. It flashes on a stinky skunk, a deflated balloon, and a pile of burnt trash. After a few moments, a ghostly figure in a red sweater appears, stumbling along a rocky path.

"Mr. Appleton," Ruth calls. "Please stop. You're going to hurt yourself. There are lots of holes in the ground."

The ghostly figure lifts a hand and waves us off. "Leave me alone!" he yells in a trembling voice.

"We're here to help you. *Please, please, stop.*"

The red sweater takes a sudden tumble and hits the ground with a thud.

"Shit!"

Ruth takes off running, and I hobble behind, my knee shrieking for relief. By the time I reach them, Ruth is on her knees next to the man, speaking to him in a calm voice. "That's not true," she says. "I promise no one is going to hurt you."

My flashlight lights up a skeletal face with a mouth stretched wide in horror. "*They will*," he sobs. "I know it. They're going to kill me, and I don't want to die."

"Of course you're not going to die." Ruth pats him on the shoulder. "Now tell me. Does anything hurt?"

"I . . . I don't think so."

"Okay, then. Let's get you up." Ruth helps the man to a sitting position, and I use my hands to brace his birdlike shoulders.

"There. Good job. Now, Zach and I will help you to your feet."

"*No!*"

Ruth's voice grows firm. "If you don't get up, we'll call an ambulance, and they'll take you to the hospital. They may want to keep you there. You aren't acting anywhere near normal."

Mr. Appleton hesitates. "No ambulance," he says. "I'll go with you if you promise you won't let them kill me."

I was a detective for long enough to know I'm hearing real fear in Appleton's voice. I help Ruth pull him to his feet. "Who's planning to kill you?" I ask, linking my arm through his. He turns to me, and his ancient breath blows warm against my cold cheek.

"*I can't tell you.* They . . . he will kill me. Tonight's my pink slip night."

"Pink slip? Wait." Ruth pauses and turns to the man. "Do you mean pink Post-it Note?"

"*I don't know what you're talking about.* Just take me somewhere safe."

Ruth frowns and then nods. "Of course we will. How about the infirmary? You'll be safe there."

"You promise?"

"Yes. Zach will protect you. He used to be a police detective."

Mr. Appleton eyes me. "You have a gun?" he asks.

I pat my hip. "Of course," I fib. "I'm carrying right now."

"So you'll stay with me until the sun comes up."

Ruth signals that I should agree. "Sure, I'll stay." That's my second lie. I won't be sitting by anyone's bedside. I still have rounds to do, paperwork to complete.

We help Mr. Appleton into the van, and moments later, we're back on campus. Then we take him to the infirmary, where he's tucked into bed in a private room and the attending nurse gives him something to help him relax. By the time we leave, he's sleeping like a baby, if babies snore like rumbling trucks. Once outside we make our way back to the administrative offices. "What was that about?" I ask as we stroll along.

"Paranoia is a common symptom of dementia. I'll have to contact Simon's family. He's no longer suited for independent living."

"No . . . I mean, he said something about a pink slip, and I could tell it bothered you."

"You could? Huh. Wasn't it dark out?"

"Come on, Ruth. Open up. We've known each other for a long time."

Ruth gnaws at her lower lip. "All right. I do have something to tell you. But it'll have to wait until we get to my office. I don't want anyone to hear."

"There's no one around."

"Still . . ."

We walk the rest of the way in silence, and after we enter Ruth's office, she takes a moment to lock the door.

"Afraid of Russian spies?" I ask, trying to lighten her mood.

She doesn't crack a smile but heads to her chair and drops into her seat. "I want to show you something." She reaches into her top drawer and hands me a half dozen pink Post-it Notes.

"Do these have some sort of special meaning?" I ask, carefully examining each one.

She shrugs. "Maybe a joke? A riddle? A threat? I'm not sure. They were found next to the bodies of deceased guests."

I finger the slips of paper. "Do the dates have meaning?"

"They correspond to the day of death."

"And the signatures?"

"Seem to imitate the handwriting of the deceased."

I look up and study Ruth, trying to read her demeanor. "Were the deaths unusual?"

"No. All of the deceased were quite elderly and dealing with critical health issues. And each cause of death was consistent with preexisting conditions."

"Have you reported this to anyone?"

She drops her gaze. "No. I haven't."

"Why not?"

Ruth takes a deep breath and exhales. "When the first few appeared, I was the genuine VP of operations. I reported directly to Bob. He didn't like to be bothered by day-to-day problems, so he delegated most everything to me. And quite honestly, I thought we were dealing with some sort of prankster. A disgruntled employee looking for a way to stir up trouble at the campus. But the notes keep piling up, and now Simon mentions something about a pink slip . . ."

"Maybe it's a coincidence."

"What if it's not?"

I nod. "So, who else knows about this?"

"Only Selena, I think."

"Selena Ornelas?"

"Yes."

I finger Kate's envelope in my pocket, thinking Selena sure gets around. "So what do you want from me?"

Ruth's hands tremble the slightest bit. "What if you did some investigating on the side?"

"What would I be looking for?"

"Someone trying to cause trouble by making ordinary deaths seem like something more sinister."

"For what purpose?"

"A rumor like this could destroy Serenity's reputation. Dampen or eliminate sales. Guests could break their contracts. Claim it's not safe to live here. It could ruin us."

"So, a form of industrial sabotage?"

"I guess you could say that."

I nod, considering her request. "I don't mind helping, but wouldn't it be better to tell your boss about the situation?"

She shakes her head. "If Kai finds out my part in this, I know he'll have me fired. And I can't afford to lose this job. So, will you help me, please?"

Ruth hasn't asked me for much over the years. It wouldn't hurt me to help her now.

You sure? Tina asks. *The bitch ruined our lives.*

I tap my head a few times. "Sure. I'll help you. Give me some time to come up with a plan."

III. ENVY

Therefore, rid yourselves of all malice and all deceit, hypocrisy, envy, and slander of every kind. Like newborn babies, crave pure spiritual milk, so that by it you may grow up in your salvation.

—1 Peter 2:1–2

The Angel

I'm running out of willing disciples. It might be time for me to move on. Or we'll need to expand the applicant pool. Give the Goodnight Club a boost.

I had a crossing planned for tomorrow. Martha Williams was all set to pass. Submitted a pink slip months ago naming the specific time and date. She wasn't suffering from some painful illness. Just the downhill slide of age. She'd been a runway model in her youth. Graced several covers of *Vogue*. Traveled the world with the jet set. Aspen. Ibiza. Gstaad. Swept through a series of affluent marriages, which allowed her to end her days in style.

Martha's fading looks were her cancer, her most difficult cross to bear. Seems vain to me, but I'm not attractive, so who am I to judge? When the men stopped looking, the surgeries began, and there were one too many of those. The last one left her sniffing nonstop like an overbred pug-nosed dog. How I shivered when I received her pink slip, hoping her secret would top them all.

I had tucked away a few doses of epinephrine. It's such a lovely way to go. The stimulant gives some minor palpitations before the heart muscle rebels and stops. I was counting down the hours for our appointment when Martha suddenly reneged. Seems she no longer desired her crossing after she snagged the love of a man.

I've only had one true crossing this season: pint-sized Mary Panini. Her secret more than disappointed—it was as boring as they come. She had barely tolerated her husband's advances, was never interested in sex. Held her frigidness close to her heart and faked every encounter they ever had. In the end she, too, had hesitated, decided her life wasn't all that bad. I gave her a little nudge. I do that now and then.

I'm pondering my cheerless future when my cell phone begins to hum. "Yes?"

"We've lost another disciple." My ambassador's voice is muffled and low.

"Who?"

"Harvey Higgins."

My fingers nearly crush the phone. "How?"

"Heart attack."

"You're sure?"

"The EMTs confirmed."

I take a hissing breath. The fattest of my disciples was scheduled to make his crossing on Monday of the coming week. I was picturing a juicy secret, a seven out of ten in my book. He'd been the pro at a local tennis club, and there were rumors he fondled the girls. The stories were squashed when he married an heiress and hired the most expensive lawyer in town. "Any sign of his pink slip?" I ask, trying to bring structure to my thoughts.

"Not yet. Should I search?"

"No need." I don't mind my pink slips living out and about. A strange quirk, I'm aware. But it satisfies some inner craving—a need to flaunt my craft. Of course I'll have to control my urge to swagger if suspicion ever closes in.

"Anything else?"

I hesitate, an idea blooming with the gradualness of a budding rose. The destitutes must be in a bit of turmoil. I bet I could nudge some along. And who will care if their ranks grow thin? Not corporate, that's for sure. "There is something," I say, a smile carving lines in my face. "I'd like to do some outreach with the destitutes. They must be nervous about the eviction rumors. Perhaps we should compile a list of the more lucid. Meet me tomorrow night?"

"Same time and place?"

"Yes." I set down my cell phone and brew a cup of coffee, which I savor with lifted spirits. God always supplies the answers if you listen close enough.

RUTH MOSBY

One

I wander alone inside a tunnel sunk deep into an ocean-bound cliff. Darkness coats me in a tingling fear; a rotten stench claims my nose. Crabs skitter along the walls, and eels slip between my feet. I turn a corner and hear the crash of the ocean. Escape is moments away. Then a shadow looms above me, its eyes glowing swampy red. I open my mouth to scream, but no sound escapes my lips. The tunnel shakes with the weight of the beast, and I melt beneath its stare.

"Ruth?"

The morning sun streams into my office, bouncing off a mesh of melted scars. For a moment I think Ember's my monster, but then I realize where I am.

"You were crying out," she says, her good eye plagued with concern.

"I had a nightmare," I reply, my head still groggy with sleep. "What time is it?"

"Eight."

"Eight!" I jump up, head reeling. Dear God, my review's in a little over an hour. I'll barely have time to shower and change. "Did you happen to bring the keys to the rental?" I sweep my hand over my aching eyes.

"Yes, I saw your text." She drops the keys on my desk. "I also brought you a bagel and coffee."

"Thank you." I grab my emergency makeup kit and change of clothes from the back closet. It's not often I sleep at the office, but I like to be prepared. "I don't have time for the bagel, but I'll take that coffee."

"You should eat," she says. "I worry about you."

"No need to worry; I'm fine." I try to act like her words don't touch me. But deep down, they really do. When was the last time anyone showed me the least bit of concern?

"Can I get you anything else?" she asks.

"No, thank you. This is great." In the past few months I've grown close to Ember in a coworker kind of way. She can't be a real friend since I'm her supervisor and more than twenty years her senior. But I've come to enjoy our occasional chats, and she seems to feel the same way. I take a gulp of the bitter brew and then another, hoping it will clear away the fog. "One thing," I say, recalling last night's events. "How's Simon Appleton today?"

"He was sleeping peacefully when I checked on him earlier this morning."

"Good. Can you call Dr. Lawrence? Let him know we have an emergency? We need to get Simon a dementia diagnosis. I want him outfitted with a monitor today."

She nods. "Of course. No problem."

"Thanks." I turn to leave, then pause. "Ember . . . ?"

"Yes?"

"I really appreciate your help."

"Anytime." She smiles at me, the good side of her face beaming. It's amazing how she can work all night and still look as fresh as a rose.

I hurry out of my office and down the hallway, praying I don't run into staff or guests. When I get outside, I spy Kai's new BMW roaring down the roadway, so I dart behind a trash bin until he's passed. I don't want him to see me looking like this. I've lost enough power as it is.

I arrive at casita 3 and unlock the thick hardwood door. It's one of five studios we rent to family and friends who visit from out of town. When empty, they can be used by senior staff. After stripping off my clothes, I step into the warmth of the shower and lean against the porcelain tiles. I stay that way for several moments until I remind myself of the time. Then I wash my hair and shave my legs before dialing in a blast of cold water to slap myself awake.

I'm dressed and applying my makeup when my cell phone begins to buzz. I'm about to send the caller to voice mail when Adam's face flashes on the screen.

My son's contact photo is from his freshman year of high school, his blond hair tousled like a child's. His smile is warm, his eyes engaging. There's none of the pallid thinness that defined him once drugs took over his life. My hand hovers over my cell, and I consider. He hasn't called since before the wedding. Why would he reach out now?

A feeling of impending disaster shoots a load of fear through my veins. It brings back a time when every Adam phone call was a harbinger of doom. I can't do this, I think. Not now. I'll return his call when I feel more in control. Then if it's the enabler he's after, it'll be easier to turn him down.

Getting back to work on my makeup, I scowl at my reflection in the mirror. I look tired. Exhausted. Worn out. A woman on the backside of life. I try smiling, and a decade is swept from my face, but then the lines slip back into place. Maybe I should try Botox or fillers. Have my face lasered or escape to a spa. If I want to ever date or keep my job, I can't afford to look so old.

I finish applying my makeup as evenly as I can. Then I blow-dry my hair and adjust my black pantsuit, which is a little big on me now. In the past year I've dropped ten pounds, and now my cheekbones protrude like razors; my collarbones jut like knives. This look might have suited me a decade ago, but now it makes me feel old.

I glance at my Fitbit—9:20 a.m. I'll have to hurry, or I'll be late. I pack up my things, head back to my office, and try to focus on my upcoming review. How will I respond to the negative feedback without ringing Kai's skinny neck? Should I play it cool and not utter a word? Or tell him where he can go? Of course, the former is the answer if I want to keep my job.

I'm about to leave my office with my review in hand when Selena steps through the door, looking worried. "Good morning, ma'am," she says.

"Good morning. I'm sorry, but I'm in a hurry. Can we talk later?"

"This will only take a moment. I heard there was a code blue last night . . ."

"Yes. Simon Appleton. But we retrieved him without injury, and he's resting in the infirmary. Now if you'll excuse me . . ."

She raises a hand as if to block my way. "He's not resting, ma'am."

That stops me. "No?"

"He's passed."

"What?" My review slips from my fingers. "What do you mean 'he's passed'?"

"He's dead."

My pulse begins to race. "He was fine when we left him early this morning. And Ember checked in on him after that."

She nods. "Nurse Milo said he wasn't breathing when he found him. He tried CPR, but it was too late. It seems it was his heart."

"That's impossible." Or is it? I have a sudden thought. "Did you find anything?"

"You mean . . ."

"A Post-it Note?"

"No. Not this time."

I take several deep breaths. Relieved. I think. "All right. Follow protocol and inform the family."

"Should I tell them about the code blue?"

I consider. "They'll be dealing with more than enough. No need to concern them with their loved one's final hours."

She stares at me a moment and then nods and leaves the room.

Two

I'm seated on one of two orange pleather chairs that reside in Kai's outer sanctum. Within a few weeks, Bob's office suite has been transformed from old world comfort to industrial chic. I can't imagine our guests spending much time here. Of course, that might be the point.

"Mr. Gilchrist should be free any moment," Uma says in her clipped Jamaican accent. She gets to her feet and drifts to the water cooler. "Would you like a glass of natural spring water?"

"No, thank you." Can spring water be unnatural?

Kai's wafer-thin receptionist blends into the room like a three-karat diamond complements its platinum setting. She looks like a Hollywood ingénue with braided hair piled high on her head. Her exotic green eyes are lined in swoops of cobalt blue; her white linen dress hugs every minor curve. Why a girl with her looks would be working at Serenity Acres, I honestly don't understand.

I glance at my Fitbit and sigh. Kai's fifteen minutes late. "How much longer?" I ask.

"Not much." She takes a seat behind her desk.

Worries swim in my head like sharks feeding on chum. I can't seem to keep them at bay. I chew over Adam's phone call, Simon's sudden death, and the pink Post-it Notes.

Focus, I order, unfolding my review and scanning through the report. But the harsh words that pop off the pages only stoke my growing angst. I work my hands together like I'm kneading a lump of dough. *Calm down. Be strategic. Take control. You know Kai's critique will go for the jugular, that the animals have overrun the zoo. But there's a good chance Bob's prediction is right. That Kai will be gone within the year. So lock up your thoughts and envision yourself as sharp, suave, noncombative. The perfect member of any management team.*

I fiddle with my Fitbit and then focus my attention on the abstract paintings hanging on the walls. Swirls of red, orange, and purple, so bright they hurt my eyes. I'm guessing they're expensive originals, but as a trailer-trash kid from Fresno, how would I ever discern? I check the time.

"It's been twenty minutes," I say.

"Sorry," Uma responds, scrolling on her cell phone.

"Is he in his office?"

"Yes."

"Does he know I'm here?"

"Of course."

I'm guessing this is Kai's form of a power play. A way to underscore who is boss. Another five minutes go by, and my good intentions go to hell. I get to my feet. "I have work to do back at my office. Kai can buzz me when he's ready."

Uma frowns and sets down her cell phone. "I don't think you should leave. Mr. Gilchrist doesn't like to be kept waiting."

My shoulders snap back, and I face the girl. "*He* doesn't like to be kept waiting?"

"No."

"Do you have any idea who *I* am?"

She shrugs and picks up her notepad. "Ruth Mosby. You work in operations."

"I'm the *VP* of operations."

"Oh."

Oh? I want to slap her. Does she know nothing about respect? "Have him call me."

She shrugs. "If you leave, we'll have to reschedule." She points a perfectly manicured finger at the desk calendar. "I won't be able to fit you in until next Friday."

Next Friday? I can't spend another week stewing over this damn review. *Hell.* I return to my seat, seething. It's another ten minutes before the inner door opens and Kai exits with a replica of the Pillsbury Doughboy.

"Thank you, Presley," Kai says. "I'm looking forward to Thursday golf."

"Ditto that," Presley responds with a goofy smile.

Presley? That's the name of the new VP of ops at Peaceful Pastures. After news of Kai's promotion got out, I discreetly applied for that position and never heard back. How is it possible I didn't rate an interview and this Presley kid got the job?

The two men engage in a few minutes of banter before Presley exits the door. Then Kai signals I should follow him into his office. "Sorry if I kept you waiting," he says without the slightest inflection of remorse.

If? I've only just stepped into Kai's office, and already my good intentions have faded away. "What's a representative from Peaceful Pastures doing here?"

"You mean Presley? He's a good guy. We were having a nice chat."

"But they're our sworn enemies. They stole our trade secrets."

"Trade secrets?" Kai laughs. "Who do you think we are? Microsoft? We have no trade secrets. Employees, maybe. But that can go both ways. They have a few I'd like to poach."

That stops me. Was he interviewing Presley? Is he thinking of replacing me? Kai's cell phone dings, and he glances at it before tapping out a short message. "I'm in a bit of a hurry," he says, not looking up. "Why don't you take a seat, and we'll go over your review."

I sit on the edge of an uncomfortable couch upholstered in shiny purple velvet. It's fronted by a coffin-like glass table on which sits two copies of my 360 review. "Spring water?" Kai asks, pouring himself a glass from a crystal dispenser.

"No, thank you." Ding. His cell phone dings every few seconds, announcing incoming emails and texts. The noise is rude and distracting, each ding a tweak to my raw nerves.

Kai takes a seat across from me in one of two lime-green chairs. "You've read your 360?" he asks, scrolling through his cell. Ding. Ding.

"Yes." I think of the nasty contents and begin to sweat. "I *will* have that water," I say.

Kai sighs and sets down his phone. Ding. He retrieves a glass and pours the water, and after returning to his seat, slides it toward me. "You doing okay?" he asks. "Your face is turning red."

"Just thirsty." I take several gulps of water. Ding.

"We could reschedule for another day." Ding.

"Would you mind turning that off?"

"What?" Ding. Ding.

"Your phone."

He looks at me like I'm crazy. "Really?"

"Really."

"Okay." He fiddles with his cell phone and sets it down with a clank. "Better?"

"Yes."

"All right then." He crosses his legs and settles back in his chair. "So . . . you've read your 360."

"Weeks ago."

"Sorry about that. I've been incredibly busy. So tell me your thoughts."

My thoughts? I pick up a copy of the review, give it a shake, and for a moment I almost spew. But then I remember I need my job and work to temper my words. "I find the new review format to be awkward."

"Awkward?" He blinks a couple of times. "In what way?"

"It seems strange to have the staff judge me. I'm their boss, not their equal."

"Oh, that." Kai offers me a sympathetic look. "I realize some of the comments were harsh, but you shouldn't take them as a personal attack. Look at them as a chance for you to grow as a person. I found mine quite helpful."

I rattle my pages. "So you had a 360?"

"I did, yes."

"Why wasn't I asked to give feedback?"

He taps his feet against the coffee table in that irritating way he has. "The secret of a successful review is to avoid feedback from coworkers who might hold a . . . well, a . . ."

"A grudge?"

Kai rubs his stubby beard, looking unconcerned. "Yes, I suppose that's the right word."

I have to resist the sudden urge to claw the insolent look from his eyes. "You realize I've worked here for eighteen years."

He lifts a hand as if swatting away my comment. "I know your work history, Ruth. I've read through your file."

"Then you'll know I've always had exemplary reviews. I can't remember when I didn't receive a five out of five."

"And who prepared them?"

"Bob, of course."

His gaze fixes on a point above my head. "Exactly. One person's opinion, easily swayed. That's old school, don't you think?"

No. I don't think.

"The 360 is more comprehensive. It captures any unseen flaws. For example, it's apparent that many of your coworkers take issue with your management style."

"I don't have any *coworkers*," I say. "I have direct reports. And I have you."

"Not quite. We've made some changes . . ."

"So I've heard."

"Really? We haven't announced them yet."

"But some people know . . . like Finn?"

He nods. "Yes. Security now reports to the mother ship."

"And I no longer handle code blues?"

"We thought it best."

"We?"

He stops his tapping and leans forward. "You have to understand. Lost Horizons prefers a flattened reporting structure."

"Meaning?"

"Meaning they think we have too many layers of management."

"Are you telling me I'm being demoted?" I wipe the sweat from my brow.

"No. I'm telling you most of the department heads will soon report to me."

"So what will the VP of operations do?"

"We're working on that. But don't worry. I think you'll find the new structure liberating. It will allow you to focus more time on important work."

I have to grasp my hands together to still the shaking. "And what will that work be?"

"To be determined. You must understand, we are in a period of transition. You'll need to be flexible. I know that may be harder as you get . . ."

"Older?"

"More entrenched in your position."

I search his face. "Am I being fired?"

"Of course not."

"Laid off?"

He gives his chin another rub. "I can't promise you anything 100 percent. You're an at-will employee, but at the end of the day, I believe you will have a job. Maybe not the one you have now, but it should be something close." Glancing at his cell, he frowns. "On another subject, there are some changes coming to our leasing policies, and I'm going to need your full support. Corporate's lawyers have spent weeks reviewing our lease agreements and agree with me that we are within our rights to evict the destitutes."

I lean forward. "But eliminating forever care goes against our policy."

"Actually, it doesn't. It's clearly a benefit, not a requirement."

"But we've signed contracts that can't be broken."

He offers me a satisfied smile. "There's a loophole."

I think back on my conversations from the past. "But we've made promises . . . verbally . . ."

"Who made promises? I didn't. And if you or Bob did, you were wrong."

I open my mouth and close it. I then try another tack. "But it would be a publicity nightmare if word got out."

"Our marketing team is working on the appropriate spin."

"Spin?" I almost spit the word.

Kai gets to his feet and strolls to the window. He peers outside with a bored look. "Let me be clear. We are fully within our rights to execute the terms of our leases, and we plan to do so. Either you're on board with management's plans, or you're not. Your choice."

"And if I'm not?"

He turns toward me with a grim look on his face. "Then maybe this isn't the right place for you."

"Are you threatening me?"

"No. I'm asking you to be a team player. Either you support management's decisions, or you don't. It's your choice."

There's so much I want to say, but I bite my lip and nod.

"Does that mean you'll support us?"

"Yes."

"Good. You realize you will personally benefit from this change. It could add thousands to your bonus."

And even more to yours, you scum.

"The policy won't be instituted for several weeks. In the meantime, I'd like you to review the files and rank the destitutes by monies owed. That will determine who goes first."

I swallow my next words and get to my feet and stride to the door. "One more thing," Kai says. "We'll want to file legal proceedings against the deadbeats' estates in case there are any assets left in their trusts. You'll hear more about this in our next management meeting." He picks up his cell phone. "Now if you'll excuse me . . ." Ding. Ding. Ding.

Three

I arrive home just before sunset, so tired I'm ready to pass out. A hot wind is blowing; dried leaves skitter through the shadows. A barbeque smokes nearby. My stomach rumbles. Did I eat today? I don't think so. I try to recall what I might have left in the fridge.

I unlock the door and pause. There's a light in the kitchen, a murmuring in the house. Someone is inside. My feet root to the ground, and I grapple for my cell phone. I'm about to call 911 when Adam steps into the living room with a longneck beer in hand.

"Hey, Mom," he says in a nonchalant way, like it hasn't been a year since we've spoken.

"You scared me," I respond, pulse racing. Adam is dressed in jeans and a ratty T-shirt. He's thinner than I last saw him, and paler. His sandy hair skims his shoulders. But no matter, he's still my handsome boy with the mischievous glint in his eyes.

"Sorry," he says. "Didn't mean to. Got the key from the planter box." He sets down his beer and flicks on the light and gives me an awkward hug. I hold him tight for a moment, feeling happy. Then I catch a whiff of pot and pull away.

"What's wrong?" I ask, not really wanting to know.

"Nothing's wrong. You didn't get my voice mail?"

I glance at my phone. "It's been a crazy day. I never checked."

"Same old mom. Busy, busy." He grabs his beer and sprawls across the old leather chair he always claimed for his own. "It's no big deal. I'm only here for a few days."

"Where's Nikki?"

"She couldn't get off work." He flicks on the TV.

"Turn that thing off and talk to me. Please."

"About what?"

"Something. Anything."

He flicks off the TV. "There. Now, what's up?"

"Have you . . ." I want to ask if he's heard from Alice, but my words are cut short by a sight that hurts my eyes. "Tell me those aren't tattoos."

"You don't like them?" He curls his right hand into a fist so that the four crosses stand out.

"Oh, Adam! How could you?"

"What? Everyone has them. It's no big a deal."

I can't keep my voice from rising. "Everyone *doesn't* tattoo their hands. In HR, that's called a *job stopper*. You'll never be hired for any decent position."

He takes a slug of beer. "You mean, I'll never work in an office job? That's a bonus, not a problem. In fact, I'll tattoo my other hand if I can avoid that shitty world."

"But, sweetheart . . ." My words escape me, so I leave it at that. But now I'm worried. Do his eyes have the glassy look they get when he's using? Are his hands shaking the slightest bit? Yes, I think they are. Dear God, not this again. "How's work?" I ask, trying to change the subject and get information at the same time.

"Work sucks." His eyes focus on the blank TV screen. "And I hate living in Palmdale."

"Why's that?"

"To start with, it's boring as hell."

My worries amp up another notch. "But you still have your job?"

"Why wouldn't I?" he snaps. Only five minutes in and exasperation already coats his voice. He may be thirty-one, but it's high school Adam who's come home.

"No reason. Just asking. I haven't seen you in a long time."

He mumbles something I'm not sure I want to hear. "You go ahead and watch your TV," I say. "I'll change and make us dinner. Is there anything special you'd like?"

"No, thanks. Not hungry."

"You sure?"

"Yep. I'm going to hang out with some friends a little later. Probably get a bite."

"Which friends?"

"You don't know them."

I hope not. Adam's high school friends are trouble. They're from the wealthy Montecito crowd. I was proud of that at the beginning. Didn't understand how excess money often went hand in hand with drugs. Or that grandiose mansions were sometimes parentless, staffed with servants who looked the other way. Adam's best friend died from an overdose. Another buddy is serving ten years. At least two are in and out of rehab. I don't know about the rest.

I never had that problem with Alice. She didn't run with the popular crowd. She had only a handful of friends, all involved in theater or dance. I had urged her to expand her network like her brother. But, of course, even then she knew better than me.

"Where are you meeting?" I ask.

"Ted's."

"Is that a good idea?"

Adam squeezes his eyes shut in that way he has and shakes his handsome head. "Come on, Mom. Don't freak. I'll only have a couple of drinks, and I'll walk home or Uber." When I don't say anything, his voice grows more exasperated. "I'm here for a break, okay? I don't need any pressure." He snaps on the TV, and his eyes glaze over in two seconds flat.

"Adam, please . . ."

"What do you want to know?" he asks, not taking his eyes off the screen. "My job sucks, and so does my life. That good enough for you? Can I watch for a while?"

A dagger twists in my heart, bringing a stab of sadness and pain. It's been stuck there for as long as I can remember, and I've done my best to ignore the thing. My throat tightens; my knees grow weak. I want to crawl in my bed and cry. Instead, I finger my Fitbit, freeze-dry my feelings, and hurry out of the room. After changing into shorts and a T-shirt, I make my way to the kitchen.

There's a pile of dishes in the sink and the scent of burned pasta in the air. An empty six-pack in the recycling, another six-pack in the fridge. I flash back to my unwanted childhood memories—the alcohol, the arguing, the mess. I step onto the back porch, grip the rail, and work to push the panic away.

It's after eight and dark out except for the rising of a full moon. I hear Zach out on his porch again, strumming a mournful tune. I check my Fitbit. I'm short six thousand steps, a problem I can actually solve. I'll head for downtown and loop up toward the mission. The thought brings me a sense of calm.

"What're you doing, Mom?" Adam steps out onto the porch and pops open another beer.

"I'm going for a walk," I say, pushing past him.

"Now? It's dark out."

"So?" I lace up my running shoes and grab a bottle of water.

"It's dangerous to go walking alone at night."

"This is Santa Barbara, not Palmdale."

"So you think there's no crime?"

"Nothing has happened to me yet."

He stares at me like I'm crazy and then whips his wallet from his pocket. He pulls out a credit card and hands it to me.

"What's that for?"

"To protect yourself."

"But how . . . ?" I turn it over.

"Careful. It's a knife."

I take a closer look at the card. He's right. This is no credit card. But it isn't a knife either. "I don't get it."

"It's a credit card knife. I'll show you how it works." He pulls a second faux credit card from his wallet and makes a few quick moves and produces a knife. He holds it up.

"Could that kill someone?"

"Probably."

"It can't possibly be legal."

"Sure is. They sell them online for five bucks a pop."

"For what purpose?"

"For protection, Mom."

"Protection from what?"

He rolls his eyes. "Just do me a favor and carry it when you go walking, especially if you're out at night."

I finger the cold metal. "I wouldn't know how to use it. I'd probably hurt myself."

"Practice a couple of times." He returns his knife to its credit card state and hands it to me. I stare at him, wondering what would make him carry such a thing. Then I make the folds like he indicates, and in a few seconds, I have a knife.

"Try it again," he insists.

I break down the weapon into a card and then fold it back into a knife. The process reminds me of the origami I used to enjoy as a kid.

"Perfect," he says with a satisfied smile. "You've mastered the art of self-defense."

"If I could get up the nerve to use it." I shove the knife in my pocket. "Anyway, I'm heading out. I should be back in an hour."

"All right. I'll probably be gone by the time you get home. No need to wait up."

"I won't." I step out onto the porch.

"Mom?"

"Yes?" I turn back to see Adam's face loaded with concern. His arms are folded, his eyes fixed on his feet.

"I wanted to say I'm sorry."

For some reason I feel embarrassed. Did I manipulate those words from my son? "No problem. I shouldn't have peppered you with so many questions right when you got home."

"Not about that . . . I mean, that too, but . . ." His sad eyes fix on mine. "I'm sorry about the wedding. How it all turned out." His voice breaks. "You see, Nikki . . . well, we visited Dad a couple of times, and she and Gigi hit it off. And she had gotten this stupid idea in her head that you didn't like her . . ."

My face grows warm. The idea wasn't so stupid.

"Anyway, somewhere along the line, she and Gigi got to be Facebook friends. I didn't even know she'd asked Dad to walk her down the aisle, and when I found out, well, I know now I should've stood up to her. I was an idiot."

My heart dagger twists a couple of times. It's hard for me to say the next words. "Of course you should've invited your father and his . . . his wife. I was the one that behaved badly. That was immature of me."

His face brightens. "So you're not mad at me anymore?"

"I was never mad at you, just hurt. But that was wrong. I hope you can forgive me."

"Of course I can, Mom. I love you. You know that. And I really appreciate everything you've done for me." He opens his arms and gives me an awkward hug. My heart melts. The dagger recedes.

He tilts his head. "That Zach playing?"

"It is."

He releases me with a smile. "Cool. I'll go say hi."

I stiffen, my good feelings draining. "Why would you do that?"

"He said he'd give me guitar lessons when I got back."

"He knew you were coming home?"

"Of course he did."

Of course? I want to ask more questions, but Adam hurries down the steps. The side gate squeals open, and moments later, Zach's guitar pauses, and a burst of laughter spills from his yard.

Four

The next morning I find Zach out on the sidewalk fiddling with his plastic fence. He's dressed in black shorts and a rumpled T-shirt, his graying hair stuck up every which way. I paste a smile on my face and try to sound lighthearted. "I thought you had to upgrade your fence."

"Yeah, well, I will when I have the money. What's the city going to do? Jail me?"

"True." I watch him for a few minutes. I can't help noticing that his looks have improved. His skin glows tan, and he's lost a few pounds. The job must be good for him. "Can I speak with you for a moment?"

Zach straightens. "Sure, I'll come over."

"Better if I come to your house. Adam's sleeping, and I don't want to wake him." And I wouldn't want him to overhear what I have to say.

Zach glances at his front door. "All right. But it's a little messy inside."

"That's okay." I've been in Zach's backyard plenty of times, but it's been years since I've stepped into his house, so I'm shocked by what I see. Boxes are stacked high against the walls. Old magazines spill across the coffee table. The TV is one of those boxy kinds with a jagged crack along its side. I brush a cobweb from my face and wince at the musty smell. Messy is an understatement. The place is a hoarder's dump.

Zach turns and shrugs. "Sorry. I'm working on cleaning it up."

"I can give you the name of a good housekeeper."

"Sure." He looks more than a little embarrassed. "Let's talk in the kitchen. It's cleaner in there." I follow him past Hunter's old room, and a chill runs up my spine.

The kitchen is not any less messy, but at least there's an almost cleared table and two chairs. I carefully take a seat and peer through the window coated in years of grease and grime.

Zach eyes me sheepishly. "Can I get you anything? Coffee? Water? I might even have tea." He throws open a cupboard door, and a box of macaroni tumbles out and splats onto the floor.

"No, thanks. I'm good."

He leans over with a groan and picks it up. "You sure?"

I glance at the unwashed dishes. "I'm sure."

Zach mutters to himself before settling in his chair and giving his knee a good rub. "Okay then. What's up?"

I take a deep breath and start in. "Simon Appleton is dead."

His eyes grow wide. "Simon? The old man? You're kidding me. How? When?"

I fill him in on what Selena told me, and he can't stop shaking his head.

"Poor guy," he says. "This is crazy."

"I know."

He kneads his hands together. "But no Post-it Note?"

"None found." A silverfish races across the floor. I grimace and lift my feet.

"So you think his dying is just a coincidence?"

I nod. "He wasn't in the best of health, and his late-night escapade couldn't have been good for his heart." I glance up at a stream of ants scurrying along the ceiling. Zach's gaze follows mine, and he stumbles to his feet. "*Damn!* I thought I got rid of those things. They've been invading my house all summer." He grabs a can of insecticide from beneath the sink and attacks the ants with the spray.

"I'll be outside." Holding my breath, I step out onto the narrow back porch and wait for Zach to finish his battle. The sky is gray with a low morning fog; moisture drips from the rafters. I take a seat on a rickety bench sheltered by the eaves and pick at a piece of peeling paint. Zach's yard looks as shabby as mine, worse when you consider the piles of rusty tools scattered throughout the weeds. A dove coos mournfully from the bushes, and a darkness shrouds my heart. I have a sudden urge to move elsewhere. Forget my job and start over. Buy a cottage high in the mountains where the air is fresh and clean.

"There," Zach says, slamming the door behind him. "That should do it." He settles next to me, wincing.

"You've got to get that looked at," I say. His knee is swollen and red.

"I will once my health insurance kicks in."

"But that's weeks away."

"I don't have much choice, do I? Anyway, I'll be fine. Weird about Appleton, though."

"Really weird."

"I mean, the guy predicted his own death."

"Maybe his heart was already giving out."

"Maybe." Zach eyes me thoughtfully. "Anyway, I've been thinking on what you told me about the Post-it Notes. You want me to involve the police? I could call in a few favors. I still have a detective friend that works there."

I shake my head. "If you do, I'll have to tell them I've known about the notes for months. That'll end my job, or maybe something worse."

"You don't think Kai would understand?"

"Kai?" I choke down a laugh. "All he would understand is that he's found his reason to fire me."

"Is it possible you're exaggerating?"

"I'm not. He'd get rid of his mother if it meant a bigger bonus. He's even making plans to kick out the destitutes."

"The guests that've run out of money?"

"Yep."

"Why would he do that?"

"I believe it's to increase his bonus. He gets a percentage of any profits over and above the projected net."

Zach nods. "Interesting . . ."

"What do you mean?"

"I happen to know he needs the money."

"How so?"

"The kid's broke. Beyond broke. Drowning in debt."

"How would you know?"

"Night I moved him into his new digs. Didn't mean to snoop, but some papers fell out of a file. Student loans gone to collection. Overextended credit cards. That kind of thing."

"But he just bought a new car."

Zach shrugs. "Maybe someone cosigned."

"Maybe." I try to pin the new information on my perception of Kai. It makes a lot of sense. "So what you're telling me is that I need to be even more careful."

"Why's that?"

"If he gets rid of me, he can add another hundred plus to the bottom line."

Zach frowns. "I think you're stretching."

"I doubt it. And I don't want to give him cause. So let's keep the Post-it Notes quiet for now. Have you nose around instead."

"All right." He points to the far corner of his disaster of a garden. "Check it out. Quail."

A family of quail is rummaging near his ramshackle woodshed. Mom. Dad. Three babies. Their plumes swaying back and forth. I read once that they fall prey to every kind of predator and rarely live more than a year. It's sad to ponder their short lives, but for a moment I do just that. Then I shake off the gloom and mentally tick off a list of my Saturday chores. Groceries, dry cleaning, laundry. Maybe a pedicure after that.

"By the way," Zach says, interrupting my thoughts. "Adam and I had a good talk last night."

"You did?" I turn to him and search his face. "What about?"

"Life."

"His or yours?"

"His."

"And . . ."

"He's got a lot of shit going down."

"I figured."

"He wanted me to tell you about it."

"He can't do that himself?"

"Seems he's a little embarrassed."

"So, what's going on?"

"To start with, his marriage has broken up."

"What?" I nearly fall off the bench. "You mean it's over?"

"Sounds like it."

I finger my Fitbit. "But they've barely been married a year."

"Yeah. Well. Things haven't gone so well."

"I knew it. I never trusted Nikki. My God, how much time has she spent in rehab?"

"About as much time as your son."

I let that remark slide and picture Adam's thin body, his ragged hair, his pallid face. My heart speeds up when I ask the next question. I'm hoping against hope. "Is Adam using again?"

Zach takes a moment to answer. "I don't think so. He says that's part of the problem. He isn't using, but she is. She fell off the wagon a few months ago, and they've been fighting ever since."

My thoughts whirl back and forth. "How about his job?"

"He got fired last week."

"Why?"

"Missed a few days of work."

"Was he sick?"

"No."

"So he *is* using."

"Actually not. He missed because he was in jail."

"Jail?" The word hits me like a blow to the head.

"Yeah. He and Nikki had a fight. Must've been a bad one. The neighbors called the police."

"Dear God. Did he hit her?"

"He claims she tripped, but she's saying otherwise. He's being charged with felony battery."

"Felony?" I picture future job applications and the accompanying background checks. A felony would destroy his life. "That can't happen," I say.

"He can try to plead it down. But he's going to need a lawyer. A good one."

"How much will that cost?"

"Five thousand for a retainer. Another five for court."

I picture my bloated credit cards and my meager emergency savings. "Does he have the money?" I ask, knowing the answer before I speak.

"Course not."

"Maybe his dad can help."

"He already asked. Doug said no."

I feel a sudden rush of anger. "So he feels comfortable telling Doug about his problems, but he won't say a word to me?"

"That's not the point."

"What *is* the point?"

"He's going to need your help."

"You mean he's going to need my money."

"With his checkered background, if he doesn't fight this thing, the felony conviction could stick. He could even spend time in jail."

The quail family has reappeared next to a wild tomato bush. They're pecking at the rotten red fruit hanging from the vine. "You don't understand, Zach. Adam's rehab trips were more expensive than Alice's college education. Financially, I'm a mess. I don't have any more to give him."

"I guess I could lend him the money."

"Do you have any to lend?"

"Only my emergency savings. But I'd have to get it back."

"How can Adam pay you back if he doesn't have a job?"

Zach gives his knee a good rub. "There's an opening in the kitchen at Serenity Acres. What if you helped him get hired?"

"Me?"

"Yeah."

"Are you crazy?"

"Don't think so."

I fix my gaze on the quail family. "Well, I don't think it's a good idea."

"Because?"

"Because . . ." I try to add structure to my jumbled thoughts. "Because it's never a good idea for family members to work at the same business."

"Who says?"

"Everyone says."

"Everyone? Come on Ruth. Give your kid a break. You won't be working in the same building. You'll never see him, let alone speak to him. We owe it to him. You know that."

Zach's words make me feel small and mean. "What about the background check?" I ask. "I doubt he'll clear it."

"He hasn't been convicted yet."

"And his new tattoos? You know they're against the rules."

136

"Bunch of the kitchen staff have them. Who gives a shit? Not like any guest ever sets foot back there."

I take a deep breath and exhale. "Okay. I don't like the idea, but I guess it's better than Adam sitting around."

"Way better." Zach grins, his blue eyes sparkling. "I told Adam you'd find a way to help him."

"He didn't think I would?"

"He doesn't know you like I do."

I nod, pleased at his words but filled with unease. I've always made a point to keep my work and home life separate. It concerns me to change that now.

Five

I have enough problems in my life without adding Carlyn to the mix. But she's been calling and texting for months now, and I've run through every viable excuse. So I left work shortly before ten and drove to the nearby Koffee Klatch, where I ordered a cup of black coffee and took a seat at a corner table. Now I fiddle with my Fitbit and wait.

The Klatch is one of those dreary places that was trendy in the nineties but has since grown old and tired. The glass showcase is covered in fingerprints, the linoleum floor yellowed and cracked. The gray walls could use a fresh coat of paint; the bay windows need a good wash. Even the customers seem down on their luck—no wannabe artists milling about. Just a couple of unkempt men slouched behind their computers in the shadowy back of the room. I chose this place on purpose. I doubt I'll see anyone I know. I take a sip of coffee and grimace. It's bitter, like it's been brewing for hours. I could sweeten my drink with cream and sugar, but the calories would add more steps to the end of my day.

I glance at my cell phone and wonder. It's not like Carlyn to be late. Or at least it's not like the old Carlyn. What do I know about the new one? The one who's been accused of manslaughter and has spent weeks if not months in jail?

I met Carlyn in my early twenties at a barbeque at Zach and Tina's. Zach was friends with her older brother; Carlyn and Zach had dated a few times. We discovered a joint fondness for jogging, so we agreed to train for a Wine Country 10K. That training led to a friendship, and we remained close throughout the years.

Model thin and movie-star pretty, Carlyn met and married Buddy, a wealthy trust funder who dabbled in expensive wine and cars. He built them a mansion along the fashionable banks of Montecito's Cold Spring Creek, and after several rounds of IVF, Carlyn gave birth to twins. Their daughters grew up to be drop-dead gorgeous and local volleyball champs. No drugs for either of those girls. No penchant for teenage depression. They breezed through their high school years and snagged sports scholarships to Stanford.

I flick a crumb from the table and gaze at an elderly woman who wanders in for a cup of tea. She's wearing a ragged yellow dress with an unraveled hem that dips below her bony knees. The way she pries her change from her wallet makes me think of our destitute guests. I've prepared Kai's ranking as ordered, but I have yet to forward it on. One of the things stopping me is the name that tops the list. As the oldest of our residents, how will Eleanor Kingsley find a new home?

I get angry every time I think of Kai's directive. He may have found an "out" in the contract, but it's against everything we stand for. When our guests shelled out deposits topping a million dollars, they were assured of their access to forever care, their lifetime of housing and support even if their finances took a turn. That's why we're so damn picky at the time of entry, why we demand healthy guests with even healthier financials. This is a common practice in an industry that bitterly competes for the wealthiest of patrons. The top 10 percent of 1 percenters can go anywhere they choose.

Lost Horizons advertises their own form of forever care. So how they can support Kai and his pathetic decision, I honestly don't know. What I *do* know is we promised to care for each and every one of our guests until they take their last breath. Not "we." "I." *I* personally promised everyone I signed up. I looked them straight in the eye. When guests find out we've reneged on that key benefit, they'll never trust management again, let alone trust me. My reputation will be in tatters; my career will end in shambles. *Dear God.* I take a sip of coffee and work to calm my nerves.

A disheveled woman enters the Klatch dressed in black stretch pants and an oversized sweatshirt. I look away and then do a double take. Carlyn? The woman lifts her hand and waves, and I force a smile and wave back. She makes her purchase and heads for my table with coffee and doughnut in hand. I can't believe how much older she looks. Has it only been a year?

"Hi there." I get to my feet and move in for a hug, but Carlyn takes a step back. I return to my seat, smile frozen. "How are you?" I ask, trying my best to mask how awkward I feel.

Carlyn settles into her seat with a tilt of her head and sarcasm narrowing her eyes. "How do you think?" Her blonde hair has gone gray and limp. There are patches of scalp peeking through. Her once sparkling eyes are sunk in shadows, her face bloated with newfound weight.

"I know it's been a tough year," I try.

"Tough eighteen months," she responds, her gaze raking my face.

"Of course. And I'm sorry I haven't reached out." I take a sip of my now tepid coffee and begin to chatter away. "I've been incredibly busy. Work has been crazy. And of course Adam got married last June." My voice fades. I've hit my first snag. Carlyn is Adam's godmother. "The wedding was quite small," I try, "held on a beach in San Diego. They invited only a few of their closest friends and family." I don't mention I didn't attend.

"Text me their address, and I'll send a card." Carlyn takes a bite from her cream-filled doughnut, and sugar dust coats her chin. "How about Alice? She doing well?"

"Fantastic." My tone registers false in my ears. "She's traveling with a band on the East Coast. Atlas Shrugged. They're hugely popular. They might even win a Grammy." Why I said that, I have no idea. It's not like me to stretch the truth. "How's Buddy?" I ask, ready to change the subject.

She tilts her head and eyes me curiously. "You must know he left me when the shit hit the fan."

"Why, no . . ."

"Surprising. It's all the chatter in Montecito. In fact, he's moved in with Eileen Van Meter."

"Arthur Van Meter's widow?"

"Yep. The former wife of the evil conman himself. Can you imagine their pillow talk? 'My spouse was the worst criminal ever. No, mine was.' They're the perfect pair. In fact, the twins traveled with them to Europe on their summer break. Just one big happy family."

I nod. Things are worse than I thought. "And where are you living?"

"In a friend's rental apartment on the lower east side. Dear woman took pity on me. Otherwise, I'd be homeless."

"I'm so sorry. I didn't know."

"It is what it is." A couple of strands of gray hair float to the table, and Carlyn pats her head. "I've been losing it," she says.

"Losing what?"

"My hair. My doctor says it'll grow back when my life gets back to normal. But I don't see that happening anytime soon." She flicks the strands from the table. "And to think I used to worry about covering my roots. What I wouldn't give for a full head of hair."

"I'll bet your doctor's right," I offer. "I bet it grows back sooner than you think."

"Glad you've turned into an optimist. Me? I've gone the other way." Carlyn sniffs. "It's been hard, you know."

"I can imagine."

"Can you?"

"But things have a way of working out."

"Do they?"

What can I say that doesn't sound false, because false is how I feel. "I'm sorry I haven't reached out," I try. "It's not just the kids. There's been a lot going on at work." I drop my voice, trolling for sympathy. "I have a new boss, and he's young and angling to get rid of me and . . ."

Carlyn lifts a hand and waves it as if she is waving away my words. "Don't worry. You're not the only one who's shunned me."

"I haven't shunned you." I start fiddling with my Fitbit like I'm trying to get the thing to work.

"No?" She picks up a spoon and stirs her coffee. "I've been dumped by all my friends. My coworkers. My husband. My daughters." She looks up. "You do know Buddy and the girls were out of town when it happened."

"On a ski trip, right?"

"Right. I guess that part was all over the news. The part that wasn't was that Buddy ordered Yolanda to clean the house while he was away."

"He did?"

"He'll never admit it, but yes. Ash from the Thomas Fire had leaked into the house and was wreaking havoc on his sinuses. He told her he wanted it cleaned up, ASAP. So in a way, he's partly responsible for her death, but he refuses to take any share of the blame. Anyway, that's a story for another day. Back to the subject at hand. Truth is, I've been dumped by almost everyone I know."

"I didn't . . ."

"It's not that I blame you." She sets down her spoon and examines her ragged nails. "If the tables were turned, I'd probably do the same. I mean, who stays friends with a person accused of manslaughter, especially when there's an innocent woman involved?"

I shift uncomfortably in my seat, and she fixes her gaze on mine. "I know what you're thinking. Yolanda wasn't a woman. She was a child.

All of fifteen. But I swear I thought she was twenty, and she had the papers to prove it. How was I to know her documents were forged?"

I open my mouth to answer, but there's nothing I can say. It's true. We all make mistakes. But the night before the mudslide, Carlyn evacuated with her gal pals to the safety of the Fairmont, leaving her housekeeper behind. It's as if she abandoned the girl on a sinking ship. A terrible thought, but true.

"No one could've predicted the mudslide," she says.

But in fact, they had. With the hillsides newly blackened by fire, an approaching storm triggered mandatory evacuations. The local Office of Emergency Management warned that the forecasted heavy rainfall could inundate the area creeks. And unfortunately, they were right. In the early-morning hours of January 9, a catastrophic mudslide swept down from the mountains, devouring everything in its path. Two dozen people died in the slide, including Yolanda Hernandez.

Carlyn shakes her head with a look of disbelief. "I had hoped . . . had believed . . . Yolanda had escaped."

But she hadn't. And when Yolanda's father came looking for his daughter, Carlyn had lied and said she'd dropped the girl at a Red Cross shelter the night before the slide. She kept the lie going after repeated questioning, first by emergency personnel and then by the police. Weeks later, a disaster volunteer found Yolanda's torso wedged under a pile of boulders at the bottom of the creek. Carlyn was arrested and charged with perjury and manslaughter. Her story made the national headlines for weeks. "Selfish Montecito Housewife Implicated in Teenager's Tragic Death."

"Anyway . . ." Carlyn takes a deep breath. "I'm here at my lawyer's request. I need a few character witnesses. People who can vouch for my integrity at the upcoming trial. And you've known me longer than most."

I fix my gaze on a dusty light fixture, pondering how best to answer. The trial is sure to be in the news, and Kai would learn of my involvement. The bad publicity could seal my fate, another chance to lose my job. "But what would I say?" I ask.

Carlyn's cheeks turn pink, and her eyes begin to water. "Oh, Ruth. Couldn't you tell the truth? That I'm a good person. That you've known me for decades and I've never once done anything wrong?"

"I guess . . . but . . ."

"But what? One moment of thoughtless stupidity is meant to destroy my entire life?"

"Well . . ."

"I was scared, Ruth. Horribly scared. Have you ever felt that way?"

"Of course."

"Then you'll help me?"

"I'll . . . I'll think about it."

Carlyn wipes her eyes with the back of her hand. "I swear, Ruth. I swear to God I had no idea the house would give. And if I didn't admit the truth at first, what did I truly do wrong? My speaking up wouldn't have changed the outcome. I didn't kill Yolanda. I did something stupid. Something selfish. Something I'll always regret. But who goes through life without making mistakes? Huh? Tell me? I mean, most people get to hide their secrets, while mine got spread around the world." She reaches out and takes my hand. Her fingers are as cold as ice. "So will you help me . . . please?"

My cell phone chimes, and I glance at it, relieved. "I'm sorry," I say, withdrawing my hand. "I have to leave. There's a problem at work."

Carlyn's eyes narrow. "Of course there is. You're *such* a busy woman."

"It's just . . ."

She tugs a business card from her wallet and slaps it on the table. "Leo Silverstein is an old friend and a damn good lawyer. He's doing his best to help me but needs some community support. Just talk to him, please? Will you do that? Will you please give him a call?"

I pick up the card, avoiding her eyes. "If I can find the time . . ."

"The time?" Carlyn's shoulders droop. "I thought we were friends."

"We are friends."

"But you're not going to call him, are you?"

"I said I'll think about it."

"Of all people . . ."

"I really have to go."

Carlyn leans forward, hands gripping the table. Her face has changed. Hardened. It's like I'm speaking to someone else. "We're a lot alike, you know." Her breath smells sour. I lean back.

"What do you mean?"

"I mean we both have our secrets. Only yours hasn't been exposed to the world."

"I don't know what you're talking about."

"Sure you do. And if your secret comes to light, you may not go to jail, but you sure as hell will lose what's left of your friends and family."

I get to my feet. "I have to go."

"We're more alike than you care to admit. Our sin is not about what we said but what we didn't say."

I take a few steps back.

"Zach told me," Carlyn calls out in a loud voice. "What the two of you did. How you kept it a secret. My God, when I think of poor Adam and the guilt resting on his shoulders. No wonder he's had issues. Who wouldn't?" She leans back, arms folded. "You think you know someone, and then they disappoint."

The world around me slows. "You're talking nonsense."

"Am I?"

"Zach must've been drunk."

She shakes her head, and several strands of hair drift into her lap. "He wasn't drunk. He was perfectly sober. In fact, I've met with him several times. He's the only one from our old group to reach out. I'm very thankful for that."

"I don't understand . . ."

"Then let me help. He told me your secret over lunch. Said he understood what I was going through. How split-second decisions can change a life. And how keeping them secret can make things worse. Then he shared *your* secret with me."

I turn and rush out of the café, my heart slamming against my chest.

Six

After pulling into a shady spot in the staff parking lot, I fumble for my cell phone and leave a voice mail. "Call me, Zach. *Now!*" Opening my car windows, I fume as I wait. *How could he? Why would he?* I hit redial.

"I swear to God, Zach . . ." I look up to see Ember rushing past my car, a look of horror on her face. A wild-eyed hippie follows, dressed in a tank top and shorts. "*Wait!*" he cries. "I just want to talk." The duo disappears into the pool pavilion, and I hang up on Zach and call in a code orange. Then I rush to the enclosure, where protocol dictates I wait for backup. But when I hear raised voices, I head inside to find Ember standing frozen on the empty pool deck, the intruder down on his knees. "*Please listen,*" he cries, his hands folded as if in prayer.

I weave between the wrought iron furniture surrounding the tranquil turquoise pool. "What's going on here?" I call. "Ember, are you all right?"

The man gets to his feet and turns to me, muscles bulging. "This is a private conversation. Get out." I'd be frightened if it weren't for the tears streaming down his face.

"Ember?" I call. "Do you know this man?"

She nods and wipes her eyes with the back of her hand. "His name is Bodie. I don't want him here."

I do my best to sound tough. "This is private property, Bodie. I don't know how you got in, but you're trespassing."

"I'm not leaving without my Joy."

Joy? "Security is on their way. Leave now, or they'll have you arrested."

The man fists his hands like a boxer, his body throbbing with a threat. "I just want to talk."

I glance at Ember, and she shakes her head. "She doesn't want to speak with you," I say.

"It's none of your business."

"Actually, it is my business. I'm in charge here. I'm Ember's boss."

"Get out!"

"That's it." I lift my cell phone. "Security is on their way, and if you don't leave the premises immediately, I will call the police."

Bodie turns to Ember. "Come with me," he begs. "Please. Just this once. I can't stand it anymore. We have to talk."

Ember is trembling so hard her voice vibrates. "I can't, Bodie. I won't. You know you're not allowed near me."

Bodie grasps at his hair like a crazy man. "I'm clean now; I promise. And I'm so, so sorry." His voice breaks into sobs. "I can't live like this. You've got to forgive me."

"All right. I forgive you. Now leave."

"That's not good enough."

"It's all I have."

I feel like I'm in the midst of some tragic Shakespearean play. "Please do what Ember asks," I say, wanting this incident to end. "Leave before someone gets hurt."

"Her name's not Ember," Bodie cries. "It's Joy." He leaps and grabs Ember, and her body goes limp as if she has melted into his arms.

"Let go of her," I order.

"Get out of my way."

"What going on here?" a man calls from behind. I turn to see Ted Barnet, the new security guard who arrived with Finn. He's short and has the squared-off look of a bulldog that has too many teeth in his mouth. He's holding a gun. *A gun?* Since when do we have guns on campus?

"We have an intruder," I say. "But don't hurt him."

"I won't hurt the asshole unless he doesn't do what I say."

Bodie takes a few steps forward, Ember whimpering in his arms. "I'm not going to hurt her. We just need to talk."

"Stop or I'll shoot."

Bodie freezes.

"There won't be any shooting," I say.

"Not if this asshole listens to me."

Bodie holds Ember tight. "I have a right to speak to my wife."

Wife?

Barnet waves his gun back and forth and fixes his gaze on me. "What is this?" he asks in a shrill voice. "Some kind of lover's quarrel? He do this before? He the one that messed up her face?"

"I don't know." I fix my eyes on Bodie. "If you care for Ember, er . . . Joy, then let her go. If you do, we'll let you leave quietly. If you don't, you'll be arrested."

"Or shot," Barnet mutters.

Bodie shakes his head. "I'm not going to leave her."

"Then you'll be charged with kidnapping. Is that what you want?"

"Please," Ember says, beginning to struggle. "Please, Bodie. Let me go."

Bodie seems to consider her request, his eyes glistening with tears. "All right." He carefully sets Ember on a lounge chair. "But you'll talk to me now, won't you? You'll return my calls?"

"No, Bodie," she says in a soft voice. "I want you to leave me alone."

"Come on," Barnet says, waving his gun at Bodie. "Get your ass moving, or I swear I'll shoot."

"Here. Drink this. A little water will help." Ember and I have made our way to the memorial garden, where the shade makes the air feel a little cooler. Ember slumps onto the cement bench, looking faded and drained. She reaches for the unopened water bottle I store in my car for emergencies. After taking several sips, she sets it down with a painful smile.

"I'm sorry about all that," she says in a tiny voice. "I don't know what got into Bodie. I promise it won't happen again."

I ease down next to her, and we sit quietly for several moments. Part of me wants to give her a hug, but I am her supervisor, after all. So I settle for patting her hand. She doesn't react in any way.

"I'm afraid I need to ask you a few questions," I say after a while. "Since the confrontation involved security, there's no way to get around a formal report."

"I know," she replies in a resigned tone.

"We can wait until later if you prefer."

"No. I'd rather get it over with."

I hesitate, wondering where to start. "Is your real name Joy?" I ask.

"It is . . . I mean, it was. I changed it to Ember after . . ." She takes a deep breath. "I changed it legally so I'd never forget. And because Joy wasn't who I was anymore."

"And Bodie's your husband?"

"He *was* my husband. We're separated. Divorced."

"Oh . . . I'm sorry. I mean, if you are."

She shrugs. "There wasn't a choice."

"And is he . . . I mean, is this behavior normal? Is he violent?"

She shakes her head. "No. At least I don't think so." From where I'm seated I can see only the healthy side of her face, and once again, I'm stunned by her beauty, even when she's in obvious pain. "I haven't seen him in over three years," she continues. "Not since . . ."

"Not since . . . ?" I repeat softly.

"Not since the trial."

"So he's a criminal?"

"Not a criminal. I mean, he did spend a year in prison for manslaughter. And I'm sure he's on probation now. That's why I know he can't see me. Why he can't be here."

"Do you mind my asking what he did?"

"No. But I ask you to keep this confidential. I don't want anyone else to know."

I think of my report. "I'll do my best."

"Thank you." She begins to tell her story, and I enter the saddest of pasts.

Seven

"Bodie and I were married young," she begins. "We were only eigh-teen, but we'd grown up together in a commune. Not a religious cult, although yoga and meditation played a part of our day. Our commune was founded by a group of highly educated professionals that included my parents. They had a dream funded by enough money from a stock syndication to build a violence-free, self-contained community on two hundred acres of rolling farmland outside of Humboldt."

She smiles like the memories are good, and her voice begins to relax. "It wasn't a bad way to grow up. There were no TVs or cell phones or computers, but we did have plenty of books. Our electricity came from wind and solar, our water from a natural spring. Our bathroom was an outhouse, and we bathed in a nearby creek. We were vegetarians but not vegans. We raised cows, chickens, and goats. None of them was ever slaughtered; it was against the antiviolence code. We grew our own fruit and vegetables, grapes for wine, and marijuana for smokes. There was no formal education—if a child took an interest in a subject, one of the adults might help them along. Otherwise, we were left on our own to explore nature. The commune was all about developing a new way to coexist."

"So, who taught you to read?"

She shrugs. "I don't remember. It seems like I always could. I had a passion for books, mostly classics: Wharton, Dreiser, Lawrence. That's all the library held. That and a mountain of do-it-yourself manuals."

I think about the drawbacks of that sort of life. "What if someone got sick?"

"My mom was a trained physician—an ob-gyn. So she ran the health clinic, and when I got older, I assisted her. It was mostly broken bones or babies or stitches. We lived such a healthy lifestyle, there was little need for the medications we surround ourselves with out here. No problem with blood pressure or diabetes. That kind of thing."

"No birth control?"

"Only natural forms."

"So the families were big?"

"Many, yes, although I was an only child. Bodie came from a big family. He was the youngest of seven boys."

"Did this commune have a name?" I ask, thinking I should look it up.

"*Empezar.* It's Spanish for 'to begin.'"

"And does it still exist?"

She nods. "I've heard it's grown larger, although I haven't spoken to anyone there in years. Not since I left with Bodie."

"Not even your parents?"

"No. When you leave the commune, there is no going back. It's one of the tenets of their philosophy. You either abide by their rules, or you're labeled an outsider. And once you become an outsider, you can never return."

"That's harsh."

"I suppose, but I do understand. Once you visit the outside world, you're corrupted by all it offers."

"You believe that?"

"I do."

"So why did you and Bodie leave?"

Her voice drops. "Bodie's family was different than mine. His father was broken in some way. At the monthly town hall meetings, he would fight with the other leaders. Complained about the rules. He had contributed the most money to the endeavor, so he believed his family deserved a bigger home, but he didn't want to build it himself. As the years went by, he became increasingly violent. He'd get in arguments with his neighbors, started beating his boys. The commune knew what was happening, but they were too frightened to get involved."

A koi splashes in the pond, a flash of orange and black. Ember smiles. "Bodie and I fell in love when we were thirteen. We spent every waking moment together. We'd go on walks that would last for hours. Talk about things we wanted to see. Places we wanted to go. But while I was fine with dreaming, Bodie was looking for escape. And when things grew worse with his dad, well, he reminded me of a caged animal in a zoo. Not a small animal. Something big, like a panther or a lion. He'd pace back and forth, yearning for what was out there . . . not willing to acknowledge any of the good things in his life. And then on the eve of his eighteenth birthday, his dad gave him an extra harsh beating. We ran away that very night."

"What about your parents?"

She sighs. "They would've tried to stop me, so I left without saying goodbye. I gave everything up for Bodie."

I think of Adam and Alice and wonder how I'd feel if I could never see them again. It would break me. I know it. We may fight at times and not understand each other, but losing them would mean the end. "So how was life outside the commune?" I ask.

"It was good at first. Bodie got a job with a construction company in Santa Cruz, and I found work in a day care center. We rented a small apartment only blocks from the beach, and that's where our first daughter was born. Little Emma was followed a year later by Ella." Her voice turns wistful. "I was so happy. I had everything I ever wanted, ever needed. But Bodie . . . well, in ways he was a lot like his father. He grew envious of what other people had. Wanted a nicer home, a better car. He bought a television and computer, and from there he began to crave things we hadn't even known existed. And it didn't help when he fell in with the wrong crowd—local surfers that worked construction in the day and partied hard at night."

A warm breeze rushes through the garden. Ember runs her hands through her stubbly hair. "I didn't know about the drugs until later," she says. "But I knew his personality had changed. He'd be jittery when he got home, his eyes glassy. Sometimes his hands would shake. And he grew irritable around the girls. He didn't like their crying. Then one day he announced we were going on a family camping trip. I was so excited, because we rarely took vacations. But by then, Ella was two and Emma three. Old enough to enjoy exploring the woods.

"So we loaded up our van and headed to Big Sur, and from the start, everything went wrong. I soon realized our trip wasn't just a family vacation. Bodie's friends were there too. We argued about that, and it didn't take him long to spiral into one of his terrible moods." Ember takes a deep breath. "After an early dinner, he went to a friend's campsite and left me alone with the girls. I got them to bed, but I waited up, hoping we might make up and cuddle. But as the hours went by, it grew cold, really cold; the fog moved in, and our campfire died out. I could hear Bodie and his friends partying, and I got more and more upset. When he returned, it was long after midnight. I couldn't see him, but I could hear the slur in his words.

"'I thought this was going to be a family vacation,' I said. 'You've barely spent any time with me and the girls.'

"That led to a fight, and I said something mean about how he couldn't even build a fire the right way to keep his family warm." She shivers in the heat, and her voice drops so low I can barely hear her. "And that's when he took the lighter fluid and squirted it on the campfire."

"My God . . ." I raise my hand to my mouth.

"He says he didn't know what would happen. I believe him. But it happened nonetheless. My clothes caught on fire, and I fell against the tent. The tent blew up in flames and . . . and . . ."

"Oh my God. Your babies."

She drops her head in her hands. "Emma was buried when I was in an induced coma. But Ella lived on for several months. Several horrible, painful months. I would've taken my own life to save her from the pain she endured."

"I'm so sorry." A storm of emotions churns in the pit of my stomach. They begin to boil, and the steam shutters my throat. I flash on the day Hunter drowned. A day I've done my best to forget. Zach's hoarse cries. Adam's begging for forgiveness. The ambulance siren. The arrival of police. And later, Tina's deep-throated screams. I feel a crack in my porcelain exterior, and tears run from my eyes.

"I'm sorry," Ember says. "I shouldn't have told you."

"No . . . that's okay. It brought back a memory . . . something I'd hoped to forget. It should be *me* that's comforting you."

She straightens her shoulders. "I've learned to comfort myself through helping others, easing them through their pain. But I can't help Bodie. No one can. He'll have to find his own way home."

IV. GREED

Having lost all sensitivity, they have given themselves over to sensuality so as to indulge in every kind of impurity, with a continual lust for more.

—Ephesians 4:19

The Angel

It's midnight in the garden of good and evil, and I'm contemplating my betrayal. I'm shivering with thoughts of revenge. At midnight, I climb out of bed.

I putter through my library, searching for an answer to my quandary. I won't allow a reprobate to come between me and my Lord's noble work. I happen on an ancient tome and pause on a portrait of Princess Olga the Great. I had forgotten about that marvelous creature, a saint in the Orthodox Church. I sip on a flute of port and settle in my chair to read.

Olga was born in the Russian city of Pskov in the spring of 925. She came from a family of noble Norsemen, as violent a people as they come. She was wed to the infamous Prince Igor, an antecedent to the Russian czars. He was later murdered by the avaricious Drevlians, an ancient Slavic tribe.

A woman before her time, Olga wielded power with an iron fist. Sought revenge for her husband's killing in the most merciless of ways. She spearheaded four forms of vengeance; she was a woman not to be crossed. Ordered the capture of Drevlian matchmakers and had them buried alive. Tricked her enemies into sending new ambassadors and set fire to them in a shed. She then attended her husband's funeral and ordered the slaughter of five thousand guests. For her final act of retribution, she leveled a rebellious village and enslaved the surviving men.

Years later, the princess converted to Christianity and spread her new faith throughout the land. It was for that she was declared a saint by the holy Orthodox Church. She became one of only five women in history to be recognized as "equal to the apostles."

I set down my empty glass and close my book, ready to settle into a peaceful sleep. I am now secure in my premise that violence used in the appropriate manner can ultimately lead to good.

ZACH RICHARDS

One

"You wanted to see me?" It's shortly after six on a hot-as-hell evening, and the central air conditioner has blown. Ruth's office windows have been thrown open, but there's not the slightest breath of fresh air. The entire campus reeks of rotting flowers and the unmasked scent of decaying guests.

Ruth glares at me from behind her desk, her face sweaty and red as a beet. Her polished look has frayed at the edges—her hair messy, her shirt askew. She looks like a different woman than the iceberg she's become. The frown on her face deepens. It's not an attractive look.

Maybe she's having a nervous breakdown, Tina says.

"Go back to sleep."

Tina's been quiet for a couple weeks. I was hoping she might've disappeared. But isn't it just like her to butt in when another woman rides my ass.

"Shut the door," Ruth orders, and I turn and comply. I know what's coming. Can hear it in her voice. I'm going to get bitch-slapped today.

"How could you?" she asks, now standing. She seems a little wobbly on her feet.

"How could I what?" I try to keep my cool but can't help starting to sweat.

You're in for it now.

Ruth marches in my direction, and I wish myself somewhere else.

"You told Carlyn."

"Told her?"

"Don't play games with me. You told her what happened that day."

"Um . . . yeah. I guess I might've." I stumble backward until my shoulders hit the wall.

"What do you mean 'I guess'?"

"I mean . . . well, yeah. I *guess* I told her."

"You told her everything?"

Just fess up, Tina says. *Give it to her straight.*

"Shut up."

Ruth's eyes widen. "Did you tell me to . . . ?"

"No . . . no, not you. Her."

"Her?"

"Nothing. I'm just talking to myself." I tense like I'm getting ready to have a fist take off my head. "I did talk to Carlyn, but it was a while ago. I was having a really bad day."

"Was that before or after I asked you to work here?"

"Before, I think. Yeah. That's right. It was right before the anniversary, and I was . . . well, I wasn't dealing with things very well."

Tell her you were getting ready to off yourself.

I don't answer Tina this time.

"Why Carlyn?" Ruth asks. "It's not like the two of you are friends."

"We were at one time."

"But now?"

"Well . . . with everything she's been going through, I thought I might help her in some way."

"It would help her to know our secret?"

"Help her to understand everyone makes mistakes."

Ruth waves her hands like she's waving away my words. "Our situation was different."

"Was it?"

She stamps her foot. "We did something stupid, horribly stupid, but stupid nonetheless."

And so did she, Tina says.

"And so did she," I repeat.

"You can't compare the two."

"Why not?"

"Because . . ."

"Because what?"

"Because what she did was . . . was unconscionable."

"And what we did?"

"It's not the same."

"Keep telling yourself that." I fumble for the doorknob. "So, I told Carlyn. Who cares? What's done is done."

"But it's not done. She wants me to act as a character witness at her trial."

"Then do it."

"I'm not sure I want to."

"Why not?"

She straightens her shoulders and folds her arms tight. "I have my reasons."

I slap my forehead. "Jesus, Ruth. Why wouldn't you help your friend?"

Ruth's face gets even redder. "I have my reputation to think of."

Screw her reputation, Tina says.

"Screw your reputation." I repeat.

Her eyes widen. "But Kai might use this against me."

I have to stop myself from laughing. "Are you kidding me? First it's the Post-it Notes, then it's the destitutes, and now it's a friendship that might get you fired?" I run my hands through my hair. "I'm sick and tired of this crap. The whole world doesn't revolve around you." To my shock, Ruth's face crumples, and she begins to cry.

She's looking for pity, Tina says.

Hell. I can't take this. I throw open the door. "I'm late for my shift."

"Wait." Ruth swipes at her tears. "Please. I'm sorry. You're right. I'm not thinking straight. There's just so much going on . . . I'm not sleeping well. And on top of everything else, I'm worried about Adam. Have you seen him today?"

"Yeah. I brought him with me. Why?"

She frowns. "He's here? Right now?"

"HR asked him to turn in his paperwork. Seems they want him to start on Monday."

"Why didn't he tell me?"

"You'll have to ask him that." She looks like she might start crying again, so I soften my tone. "It was a last-minute call. You were at work."

"You really think it's a good idea to have him here?"

"I think it's a bad idea to have him sitting on his ass. Plus he needs to repay the legal fees I fronted."

She works her hands together. "Did he cover up the tattoos?"

"Best he could."

"What about his background check?"

"I'm sure you can figure that out."

"I'll try . . ."

I can't hold back my exasperated sigh. "Remember, you're not doing this for me. You're doing it to help your son."

"I know that . . . and I do appreciate your support of Adam."

"Thanks. But it's nothing out of the ordinary. It's what friends do. They help each other."

Her frown returns. "Are you referring to Carlyn?"

"Of course I am." I don't wait for her response. I just turn and hobble down the hallway.

My God, she's dense, Tina says. *How can she see everyone else's faults but not spot a glimmer of her own?*

I give my head a hard knock and blast through the outside entrance. I've had more than my fill of nagging women today.

Two

"How much farther?" Adam calls from behind.

"Maybe a mile."

"Shit. That's a long way."

"It's not that far." But my knee begs to differ. Should we turn and head home?

I'm on a morning hike with Adam up Rattlesnake Canyon, a steep three-mile trail that winds along a rock-strewn creek and emerges near the top of Gibraltar Road. If we can reach the end, we'll have a view of the coastline from wild Gaviota to sweet little Carp. But my knee is screaming stupid, and there's little chance we'll achieve my goal. Why I thought I could do such a thing, I honestly don't know. Guess my good memories blinded my better sense.

Years ago, Tina and I often hiked Rattlesnake, mostly in the spring when the creek was flowing and the wildflowers bloomed in brilliant hues. But today, in deep summer, there's not a single flower in sight, and the bushes are crackling dry. Still, there's a kind of beauty out here. I like how the charred remains of old trees point their blackened branches toward the heavens.

I haven't been on this trail since before Hunter's death. Hard to believe it's been that long. I remember there was a fairly short jaunt to a pretty meadow where Tina and I liked to picnic. But we've been hiking for over an hour now, and there's no pretty meadow in sight. And with each new step, my knee rebels with a fiery zap to the joint. I thought my old knee brace might give me enough support, but I was totally wrong. I also thought this might be a good way to get Adam to open up about his life, but he's not too pleased by the climb.

"Water break?" he calls from behind. He sounds out of breath.

"Sure." I settle against a granite boulder that rests in the shade of a twisted oak. It's still early, and the edges of the grayish-blue sky are rimmed in waves of pink. I inhale the scent of heather and sage and something that smells like curry. A rabbit scurries into the bushes; a hawk soars overhead.

"Isn't this great?" I ask Adam. He's dressed in baggy shorts and a ripped T-shirt like he was planning to spend the day at the beach. His ratty Converse may look hipster cool, but their soles can't offer much of a grip.

"I guess."

"You been before?"

He nervously runs a hand though his shaggy hair. "Not since I was a kid. Hiking's not my thing." He pulls a pack of cigarettes from his pocket and offers me a smoke. I'm about to wave him off, but then I shrug.

"Sure. Why not." I work at sounding jokey. "But don't tell your mom. She thinks I quit."

He snorts. "As long as you don't tell her I started. She'd be pissed with both of us."

We puff in silence, and I try to relax into the view. If only my knee would quit throbbing. "How's the new job?" I ask after a while.

Adam exhales long and slow, threads of smoke curling around his head. "Better than binge-watching some stupid show on TV. Good thing is I'm not just washing dishes. They got me chopping stuff."

"You like that?"

He nods. "I always liked helping in the kitchen, even when I was a kid." He glances at me sideways. "Might try to work up to chef."

"That's a great idea."

"Don't sound so excited."

"I'm not excited."

"I'm not a total loser, you know. I'll figure out my life."

"I know that."

"Just got to get this court date behind me."

I choose my next words carefully. The kid wears defensiveness like a coat. "How'd it go with the lawyer?"

Adam shrugs. "Fine, I guess. He thinks he can get the felony reduced to a misdemeanor as long as I don't get into trouble."

"How does he define *trouble*?"

"I can't get picked up by the police for anything. Even a speeding ticket might screw things up. But mainly I've gotta stay away from Nikki. She took out a restraining order." He pauses before saying the next words. "Can't believe she says I hit her."

"But you didn't."

"Hell no. I mean, I might've pushed her a little. I was heading for the door, and she blocked my way."

His words make me flash back on all the domestics I handled during my long-ago detective years. But he's not like one of those men, is he? The kind who hits and lies? "So what's going to happen with you two?"

"Nothing. Nikki's moved in with some fried-out tweaker. Creepy guy. I don't want to have anything to do with her. Filing papers as soon as I can."

"I'm sorry about that."

"No big deal. Things just didn't work out, that's all."

I gaze at him long and hard. For all his tough-guy demeanor, I can hear the sadness in his voice. Makes me sick to think I might be the source of his problems. If only . . .

Tell him, Tina whispers. *Come on. He needs to know.*

"Not now."

"Anyway," Adam continues. "I appreciate you covering the lawyer. You know I'll pay you back."

"I'm not worried about that."

He clears his throat. "You think . . . you think you would've started drinking if it hadn't been for . . . you know . . ."

I work to keep my voice steady. "I'm not sure. Maybe the darkness was in me all along. Why?"

He takes a moment to answer. "Just wondering . . . I mean . . . sometimes I wonder why I'm so fucked up . . . if I hadn't . . . if I didn't . . ."

A knife cuts through my gut, causing a pain sharp and deep. "You've got to get over that, you know. It wasn't your fault. You were just a kid."

"So you don't blame me?"

"Never have, never will."

"You mean that?"

"Yeah. I do." My gaze fixes on two shirtless men running up the trail. Triathletes from the look of them—slim, hard, and tan. They're about the same age as Adam, but it's as if they come from another world. I can't see their eyes behind their razor-shaped sunglasses, but I'm sure as hell we're being judged. Who comes up here to smoke cigarettes? Losers, that's who.

You're not much of a role model, Tina says as the men run by.

"Never said I was." But I snuff out my cigarette anyway.

"How come you're always talking to yourself?" Adam asks.

I shrug. "Guess it comes from living alone. Want to go on?"

"Not really." His eyes follow the backs of the runners. Frowning, he drops his cigarette and grinds it into the ground. "You?"

"I think I've had enough." There's a lone hiker moving fast up the trail. Tiny, thin, and trim. I'm thinking that a girl shouldn't be out hiking alone when I spy the familiar maze of scars. *Jesus.* Not here. Anxiety bubbles in my gut. "Let's get going."

"Wait a sec." Adam crouches to tie a shoelace.

Damn. There's no way around it. I'll have to speak to her.

Ember glides toward us with the smoothness of a lynx, her footing sure and quick. She's dressed in black shorts and a sleeveless top, with a red baseball cap perched on her head. When she catches up to us, she pauses, and a smile lights her face. "Well, look who's here. Zach and . . ." She screws up her forehead to peer at Adam. "I'm sorry. I don't believe we've met." He gets to his feet, and she extends a slender hand, silver rings glinting in the sun. "I'm Ember."

Adam reaches out like it's the first time he's ever shaken a hand. "Adam," he says with a nervous twitch. He must be spooked by her face.

"Adam. Wow. My dad's name is Adam."

"It's kind of a common name."

"It's a nice name." She turns to me, and I shudder from my head to my toes. "Are you two related?" she asks.

"Uh," I glance at Adam. "No. He's just a friend. Actually, he's Ruth's son."

"Ruth? From work?" She smiles at Adam. "She's your mom? She's great. I really like her. She's so nice."

"You think my mom's nice?" He seems surprised.

"Very."

I feel the need to explain the relationship. "Ruth and Adam live next door. We've been neighbors for going on thirty years. Adam just started working the day shift at Serenity a couple of weeks ago."

"You did?" she claps her hands together like I've said the most exciting thing in the world. "That's wonderful. I love it there. Where are you working?"

"In the kitchen," Adam mumbles. He looks as uncomfortable as I feel.

"Which kitchen?"

"Uh . . ." He glances at me.

"He's working in the cafeteria at the Champion's Club."

"Champion's Club? How lucky you are. The champions are the sweetest people. They bring joy to my heart every day." She presses her hands to her heart. "I think of them as God's little angels. It's like they're getting ready to return to heaven's womb."

I stare at her, wondering if she's a little off. How can anyone enjoy hanging around people who drool and can't remember their kin?

She reaches back and grabs a water bottle from her pack and takes a few gulps. "You hike this trail often?" she asks, wiping her lips with the back of her hand.

"Every now and then," Adam lies.

"I'm surprised I've never seen you."

"We must come at different times."

She turns and regards the view. "I hike here at least once a week. I love it. It's so peaceful, like you've traveled hundreds of miles from civilization, when in truth you're only an hour's walk from downtown." She turns back to us. "Are you on your way up or down?"

"Up," says Adam at the same time I say "down." I peer at Adam, confused. Did I hear him right? Ember looks from me to Adam and back again, and I work to clarify. "My knee's acting up, so I'm heading down. And you, Adam . . . ?"

"I'm going on."

"You are?"

"Sure. Why not?"

I shrug. Yes. Why not?

Ember reaches around and pats her backpack. "I brought some hot tea and granola bars. I was going to have a minipicnic at the meadow. I'd be happy to share."

"Sure." Adam glances at me. "You don't mind, do you?"

"Of course not. You two go ahead." I turn and stumble my way down the trail, thinking that if Ember's a lynx, I'm a three-legged elephant. I make it about twenty yards before I trip on a root. Luckily, I right myself before I hit the ground, but still, it feels like an ice pick skewers my knee. I moan and look up the trail where Ember and Adam are moving along. I get up and take a step and almost trip again.

Why so nervous? Tina asks.

"You know why."

She's such a pretty girl, but that terrible burn . . . of course, who am I to talk? After my accident, it wasn't as if there was much left of my face, was there?

"No, there wasn't."

You shouldn't have peeked, you know. That way you could've remembered me for my pretty younger self.

"Stop it."

I'm just telling you the truth.

"Go away."

Maybe you should tell Adam the truth and you'd be a happier man.

"*Shut up!*" I slap the side of my head.

You're such a grouch this morning. You need to get more sleep.

"And you need to crawl back into your cave."

That's up to you, and you know it.

"Leave me alone."

You shouldn't speak to your wife that way.

"You're not my wife."

Then what am I?

"I don't know . . . you're my . . . my crazy."

Hmm. Yes. Maybe you're right. I'm your crazy. I'll go away when you do the right thing.

Three

I finish my cup of coffee and set it down in the kitchen sink. It's just after four in the morning, and the Highlife's early shift is straggling in—Latinos mostly with tired eyes and wide-mouthed yawns. "Hey there," Pablo calls from across the darkened room. "How's the big-time detective this morning? Solve any major crimes?" The amateur comedian laughs, and I can't help but join in. It's not like he's an asshole. He's an okay guy. He's the morning sous chef and likes to start his days with a few jokes. How he figured out I'm an ex-detective, I'm not sure. But he might be part of the gossip train, and I'd like to take a ride on that.

"Have a moment?" I ask once he's done with his comedy routine. Ruth's been bugging me about the Post-it Notes, but I've run into nothing but dead ends. So I thought I'd attack this a different way. Check out Panini's doomsday club.

"Sure," Pablo says, grabbing a cup of coffee. "What's up?"

"You've been here a long time, right?"

"Ten years."

"That's what I thought." I lean against the wall to give my aching knee a break. "Ever hear of something called the Goodnight Club?"

He wrinkles his forehead in thought. "That some boring gringo movie?"

"No. It's a secret campus club. Maybe you've heard a guest mention the name?"

He shakes his head. "Never heard nothing 'bout that."

"Would you mind asking around?"

His brown eyes sparkle. "What's in it for me?"

"How about a beer?"

"Craft beer?"

"Yep."

"Sold." He gulps down his coffee, and I turn to leave, but he stops me with a wave of his hand. "Wait up. Since you're playing detective, why not check out some of the other shit going down?"

"What kind of shit?"

"Like how the new owners are trying to toss out the old people that got no money."

I act like it's news to me. "Where'd you hear about that?"

"Around. Thing is, they gotta be breaking some law."

"I can ask Ruth."

"Boss Ruth?" His smile disappears. "She a friend of yours?"

I shift uncomfortably. "She hired me. Why?"

"I'll bet she's in on it. The new management's a bunch of cheap-ass liars. There's a rumor they'll be cutting our benefits soon."

I'm about to question him further when my cell phone lights up. *Hell.* It's Adam. Kid's worked here less than a month, so he better not be calling in sick. "I'll catch you later." I turn my back on Pablo and press my cell phone to my ear. "What's up?"

"Just got here and . . ."

The tension in his voice gets my alarm bells ringing. "What is it?"

"There's a guy down. He's hurt or something. I don't know what to do."

I stumble out the kitchen door into the predawn gloom. "Is he breathing?" I bark into the phone.

"I don't think so . . . I don't know. But . . . shit . . . there's a lot of blood."

"Where are you?"

"In the back of parking lot six."

Hell. "Stay put. I'll be right there." I head for the parking lot as fast as my busted knee will allow. It takes me five long minutes to limp to the backside of the campus, hurrying as fast as I can. I round the edge of the champion's unit and head in the direction of a glowing cell phone.

"Adam?"

"Over here. Hurry." I hobble to where he points at a shadowy figure splayed across the pavement. I light up the body with my flashlight and inhale a jagged breath.

"Any idea who it is?" I ask.

"No. But that's blood, right?"

"Yeah. That's blood." I run my flashlight across the stocky man dressed in a yellow uniform. Then I flash my light on Adam. He covers his eyes with his forearm.

"You sure you don't know him?" I watch for his reaction.

"Should I?"

"He's wearing a nurse's uniform. Ever see him around?"

"Don't think so."

I have, but I can't recall his name. I crouch next to the body and examine the stream of dark liquid pooling around his head. I carefully reach for his neck. No sign of a pulse. I grab his limp wrist and try again.

"Is he dead?" Adam asks.

"Looks like it."

"But how . . . ?"

"Give me a sec."

The rusty scent of blood creeps up my nose, reminding me of gory incidents in my past. I shine the light around the man's neck and pause at a puncture wound. Looks like a stab to the carotid artery did him in. Even in the cool of the morning, my face begins to sweat. I scour the scene, but there's no weapon in sight. I get to my feet.

"He's been stabbed."

"Holy shit." Adam stumbles backward. "But who . . . ?"

"How long you been here?" Dawn has broken, and it's now light enough for me to study Adam's face. He looks pale, nervous, tired, but not guilty. Thank God for that.

"Maybe ten minutes max. I got out of my car and saw him and called you right away."

"Did you see anyone else?"

"No."

"You sure?"

"Yeah. Why you asking?"

Why? Because I've put on my detective hat, and my mind has shifted into suspicious mode. If I look at this situation as an outsider, a dead nurse and an ex-druggie might suggest a drug deal gone bad. Adam glances at his cell phone.

"I better go," he says. "I'll be late for my shift."

"You can't leave. This is a crime scene."

He backs up a few steps. "But I didn't have anything to do with this . . . I just happened to walk this way. Shit. Shit. *Shit.* I have enough problems in my screwed-up life. I don't need any more."

"Where's your car?"

He points at a far corner of the lot.

"Why'd you park over there?"

"I don't know. Why not? Anyway, I gotta go."

"I told you, you have to stay. The police will want to question you since you were the first person on the scene."

"I can't get involved in this." His voice rises until it reaches a fevered pitch. "My lawyer said if I get into any kind of trouble, I'll end up in jail."

"You won't get in trouble."

"You sure?"

I start to nod and then stop. I'm not so sure. I stand and consider the situation before coming to a decision I hope I won't regret. "All right," I say. "Get out of here. Go to work."

"Thanks," he gasps, like he's been holding his breath.

"Just keep your mouth shut, understand? Don't mention what you saw to anyone. I'll take care of this."

Adam stares at me for a moment before turning and jogging away. I wait a full five minutes before I get security involved. *"Richards. Code black."*

"His name is Milo Kushner," Finn says. "A night nurse. Tell me again how you found him." Finn's eyes are locked on mine, and I know exactly what he's doing. I've been there many times. He's caught a whiff of an untruth, so he's sniffing me like a dog. I've got to give him something, and I've got to do it soon. I repeat my story. How I'd been having coffee in the kitchen. Left to make my final rounds. Came upon the dead body. Gave security a call. He lets me finish and then shakes his head.

"Bullshit, Richards." He says my name like he's spitting nails. "Something doesn't add up."

"What do you mean?"

"I mean, if you were following the schedule, your final round would've taken you to the right, not the left."

"I started off a little early, so I thought I'd add some extra distance to my route."

"You're aware the cameras will time-stamp that."

"Of course." I start sweating at the thought of the cameras that watch this place like hawks. How stupid can I be? The cameras will out my lie. Now I've backed myself into a corner, and I can't see an easy way out. Not only will they question Adam's behavior but they'll question mine too. If you're going to tell a lie, make it a good one, the detective in me always says. I reach deep into my pocket and pull out the spare cigarette I save for when the craving gets too much. "Truth is, I came out here to smoke. I know it's against the rules, but I promise I'm cutting back."

He eyes me like I'm a loser. "So a cigarette brought you here?"

"Yeah." I'm pretending to be ashamed when Finn's sidekick comes running up. Ted Barnet showed up the same day Finn did—I assume he's corporate too. He has some sort of weird deformity. He's shorter than me by at least half a foot, and his jaw is way too large. But he's built like a tank, and if we got into a fight, I have no doubt who'd come out on top.

"I checked the security cameras," he says in his odd, high-pitched voice. "The ones in the parking lot aren't working."

"So, no view of the altercation?"

"No view of nothing."

"That's convenient." Finn rakes me with his gaze. "You were a detective at one time, right?"

"Right." Guess the guy took a peek at my file.

"What do you think happened here?"

I tilt my head, considering. "Maybe a lover's quarrel. Coworker fight. But whoever it was, they knew what they were doing."

"Meaning?"

I crouch and point at the entry wound. "This isn't a random stab. It's a carefully calculated jab."

"You sure?"

"Yep."

"What else can you tell me?"

I study the body again. "I'd say the assailant was about the same height. And see how the stab wound is clean? Not jagged. I'm guessing whoever did this used a knife with two sharpened edges. Probably a punch knife."

"You mean a push dagger?"

"Same thing."

"Aren't those illegal in California?"

"If concealed, yes. Anyway, forensics will have more to say about that."

"Would he have died right away?"

"Maybe two minutes. Three. He didn't just drop on the ground. They rarely do. Victims of stab wounds typically react by fight or flight. See how there's blood splashed around? I'd say he staggered in a circle a few times."

"So flight?"

"I think so."

"Wouldn't the killer's clothes be covered in blood?"

"Most likely."

"All right. Go get some coffee. I'll be in touch."

"Shouldn't I wait for the police?"

"That might take a while."

"You haven't called them?"

"Not yet."

"They'll be pissed if you wait too long."

Finn's eyes narrow. "You telling me how to do my job?"

"Just saying . . ."

"Then say it to yourself. And by the way, keep your mouth shut, and don't go spewing your theories."

"Theories?"

"You're no expert, and you sure as hell don't know what happened here." He jabs his finger at my chest. "Unless you do. Now move along.

You're dismissed." He turns his back to me and starts talking to Barnet. I want to say something nasty but think better of it and head off. When I get halfway across the parking lot, I pause and look back. Finn is crouched next to one side of the body. Barnet is crouched on the other. I swear they're going through Milo's pockets. Maybe *I* should call the police.

Four

I hobble straight for the Champion's Club, fumbling with my cell phone. Peck. Peck. Peck. I'm deleting all traces of Adam's call. Now I've got to find him and make sure he does the same. Shit. I'm the one acting like a criminal. But now that I've gone and lied to Finn, isn't that what I've become?

I burst through the side door and head for the kitchen, where I find Adam chopping onions near the kitchen sink. He's wearing the white uniform that denotes the kitchen staff, a hairnet pulled low on his head.

"We gotta talk," I say.

He barely looks up. "Too early for my break."

I lay my hand on his arm to stop the chopping. Give it enough pressure so he'll understand. "Say you gotta piss or whatever. Meet me outside the back door."

He opens his mouth like he's going to argue and then he sets down his knife. "All right."

Outside, I explain what he needs to do. He pulls his cell phone from his back pocket and wipes it clean. I explain a little more, and he starts pacing back and forth.

"I can't believe my shitty rotten luck."

"It is what it is."

"They say anything about the cameras?" he asks in a nervous tone. I catch a whiff of something a little off.

"The ones to the parking lot weren't working."

"Guess that's a good thing."

"Not really. They might've proved you weren't involved."

"Oh, yeah." He stops pacing. "But they'll know what time I drove in, right? That I was a little early? And that I parked on the far side of the lot."

"True."

"So what do I say?"

"That it was dark and you were tired. You didn't see a thing."

He scrunches up his face in thought. "But won't they wonder why it took me so long to get to the kitchen?"

"Did anyone notice?"

"My boss did. I was five minutes late."

"If anyone asks, say you stopped for a smoke."

"But that's against the rules."

"So what?"

"I could get fired."

"*Fired?* That's the least of your worries. I lied to cover your ass, so now I need you to play along. Understand?"

He drops his gaze. "Yeah."

I scour his face, wondering if I've done the right thing. Is there the slightest chance he's involved? Why *would* he park in the far corner of the parking lot? It does seem a little strange.

It is strange, Tina says.

Jesus. I've woken the beast. "Go away."

I can't believe you're willing to toss out your ethics. And for what? Your lover's son?

"She's not my lover."

It's Adam's turn to lay his hand on my arm. "You okay, Zach?"

And there it is. Right there. There's my reason. I'm helping the kid because he's the only person in the world who seems to give a damn about me. "I'm fine. Just tired."

"You're off shift, right? You should go home."

"I will after I talk to the police."

His face grows pinched with worry. "Think they'll wanna talk to me?"

"Maybe. Just stick to our story."

"All right. Good luck."

"I'll need it."

Thirty minutes later, all hell has broken loose. A squadron of police cars has cordoned off the parking lot, and a dozen uniformed officers are milling about. Murder is rare in Santa Barbara. Maybe one or two a year, none of which has ever occurred at an old folks' home. Within the hour, I'm seated in a chair in Finn's spotless office across the desk from Detective Sergeant Javier Ruiz.

"How are you, Zach?" he asks.

"Good, Javier. You?"

"Can't complain." I met Javier years ago at the precinct when he was a greenhorn rookie. He's a bear of a man with hulking shoulders and hands so large they can swallow a basketball. He must be closing in on fifty but still carries himself like the athlete he was—a star football player at the local high school who married the prettiest cheerleader in town. He'd be a menacing presence if it weren't for his easy smile and puppy dog eyes. Despite the growing jowls, he still has that friendly spark in his eyes I remember when he was a tenderfoot and I took him under my wing.

Man, those were good times. My life was in front of me, my dreams weren't just that. A sense of sadness gnaws at my gut, which I do my best to ignore. I'm exhausted, but I need to stay focused. Javier may play the part of a casual ex-jock, but he has a mind as sharp as a tack.

"How are the boys?" I ask, remembering two rough-and-tumble kids who fought as much as they played.

His proud smile stretches from ear to ear. "Ernesto got into UCLA. He starts in a couple of weeks."

I blow a low whistle. "UCLA. That's impressive. And the younger one?"

"Juan's a senior at Santa Barbara High. He's the starting quarterback."

"Like father, like son."

"No. Juan's much better than I ever was. There's a chance he can play Division One."

"That's pretty damn impressive. You've done well."

"It has nothing to do with me," he says with a mouthful of false modesty. "Angelica runs a tight ship."

"How long have you two been together now?"

"Had our twentieth anniversary a couple of months ago." His smile falters, and I know what he's thinking. His wedding was the weekend before Hunter passed. I know that because Tina and I attended the event. A huge party at the Paseo Nuevo with an unending supply of alcohol poured to the beat of a mariachi band.

That was fun, wasn't it? Tina whispers. *Angelica looked so beautiful in her gown.*

"Go away."

Javier squirms in his seat. "I heard you got clean. Congrats."

"Yeah, well, don't congratulate me yet. It hasn't been that long, and you know how that goes."

"At least you have a good job."

I snort. "Good job? Are you kidding me? I'm a lowlife security guard."

"Don't underestimate yourself. And Zach . . ." He clears his throat. "I'm sorry about the firing . . . I mean . . . it haunts me to this day."

I shift uncomfortably. "You only did what you had to do." During the last two years of my work life, the tables had been turned. Javier ascended the work rungs of the police department at the same time I descended into hell. In the end, he was the one who fired me. Our roles had been reversed. But I don't hold it against him. I would've fired my sorry ass too.

Javier rubs his oversized hands together. His nails are neatly groomed; a gold band glows from his wedding finger. "I want to tell you something," he says, "and then we can move on to the business at hand." His voice has that tone everyone used back then. The one that said we know you're broken, but we have no idea what to say. Maybe that never changes after tragedy strikes. You're forever labeled a victim. I wonder if his tone would change if he knew the true story behind Hunter's death.

You could tell him, Tina says. *Nothing's stopping you.*

"Not now," I reply, covering my words with a cough so Javier won't think I'm a nut.

"I was pretty damn self-righteous back then," he says, his eyes focused on his hands. "Even with everything you'd gone through, losing your . . . well . . ."

"It's okay. You can say it. Losing my family . . ." I will my eyes to stay dry.

"Yeah. Right. Well . . . truth is, I was a judgmental jerk."

"No worries. If I've learned anything, it's that we all deal with tragedy in our own way. I made the mistake of turning to alcohol. If I could go back and change that, I would."

"What else would you have done?"

"I don't know. Guess I could've buried myself in my work. Found myself a hobby. Or I could've sold everything and moved to a third-world country to do Peace Corps work or something like that."

He nods. "Well, I want you to know I've changed. Mellowed a bit. Anyway . . . now, well, I understand. I mean, if I lost my wife and boys,

I don't think I'd have it in me to live. My family is everything to me. I don't know how you did it."

I try to lighten the tension with a joke. "I didn't do *it* very well, did I?" I finish off with a strangled laugh.

Javier clears his throat, and I see a glistening in his chocolate-brown eyes. I look away, embarrassed. And then the moment is over, and he straightens his shoulders, and the interview is back on.

"So why don't you tell me what happened this morning," he says. "You were on duty?"

"Yes. Near the end of my shift."

He scribbles on a small pad of paper. "So walk me through the minutes leading up to your discovery of the body."

I wish I didn't have to lie to Javier. Every fiber in me regrets my choice. But there's no going back, so I tell my story. The same one I told Finn. But unlike Finn, Javier doesn't drill me. He's giving me the benefit of the doubt. He wants to believe I'm a good guy. Can't help but appreciate that.

Now's the time to tell the truth, Tina says. *Don't compound your lies.*

I don't attempt to answer. I focus on the problem at hand.

"Did you know the victim?" Javier asks. "Milo Kushner?"

"No. But he worked the night shift, so I saw him hanging around."

"Any evidence of drug use?"

"Not that I know of."

"But he would have access?"

"As a nurse, I would think so. But you'll have to ask Finn about that."

"I will." Javier leans back in his seat and taps his pencil on his pad. I figure this is when he figures out something is wrong.

"You see anyone acting suspiciously?"

"No."

"No staff coming or going from work?"

I shake my head.

"I'm told the cameras weren't working. That seem strange to you?"

"Could be a coincidence."

"Could be."

He stares at me hard for a moment, and I work to keep my expression flat. "Why the delay in calling 911?" he finally asks.

I shrug, relieved to see him following a different kind of lead. "Finn's choice."

"He's a bit of an asshole, right? Control freak?"

I glance behind me at the closed door. "You can say that."

"How long has he been working here?"

"Just a couple months. Showed up after the place got bought by some megacorporation."

"Military background?"

"Yep."

"I can tell. Sometimes they're the worst."

"More often than not."

He laughs. "That could be true."

"Well, good luck then."

"Thanks."

"Is that it?"

"For now. Go ahead and go home and get some sleep."

I get to my feet, more relieved than tired. "Thanks."

"Good to see you, man."

"Likewise."

"Let's get together sometime. Angelica would love to catch up."

"Sure." Of course we both know a visit will never happen. There's one too many skeletons buried in that grave to spend an evening breaking bread.

Five

I wake in my bed to the sound of drifting voices and the strumming of a guitar. Adam must be practicing on my back porch again. He's been doing that most every evening. But it sounds like someone's with him, and I'm not okay with that.

The house is hot and stuffy, and a headache gnaws at my face. I could've slept another twelve hours. Hell, I feel like shit. I get up and head to the bathroom and do a quick brush of my teeth. Seconds in, my wild-eyed reflection conjures up the earlier events of the day. Adam's frightened voice. Milo's bloody body. Javier's questioning eyes. Seems I may have gotten myself up a creek, and there ain't no sign of a paddle.

In honor of the unknown visitor, I run a comb through my hair and change into a clean T-shirt and shorts. Then I pick my way through my house of horrors, eager to join Adam on the porch. I need to find a way to get rid of his friend and speak with him alone. Maybe there's news on Milo. Maybe the murderer's been found.

"Hey there," I call out, stepping onto the back porch. And then I take a quick step back, sucker punched in the gut.

"Hi, Zach," Ember says, turning her scarred face toward mine. "What a nice place you have."

I nod and eye Adam, who's splayed across the worn wooden steps with my guitar resting in his lap. He reaches for a squat brown bottle of beer and takes a chug before speaking. "Did we wake you?" he asks.

"Uh . . . no."

"Good. Hope you don't mind us invading your space."

"Oh, no. Of course not. It's just . . . I'm going to head back inside. I've got a few things to do."

"Anything we can help you with?" Ember asks.

"No . . . no . . . you stay right there. Adam, can you step inside for a second? Want to show you something."

"Sure." After stretching his lanky body, he sets down my guitar and mumbles something to Ember. Her face lights up, and she giggles. He pats her knee, then gets to his feet and follows me into the kitchen. "What?" he asks with a goofy smile.

"Not here."

I turn and pick my way through my trash pit of a dining room and head to the far corner of the living room.

I bet he has a crush on that girl, Tina says.

"Impossible."

Why?

"You know why."

You're mean. What if I'd lived? Would you have avoided me too?

"That's different."

No, actually, it's not.

I turn to face Adam. "Why's that girl here?"

"Ember?"

"Who else?"

Be nice, Tina moans.

I slap the side of my head. "Mosquito," I say to Adam's questioning eyes.

191

He blinks a couple of times. "Well, I didn't think you'd mind if I brought over a friend. We didn't come inside. I took her through the back gate."

"I don't mind. It's just . . ." A storm of emotions brews in my gut. Of course I mind . . . because . . . because . . . shit. I can't think straight. I try again. "Why don't you take her back to your house . . . I mean . . . it's neater, right? And you got food and stuff like that."

Adam's smile fades like the receding of an ocean wave. And there's a flash of something else. Sadness, I think.

You've hurt his feelings, Tina says.

I can't argue with that.

Adam fixes his gaze on the blank TV screen, his face growing sullen and gray. "I like it better here, and I thought you were okay with that. I even brought my own beer. But if we're bugging you, we'll take off."

"It's not that . . ." How can I explain about Ember? How she brings back the horror of my past?

It's guilt, Tina says. *Pure and simple. You'll never escape it until you tell the truth.*

I tap my forehead. "I like having you here," I say. "But I'm not so sure about other people." I point at the piles of magazines. "Don't know if I want my coworkers seeing this mess. It's kind of embarrassing. Anyway. I'm sure your mom would like to see more of you. At least that's what she says."

Adam pushes his hands deep into his pockets, his voice sounding tight and strained. "I get enough of my mom every day. She's always bugging me about my future. I mean, I appreciate her letting me camp out for a while, but she never knows when to shut up. When she's not asking me questions, she looks like she wants to. If I brought a girl over . . . well, you know how she gets. She'd want to know if something was going on."

"*Is* something going on?"

He shakes his head. "No. Ember's just a friend. I can talk to her. She's had some bad things happen; I can relate to that."

"Oh." I slump against the wall, trying to take the weight off my knee. "How about this morning? Did you tell Ember about that?"

"She knows about Milo, if that's what you're asking."

"You didn't tell her you found him, did you?"

He bristles, his eyes narrowing. "I'm not stupid, you know. I told you I wouldn't say anything, and I didn't. But she worked with Milo, so of course we talked about him. It would be weird if we didn't."

"Maybe . . . but even if you think you can trust her, you can't reveal the truth. We could get in a lot of trouble for lying, so we've got to keep our stories straight."

"Of course. I know the drill. I parked my car and walked straight to the kitchen and didn't see nothing."

"And you smoked a cigarette."

"Yeah. I told the detective that."

My blood runs cold. "You met with Detective Ruiz?"

"I met with some police guy. Don't remember his name."

"Big guy dressed in a suit?"

"Yeah. He didn't seem very smart. Kept asking me the same questions in lots of different ways."

My heart begins to race. "What questions?"

"I don't know . . ."

"Try."

He shrugs. "Like why did I park way back in the corner, and am I sure I didn't see nothing at all."

I take a deep breath. "Why *did* you park way back in the corner?"

He shifts uncomfortably. "I told you before. I just did."

"That's not a good answer."

"Yeah, well. That's what I told the detective. But between you and me . . ." His voice drops. "I parked there because Ember was working the night shift. After she gets off, she usually walks that way to get to the bus. I wanted to talk to her."

"That's bullshit, Adam."

His cheeks bloom red. "Why would you say that?"

"Because you're lying to me." I bend and rub my knee. The thing's throbbing like a bitch. "Ember wouldn't walk that way to catch the bus. The bus stop is outside the front gates."

"Well, maybe she was going to her car."

"She has a car?"

He shrugs. "I don't know."

I straighten and curl my hands into fists. "Damn it, Adam. You want me to help you, you'd better tell me the truth."

Adam stares at me like he hates me, and then his shoulders droop. "Okay. Well, maybe I didn't tell you everything . . ."

I freeze. "What's everything?"

His eyes dart back and forth like he's searching for an escape. "I got there early to buy some Adderall."

"Adderall?"

"Yeah. It helps me focus."

"Who the hell's selling Adderall in the parking lot at that time of the . . ." I swallow my next words, the answer dawning on me. "Jesus, Adam. No."

"He was already dead when I got there."

The ramifications race through my mind. Holy shit. "I can't believe this . . ."

Adam glances over his shoulder like he's looking for an escape route. "It's no big deal."

"No big deal? *Are you crazy?*" It takes everything in me not to punch him in the face.

"Look," he pleads. "It really isn't. I mean, you can get Adderall by prescription. People use it all the time."

"Then why not get a prescription?"

"I don't know. More of a hassle, I guess."

"A hassle?" I try to calm myself by putting on my detective hat. "So who suggested meeting in the back of the parking lot?"

"Milo. That's his spot."

"His spot?"

"That's where he meets everyone."

"Everyone?"

"He was the campus candy man. You didn't know that?"

"Candy man?"

"As in dealer."

"How would I know that?"

"Someone in security helps him. That's why the cameras don't work."

"And you thought that person was me?"

"No . . . but stuff gets around."

I think of the men at security. Manny, Moe, and Mac. Some of the other lowlifes. Hell, it could be anyone. "Did you tell the detective about this?"

He sniffs. "I'm not a moron."

My legs are ready to give out. "We're fucked; you know that, right?"

"It's no big deal."

"*No big deal?* On what planet do you live?"

"Hell, I didn't touch the guy. And I bet he had ten other drug deals going down that morning. It could've been anyone."

I peer at his too-handsome face that may have let him off the hook one too many times. "So why didn't you tell me the truth?"

He shrugs. "I was scared, I guess. I thought you wouldn't help me if I told you about the Adderall."

"You thought right." I fumble for my next words. "You understand this looks bad, right? With your history . . . our history . . . if the police find out we're lying . . ."

"They won't find out."

"How can you be so sure?"

"I won't tell them if you don't." He takes a step back. "We'd better get going. It's kinda weird leaving Ember out there on her own."

I open my mouth to argue, but it's like the air has been squeezed from my lungs. "Go on." I dismiss him with a wave of my hand.

Well, that's awkward, Tina says once he's out of the room.

"More than awkward. If he lied about meeting Milo, what else don't I know?"

He was scared, Zach. Nothing more. You know he wouldn't kill a man.

"Do I?"

Yes, you do. Now go on and greet your guest. Talk to that sweet girl. Make her feel welcome. Offer to cook up some dinner.

"Serve a can of chili?"

Come on, Zach. Do I have to think for you too? Order pizza and a salad. Something. Anything. Try to be a gracious host.

I take a bite of pizza and try to savor the salt and the fat, but when I glance across the picnic table, the gorge rises in my throat. My young guest doesn't seem to notice. Ember just giggles and chats. An outsider might assume our odd-looking trio was the very best of friends.

You're not trying, Tina whispers. *Slap a smile on your face.*

I swat her away like a bug.

"Your garden is beautiful," Ember says, a slice of cheese pizza dangling from her hand.

Beautiful? Maybe decades ago, but now? When we first moved in, there had been a lush green lawn surrounded by more than a dozen citrus trees—oranges, tangerines, grapefruit. I flash on a memory of Hunter's happy kid face, his chin glistening with sticky yellow juice. He liked to help his mom pick the ripe fruit. He especially liked the tangerines.

"It's as if you live in a jungle," Ember continues. "Like we're not dining in the backyard of a downtown home but having a picnic out in the wild."

Jungle? I suppose that's true. The trees are overgrown and tangled, the ground drowning in rotten fruit. The lawn has been replaced by unstoppable crabgrass that has smothered everything in its path. A family of skunks has taken residence in the tool shed sagging in the far corner of the yard. Raccoons forage in the weeds; rabbits scurry from hole to hole.

Two neighborhood crows swoop across the darkening sky and settle in the uppermost branches of my neighbor's acacia. When the birds first arrived a few years ago, their cawing drove me nuts. But now I think of them as family and worry when they're not around. I pop open a second beer and take a slug, and my shoulders begin to relax. I close my eyes and picture Hunter gathering fruit in a wicker basket. Then I snap back to the present and tune in to the conversation at the mention of Milo's name.

"It's awful." Ember's expression has turned sad. "I can't believe he was killed. Who would do such a thing?"

"Are the police saying he was murdered?" I ask.

"I don't know," she replies. "But that's the gossip going around."

I'd like to hear more about the gossip. Maybe it will lead to the murderer, which will get Adam and me out of this mess. "Were you friends with Milo?"

"Not friends, but we both worked the night shift."

"Decent guy?"

"Decent? Um . . . I don't know. I suppose."

Adam narrows his eyes and mouths something at me that I pretend not to understand. "Ever hear any rumors?" I ask.

"What kind of rumors?"

"This is depressing," Adam says, draining his beer. "Maybe we should talk about something else."

I ignore Adam's words. "Rumors about Milo selling drugs."

Ember fixes her good eye on mine, and I do my best to keep a straight face. "Does this have something to do with his death?" she asks.

"Maybe."

She wipes her hands with her napkin. "Well, then yes. There were rumors . . ."

"What kind?"

"Well . . . it always seemed like he was the first to arrive when one of our guests passed. And sometimes the painkillers would go missing."

"Sometimes?"

"Many times."

"You ever catch him in the act?"

She hesitates and twists her napkin tight. "Once when Loretta Thomas passed."

"Did you report him?"

"No."

"Why not?"

"He said he was just cleaning up."

"And you believed him?"

"Not really. I guess I felt sorry for him. He seemed lonely, and I didn't want to get him in trouble."

I shiver at a change in the weather; a fog-laced breeze ruffles my hair. But I won't let the cold stop my informal interrogation. Who better to tell me the truth? "You were one of the last people to see Simon Appleton alive, right?"

"Right."

"Was Nurse Milo at the infirmary that morning?"

She slowly nods. "Yes. He was."

"Any chance he was there to steal drugs?"

She shakes her head. "No. Not from the infirmary. They keep a strict count."

"But he was alone with Mr. Appleton?"

"I think so. Yes."

I take a stab at the next question. "Ever hear of something called the Goodnight Club?"

"Um . . . no." She picks up another slice of pizza and nibbles at the end.

"Could you ask around at work?"

"Sure. Why?"

"Because I'm thinking they may have something to do with this."

"With Nurse Milo's death?"

"Possibly."

Adam makes a strangling sound and staggers to his feet. "Come on, Ember," he says. "I'll give you a ride home. It's getting cold, and there's a show I want to watch."

Six

"It's been a while," Kate says. She's perched on the edge of her favorite lounge chair, pouring whiskeys with a shaky hand. She's dressed in a green-and-orange velvet robe tonight, her fiery hair tamed in a bun. A candle burns bright on the glass end table; cherry-scented smoke sweetens the air. A sphinx moth thumps against the outdoor light, casting shadows across the ground. Its wings must hurt when they hit the glass, but I'm guessing that insect won't stop. It'll just keep on with its bumping until it finally gives up and dies.

"They've been messing with my shift," I say.

"Murder will do that."

"Um . . ." I stutter to a stop. We've been told to keep quiet on the cause of Milo's death while Javier makes his rounds.

"No need to lie to me," she says. "I may be old, but I'm not stupid. Nurse Milo didn't die from a heart attack. Rumor is he was killed."

A coyote yips from somewhere nearby. I glance at Kate sideways. "Who's saying that?"

"Everyone. There's nothing to do in this place but gossip. I'm sure you're aware of that. And we don't typically have police types poking around. People die here every day."

"Did you like him?" I ask.

"The deceased?" She shakes her head. "I shouldn't speak ill of the dead, but no. No one did." She settles in her chair with a sigh.

"Why not?"

"Are you investigating the murder?"

"I'm just an interested party."

"Well . . . most caretakers are decent people. I hold them in the highest regard." She sets down her glass with a clank. "But there are a few that are different. They're here because they have a craving for power and can't acquire it any other way. So, who better to victimize than the old and frail? No one listens to us anyway. It's as if at the end of life we age backward and people treat us like young children."

I lean forward, interested. "Tell me more about Nurse Milo."

"He was cruel but careful. Would wait until he was alone with one of the champions and turn his evil ways on them."

"Do you have proof?"

She shakes her head. "No proof."

"But guests knew?"

"Oh yes. We avoided him if we could. There was a reason he chose to work in the champion's unit. And, of course, he preferred to work at night."

"What about Kai? Did he know?"

"Our infantile executive director? I suppose it's possible. It's so difficult to find staff in Santa Barbara, it wouldn't surprise me if he turned a blind eye."

"Hypothetically, if Nurse Milo came to a bad end, is there any guest that would've had the strength and skill to kill him?"

She levels her gaze on mine. "Hypothetically, what kind of death are we talking about?"

"Let's say a quick stab to the neck."

"Carotid artery? That must've been a bloody mess."

I nod. "So is there anyone you can think of?"

She stares at me for a moment before answering. "No. Sorry. There isn't."

Something about the way she answers doesn't ring true. "You sure?" I ask.

"I'm sure." She finishes off her drink, and I do the same. I'm about to stand and take my leave when a pain-ridden howl escapes through the open door.

"Jesus," I say. "What was that?"

Kate wobbles to her feet. "It's my Gordon."

"Is he all right?"

"Unfortunately, no. My night nurse canceled at the last moment, and I wasn't able to find a replacement. Gordon should've been rotated an hour ago, but I don't have the strength to move him on my own."

"Won't one of Serenity's caretakers help you?"

She makes a face. "They used to, but the new management won't allow it. Some sort of liability nonsense."

"I'll help you."

She perks up. "Really? You'd do that for me?"

"Of course."

"Well, then. Follow me. And excuse the mess."

What mess? The house is about as immaculate as Kate Harrington, and just as well off. It reeks of the type of old money I've only seen on TV. White walls lined with original paintings giving off a Picasso-type feel. Hardwood floors burnished with lemon oil. Each piece of furniture a work of art. The only mess I can see is a *New York Times* flung open to the obituary page. A near-empty glass of red wine and a magnifying glass rest on its face. Kate takes note of my interest.

"My nightly ritual," she says in a tired voice. "When you get to be my age, it's far too often that friends and acquaintances end up in there. It really isn't a blessing to live as long as I have."

I glance at Kate. "Do you mind my asking your age?"

She smiles. "There was a time I would have slapped you for such an impertinent question. But now? Well, who cares? I'm all of eighty-three."

"So you were born . . ."

"I was born on leap day in 1936."

"Leap day? So, you only have a birthday every four years?"

"So they say. Gordon and I always made it quite the occasion. Nothing as frivolous as parties. We liked adventure, the two of us. One year we climbed Mount Kilimanjaro. Another we snuck into Cuba. We led quite an exciting life."

I make my way to the grand piano, where a number of black-and-white photos sit. There I spy a gold-framed wedding photo of what I'm guessing is Kate and her man. She has the strikingly angular face she still carries to this day. And Gordon resembles a young Cary Grant. Handsome with the kind of wide and friendly smile that turns strangers into friends.

"We had a good marriage," Kate says wistfully. "And I so depended on him. It takes everything in me to remember my husband for what he was and not the man he is today."

There's another animal groan from an interior room, and Kate's gaze returns to the present and settles on me.

"You sure you're up for this?" she asks.

"Of course. Why not?"

"It's hard for me to look at him. I can't imagine what a stranger thinks."

"I'll be fine." I follow her to the interior of the villa, where the walls are shadowy and the lights have been dimmed. We step into a bedroom, and I'm nearly overcome by a musty, fetid stench. In the center of the room, surrounded by gleaming white equipment, sits a solitary hospital bed. Gordon rests on his side, looking less living human than long-dead corpse. A white sheet covers his thin body. A series of low moans escape from his mouth.

"Hello, sweetheart," Kate calls. "I've brought Zach. He's the nice man I've been telling you about that visits every now and then. He's going to help me turn you tonight. Judy called in sick." Gordon moans, louder this time.

I have to stop myself from quaking at the sight of the withered man, his face frozen in a scream of horror. His hands are curled into yellow claws, while tubes emerge from his throat and his side. Only his wheezing moans and the blink of his eyes offer a clue that he's alive. "Is he in pain?" I whisper.

"I'm told he's not. But he has to be moved every few hours or bedsores develop. And those can be brutally painful."

"How do you turn him?" I ask, eyeing Kate's frail body.

"He no longer weighs much, and this is the best hospital bed money can buy. We strap him in like this." She pulls a strap across his shoulders and indicates I should do the same with his legs. "I used to be able to do this on my own, but it seems even the smallest task bothers my back these days."

"Don't worry. I'll handle it." I secure Gordon's legs and wait. The stench in the room reminds me of the bloom of a hundred-year flower I saw once at an orchid show. A big, black, ugly flower over which visitors oohed and awed.

It's not as bad as that, Tina whispers.

"Yes, it is." I'm surprised that my wife has made an appearance. She usually hides when Kate is around. Not sure if that means she's taken a liking to the woman or if the opposite is true.

"Tell me what to do," I say in a too-loud voice, trying to mask Tina's pesky whisper.

"Once he's strapped in tight, pull on this." She indicates a metal bar, and I apply pressure. The bed rumbles and lifts to one side, and with a quick flick of her hands, Kate turns Gordon onto his back. It doesn't seem like the adjustment should be painful, but Gordon's moan says otherwise.

"Sorry, sweetheart," Kate whispers.

I picture the man in the wedding portrait, so vibrant and alive. "What happened to him?" I ask.

"No need to whisper," Kate says. She takes hold of one of Gordon's frail hands and gives it a little squeeze. "Gordon likes to listen to conversations, don't you, sweetheart?" Her gaze slips from Gordon to me. "I think he's mostly gone. Resting in some eternal sleep. But a hospice nurse once told me that hearing is the last sense to go. So, I talk to him whenever I can. Maybe he's there. Maybe he's not. Honestly, for his sake, I hope he's somewhere else."

I nod, staring at the waxy face with the heavy-lidded eyes. "How long has it been since he was . . . ?"

"Normal?" She turns and plucks a framed photo of Gordon from a bookshelf and runs a crooked finger across the glass. He looks to be no more than forty, a trim, athletic man dressed in white tennis gear. "He was unusually healthy right up to his late seventies and so proud of that fact. Never once caught a cold or flu. And then out of the blue, he was paralyzed by a massive stroke. That was six years ago. He's been in declining health ever since." She gazes at me with liquid green eyes that glisten with forming tears. "It's cruel, don't you think? In a different time and place, he would've been allowed to pass into his next life with his dignity intact. But nowadays, our medical technology can keep a man alive even though he's technically gone."

I peer at the ropes that tether Gordon's hands to the bed, and I have a sudden sensation that the walls are closing in. I can't let this ever happen to me. "Didn't he have a . . . ?" I fumble for my next words.

"Medical directive?"

"Yeah. That."

"He never got around to signing one. But he had always been clear that he didn't want any extraordinary methods used to keep him alive."

"But that didn't stop this from happening?"

"His boys intervened with the courts."

"I remember you saying that. Do they ever help out?"

"Randall and Alfred? No. Never. In fact, they've only visited their father once in the past three years."

"But the court listened to them, not you."

"Yes."

"I'm sorry about that."

"Don't be. It's our own fault for being so arrogant about our health care that we didn't have our directives in place. The thing is, I have more than enough money to provide the highest level of care for Gordon. Think of all the people that don't."

I nod, making a mental note to get my own directive in place.

"I do hope to make a difference in eldercare," she continues. "Or at least to ease the suffering of a few. Our trust now designates that every penny of our estate will go to a local nonprofit that provides for hospice care for the indigent."

"That's kind of you."

"Not kind. I'm just thankful for all I've been given, and I want to pass it on."

"What about Gordon's sons? They okay with being written out of the will?"

She waves her hand dismissively. "Absolutely not. In fact, they've attempted to intervene by having the court declare me incompetent."

"Well, you're anything but that."

"Exactly. They lost that battle, but it doesn't mean they won't come at me again. Money does terrible things to people." Kate arranges the sheet so that Gordon is covered and then gives him a swift peck on the cheek. Then she picks up a needle and injects something into his IV. "There you go, sweetheart," she says. "That will help you sleep through the night." She nods at me, signaling we should go.

I turn to leave and then pause at the sight of a pink Post-it Note resting between a stash of prescription bottles. I bend down to see

Gordon's name scrawled across its face, but no date. I grab the note and wave it at Kate. "What's this?"

She stiffens. "Just what it looks like. A piece of paper."

"I don't believe you."

"What else could it be?"

"That's what I want to know."

"Is it any of your business?"

"It might be."

Her eyes narrow. "Let me have that. We'll talk about it once we're outside." She tugs the note from my fingers and signals that I should leave the room. Once we're back on the veranda, I turn to Kate. She seems smaller somehow, like she's shriveled. Still, I speak as firmly as I can. "I want the truth," I say. "Tell me what that pink note is about."

She settles in her lounge chair with a groan. "Why don't you top off our drinks? Better yet, toss them and make fresh ones."

I stay on my feet, arms crossed. "I don't have time for this. I just want answers."

"Another ten minutes won't matter."

"I'm not so sure."

She folds her arms and closes her eyes, relaxing with a sigh. She suddenly appears years older, her face further ravaged by time. "If you want answers to your question, you'll humor me and share a drink."

"All right," I say, irritation blooming. I freshen our glasses with two-inch pours. "Here you go."

"Thank you. Now sit, and I'll answer your questions."

I'm not in the mood to sit, but I need to know what Kate knows, and tonight might be my only chance. "Does the note have anything to do with something called the Goodnight Club?" I ask, settling into my chair.

Kate shifts a little uncomfortably and takes a sip of her drink. "Yes," she says after a long pause. "It most certainly does."

Seven

There's a pounding at my door drilling holes through my head. "Go away," I moan into my pillow, but the pounding won't stop.

"*Zach!* I know you're in there. I have to speak with you. I need you to open up."

It's Ruth, Tina says.

"I know who it is."

Just ignore her. You need your sleep.

"She probably wants my info on the Goodnight Club."

Your message said you'd meet her before the start of your shift.

"Maybe she can't wait."

That's her problem, not yours.

I glance at the clock. Hell. Tina is right. It's two in the afternoon, and I've gotten only a few hours of sleep. I sit up, and the room spins like a drunken top. I think back on the drinks with Kate. Was there one? Two? Maybe three? But then I recall the story she told me, and I stagger to my feet.

The pounding begins again. "*Coming!*" I yell. I throw on a clean T-shirt, brush my teeth, and splash cold water on my face. I glance into the mirror. At least I don't look as bad as I feel. Sure, my face is carved by the ravines that took hold in my early forties. And my eyes are partially hidden under the shadows of my brows. But I've lost some of the puffiness and fatigue that have plagued me these past few years. Seems things have gone from worse to bad.

"*Zach!*"

Better hurry, Tina hisses, messing with my mood.

"You stay out of this," I reply, getting ready to slap my head.

I'll be good, she says in a fading voice. *I won't say another word. I promise.*

I slip on my ancient Tevas and hurry to the front door. Despite the angry sound of Ruth's voice, I throw it open with a smile. Can't wait to tell her I might've cracked the case. I open my mouth to greet her, but her sour look shuts me down.

"I can't believe this, Zach," she says, rushing in.

"What? What is it? Has something happened to Adam?"

"You tell me," she snaps. "You know more about my son than I do."

I shut the door and turn to face Ruth. She's dressed in her typical work attire—black pants, matching jacket, a pink shirt to lighten the dark. Sensible flats to match her attire. She raises her fists like a boxer getting ready to punch. "How could you?" She stamps her foot, and the floor shakes.

Guilt surges through my gut. Did she find out about my drinking on the job?

"I can explain," I say.

"Can you?"

"Yes. I mean, I know I shouldn't share drinks with guests, but Kate is so damn lonely, and . . . and," I continue foolishly, "and it ended up being a good thing, because I got the information we need."

"That's not what I'm here for," Ruth says, her eyes gone hard as flint. "What I want to know is why? Why'd you do it? How could you betray us like this?"

Betray? For a moment I have no idea what she's talking about, and then my stomach drops. "Is this about Nurse Milo?"

She raises her voice so loud it reverberates through the far corners of the house. "*Of course it is.* What else would I be talking about?"

I stare at her for a moment, my mind churning like Niagara Falls. Damn. Did Adam say something to Javier? If so, I'm up shit creek.

"I can explain," I say.

"So it's true."

"In a way, but . . ."

The strength seems to slip out of Ruth, and she collapses onto my couch. "But what?"

I don't answer her right away. I'm not thinking too straight.

She looks up, her face flushed. "Go ahead, damn it. Give me an explanation that would help me understand why you of all people would tell my son to lie."

"I didn't tell him," I try to organize my thoughts. Does she know about the drugs? "He asked me for my help, and I agreed."

"Help? What kind of help?"

"He stumbled into a situation, and he wasn't sure what to do."

"You mean he found Milo's dead body."

"Yes."

"So you told him to lie."

"Not exactly . . ."

"Not exactly?" She pounds her hands on her knees. "My God, Zach. This is no joke. This is a murder investigation. You of all people should know the danger you've put him in."

"*I've* put him in?" That stops me for a moment. She obviously doesn't know about the Adderall, and it takes everything in me not to tell her.

She swipes at the sweat on her brow. "You were supposed to help him straighten out, not teach him how to lie."

"I didn't tell him to lie. Not exactly." Now I'm getting pissed.

"That's the second time you've said that. What does *not exactly* mean?"

"If you calm down, I'll tell you."

"How can I *calm down*?" She buries her head in her hands. "I never should've allowed him to work at Serenity Acres. I was an idiot to let you convince me."

I take a deep breath and grip my hands to keep myself from lashing out. "Why don't you back up and tell me what's happened. Tell me what you heard, and we can discuss this calmly."

She eyes me like I'm crazy. *"Calmly?"*

"I mean . . . just tell me what happened? Did the police find out?"

It takes her a moment to answer, and then she shakes her head hard. "I don't know. I don't think so. I was having a bad day, so I ran home for lunch, and Adam was in the backyard talking to Ember on his cell. He sounded upset, so I did what any mom would do and listened in. I heard him say something about Nurse Milo, so when he got off, I confronted him, and he told me everything, Zach. *Everything!*"

"Hell." I sink down next to her. "He told Ember?" There's a sizzling in my gut, an old ulcer coming to life.

"Who cares? What matters is that you told him to lie, Zach. *To lie!*" She pounds her knees again.

"That's not how it went down . . ."

"It's not? Then tell me your version."

"Well . . ." I think back. In hindsight it does seem like a stupid move, but what else could I have done? "It was the only way to protect Adam. At least I thought so at the time."

"Well, that was beyond irresponsible."

Tell her about the drugs, Tina says.

I want to. I really do. But that's just anger speaking. "No," I reply and continue on. "Adam happened to park in the wrong place that morning and found Nurse Milo, already dead. He was worried about the implications. Thought it might mess up his court case. And honestly, with his background, I thought it might mess him up too. So, I agreed we could keep it our secret. I didn't think . . ."

"Of course you didn't think. If you had, you would have insisted on the truth. What's going to happen when they find out he's lied?"

"They won't."

"No?" Ruth gets to her feet and begins to pace. "You really think so? Because he's scared, Zach. He told me so. That's why he called Ember."

"What's he scared of?"

"He thinks Finn is on to him."

"What do you mean by that?"

"Finn questioned him again this morning."

"Were the police involved?"

"I don't think so."

I work my hands together. "Go on. What did he say?"

"He told Finn it was dark and he didn't see the body, but Finn said he didn't believe him. And then he asked Adam about us."

I give my knee a rub. "What about us?"

"He wanted to know how long we'd been neighbors . . . if the two of us were friends."

"He figured that out?"

"It wouldn't take a genius, just a glance at our files." Ruth stops pacing and turns to me. "The thing is, if Finn is snooping around, it won't take him long to uncover Adam's history of drug abuse. Add in the felony assault accusation and the growing rumors that Milo was a dealer and . . . oh my God, you have to understand this looks *so* very bad."

The sizzle in my gut begins to burn. "That's why I agreed with Adam we shouldn't tell anyone he was there."

Ruth throws up her hands in frustration and once again raises her voice. "You were a detective once, right? If they figure out that Adam lied about his whereabouts, won't it make things worse?"

"You don't understand . . ."

"What don't I understand? Stupidity? For God's sake, Zach. How could you let this happen?"

My gut has reached the boiling point. "I didn't *let this happen*," I shout. "He did it to himself. The truth is he arrived there early to meet Milo. He went there to buy drugs."

Ruth eyes widen. "Drugs?"

"Not bad drugs. Just Adderall."

"Just? He was meeting Milo that morning? He was going to buy stolen drugs? Oh my God. This is so much worse than I thought." She begins to pace again. "It's your fault," she says.

"What?"

"Adam didn't need to work at Serenity. That was your terrible idea."

The sizzle bursts into flames that are fanned by my words. "*It wasn't a ridiculous idea!* He couldn't just sit in your house like some worthless loser and do nothing every day. That would've been the worst possible thing for him."

"He could've found another job. Somewhere, anywhere else."

"Yeah? Where?" I get up and slam the window shut. Don't need nosy neighbors listening in.

"I don't know where. Anywhere but Serenity Acres."

"Didn't we agree it would've been difficult for him to get a job?"

She plucks at her stupid Fitbit. "We didn't agree on anything. It was your idea. Damn. I should've known better. I never should've hired you, Zach. That's the dumbest thing I did all year."

"Really?" I get right up into her face. I can smell her baby powder scent. "Why did you hire me, Ruth? Huh? Let's talk about that."

"I hired you because I felt sorry for you."

"That's a lie." I jab a finger at my chest. "You hired me because you wanted to keep me quiet. You knew I was falling apart with guilt, and you didn't want me blabbing. You didn't want the real story of Hunter's death to get out."

"That's not true."

"Bullshit."

"Well, if it's the truth, I failed in my mission. You spewed to Carlyn anyway."

"I didn't spew."

"What do you call it?"

"I call it telling the truth." The flame in my gut ratchets back and turns into a hardened lump of coal. Whatever sympathy I've ever felt for Ruth, whatever caring, all of it is gone. "Come on, Ruth. Admit it. You hired me to buy my silence."

It takes a long time for her to answer. "Yes," she says. "I suppose I did."

I take a deep breath. "Well, I can't be bought, Ruth. And it's time we told our secret. It's only fair Adam should know."

"You think it's going to make him feel better to learn we were having an affair?"

"Not an affair." I'm aiming daggers at her heart. "We had a one-night stand. And it wasn't even night."

She holds her hands to her ears. "Don't say that."

I wrestle her hands away. "It wasn't one night, was it? *Was it?*"

Her eyes grow large with fear. "No," she whispers. "It wasn't."

"It was a warm spring afternoon when you were falling to pieces."

"It wasn't my fault . . ."

"Because you had just learned your dick of a husband was having an affair."

Ruth yanks her hands from mine. "I've had enough. Don't say anymore."

"And to be honest, there was no love on my side. It was barely lust. I felt sorry for you, Ruth. I felt pity. Doug treated you like shit."

"Stop it."

"You were upset. I was upset. We added booze to the mix, and hell if I didn't do to my wife what Doug did to you. Only I had no excuse, because I loved Tina." I grab Ruth's hands again and hold them in mine. She struggles like a captured animal, but I refuse to let go. I can no longer see her clearly through the tears that blur my eyes. "We're doing this, Ruth. Today. We're not going to let another hour go by without facing our truth."

"No!"

"Because I can't stand it anymore. I want people to know. I want Adam to know."

"Leave Adam out of it!"

"How can I, when every day I wonder if his problems stem from our lie?"

"We didn't do anything to him. He . . . he was the one that left the yard to watch TV."

"He was eleven, Ruth. Only eleven. We were the adults. We made the mistake. And we laid every bit of blame on that young boy's back."

Ruth's voice drops to a whisper. "Please. Please don't do this to me. My life is already a mess. This will only make things worse."

Come on, Tina interjects, *do it. I've been waiting two decades for this.*

I let go of Ruth, and she drops onto the couch. I stand above her, arms folded. "The truth is, if we hadn't gone to your bedroom that day, Hunter would still be alive."

And me, Tina says. *Don't leave me out of the equation.*

"And Tina," I say. "Both of their lives rest on my back."

And they rest on hers too.

"And they rest on yours too. And then to let a kid take all the blame for a drowning? It's no wonder Adam turned to drugs to deal with his guilt. I turned to alcohol. And you . . . you turned into a block of ice."

"We didn't let him take the blame," Ruth moans, dropping her head in her hands.

"Hell we didn't. You told the police we put him in charge for only a few minutes so we could check on some paperwork. Remember? Remember that? You said we ran into the house to grab a copy of your plans for the remodel. That we'd put Adam in charge for no more than five minutes, and you couldn't understand why he wandered away. But it wasn't five minutes, was it? It was over an hour. Who would blame the kid for heading inside? He was hot. He was tired. He was thirsty."

She looks up, eyes narrowing. "You went along with my story."

"That's true. I did. And I take full responsibility for that. You came to the hospital and begged me, and I agreed to back you up."

"I was trying to help both of us," Ruth says. "If Tina had learned the truth, it would've made things worse."

She's wrong, Tina says.

"*You're wrong!*" I yell, the rafters shaking. "Maybe if we had told her the truth, she would've focused her anger on me. Maybe her 'accident' never would've happened. Maybe she would've found her way to a decent life." I raise my fists in the air. "And that would've been better. Don't you understand? Anything would've been better than how it turned out."

"Please stop," she whispers.

I sink next to Ruth, anger melting. "Remember that afternoon, Ruth. Remember? Doug was out of town at a conference. You were sure he was with his gal. Alice had spent the night at a friend's. And Tina was at a play in LA. It was hot, so Adam had filled up a plastic pool and was sailing his toy boats around. He was a nice kid. Really nice. So he had no problem sharing the pool with a toddler. If only he had been a selfish brat."

"*Stop.*"

"You were needy, and we got drunk, and I took you in my arms."

"*No.*"

"And I kissed you, not once. I kissed you several times."

"*Please.*"

"And then you nodded toward the inside of your house."

"*No.*"

"Watch Hunter," you said to Adam. "Mommy and Zach will be right back."

I hate this part, Tina sniffles. *It really breaks my heart.*

"And then we climbed into your bed. Remember, Ruth? Remember?"

She looks up, tears streaming down her cheeks. "Please don't do this. I'm begging you."

I understand what she's asking, but there's no way I'm going to stop. "And then somewhere along the line I noticed how quiet everything had grown. Remember? Remember the quiet? I can't get it out of my head. I knew before I even jumped up that my little boy was dead."

"I'm so sorry," she moans.

"And then when I pulled him from the water . . ." My throat closes.

"*Stop*," she begs.

"Mom?" I look up and see Adam standing limp in the doorway, Ember's melted face peeking around his back.

V. GLUTTONY

For drunkards and gluttons become poor, and drowsiness clothes them in rags.

—Proverbs 23:21

The Angel

Death be not proud. That's a lovely but troublesome phrase when you can't get it out of your head. And that's what's happening to me right now. My thoughts are spinning wild. It's not like I'm looking for justification. I know I did nothing wrong. God placed me on earth to do his bidding; who am I to thwart his will? But I could have handled matters differently. I admit to making a mistake. I didn't expect to operate in such an obvious manner; the death shouldn't have happened that way. I was planning on a quiet overdose in his morning coffee or evening snack. A drug death wouldn't have surprised anyone after his history came to light. But Milo's passing was more than messy, and now outsiders are snooping about.

Of course, I shouldn't have gone through with Appleton's crossing; I should've waited until he returned home. But he had set a time and a date, and I can be quite compulsive when it comes to my heavenly work. Unfortunately, I didn't notice the scoundrel hiding behind the bathroom door. Milo watched as I administered the epinephrine. Revealed himself before I left the room. Threatened to expose my secret unless I conceded to his demands.

I'll allow my temper took control of my actions and clouded my better judgment. I attended his clandestine meeting hoping a payoff might delay his next move. I offered him money in exchange for his silence to give me time to construct a plan. But the wretch snubbed my proposition—wanted more than my meager savings would allow. So when he reached for the initial payoff, I lunged for his portly neck. I honestly had no choice in the matter. It was eradicate or be exposed.

RUTH MOSBY

One

Thursday, September 26

"Mom?"

The look on Adam's face brings back memories of his early childhood. That time before a newborn gains control over his fleeting facial expressions. I remember watching as my baby boy tested the boundaries of every human emotion, from happy to sad, proud to embarrassed, courageous to scared. He does that now until his face settles into an angry mask. My throat goes dry; my stomach curdles. I finger my Fitbit and pray.

Zach gets to his feet, then freezes. No one says a word. The silence is all-encompassing, the earth about to shake. My gaze pivots from Adam to Zach, soundlessly begging for help.

"*Mom,*" Adam repeats, his hands clenched by his side. His face has grown swollen and red. I think it might split. He eyes me like I'm a monster. I want to tell him I'm not.

"Honey," I say, slowly standing. "I can explain."

"Explain?" he says. "Explain what?" Ember steps into the room and takes Adam's hand and whispers in his ear. "No," he says, shaking her off. "You don't understand."

Zach takes a step forward, clearing his throat. Adam takes a step back. "I'm sorry," Zach says in a pleading tone. "We should've told you a long time ago."

"So why didn't you?"

Zach mumbles something to himself. "I wanted to," he says after a moment. "I really did."

"*Wanted to?*" Adam thrusts his fists in the air. "Wanted to what?"

"Wanted to explain . . ."

"Explain? There's that word again. Explain what? How you fucked my mom when she was married to my dad?"

Zach looks like he's been struck. "Adam, please."

"*Fuck you.*" Adam spins in circles, looking like a trapped cat. "Fuck the both of you."

"Don't use that language," I snap, although I really don't care. I'm frightened my secret has escaped from the bottle, and there's no chance of putting it back. Adam stops spinning and glares at me.

"Don't use that language? Really?" He jabs his finger in my direction. "Who are *you* to stop *me*? You're a liar and a whore."

"*Adam!*"

"Don't look at me like that. It's true and you know it."

"Adam," I repeat, my heart racing. "You've got to settle down."

"Are you kidding me?" He rakes his hands through his hair. "You let me believe it was me and only me that was responsible for Hunter's death."

"We didn't do that . . . we just . . ." My voice fades, and Adam jumps back in.

"That day has haunted me for twenty years. Even when I was using, I never got it out of my head. If I hadn't gotten bored. If I hadn't watched TV. If I'd only paid attention. But I didn't. And Hunter died, and so did Tina, and I've spent years blaming myself."

"You have?" I'm overcome by a wave of crushing guilt. "I'm so sorry. I didn't know. You never said anything."

"I was only a kid. I couldn't express myself. Just felt guilty and ashamed."

"But we took you to a counselor . . ."

"You took me to some old lady that smelled like cigarettes and pee."

"She came highly recommended."

"Guess she fooled you."

"She told us you were handling things fine."

"Did she?" Adam belts out a crazy laugh. "Then that old lady didn't know shit, 'cause I wasn't 'handling things fine.'"

"Oh, Adam." I think back on my little boy, wishing I could take him in my arms.

"And to top it off, there was the arguing. You and Dad going at it night after night, and all because of me."

"It wasn't because of you."

Adam slams his fist against the wall. "*I thought it was.* That's what counts, right? I couldn't escape feeling guilty. Not anywhere. At school it was even worse."

I swallow. "How on earth could that be? You were in fifth grade. How would the children have known?"

"*Hello!* Everyone in town knew the story. And there are mean kids in the world, Mom. Not many, but it only takes one to get things going. And in my case, a couple of them started calling me *baby killer.*" He places his hands on his hips. "Did you know that? Huh? Baby killer. That was my nickname for years."

I put my hand to my mouth, a siren screeching in my ears. "I'm sorry," I say. "I wish you had told me."

Adam sinks to his knees. "Do you? And what exactly would you have done with the information? Sent me to another counselor? Told me a new pack of lies? Because I find it hard to believe you would've told the truth." He begins to sob, a low guttural sound. Ember tries reaching out, but he jerks his shoulder away. "Do you know that *baby killer* followed me all the way through high school? It's true. I even heard it on the soccer fields. That's why I quit the team. In the end, the only thing that made me feel better were the drugs. Yeah, that's right." He points from Zach to me. "You two played a part in making me an addict. Can't thank you enough for that."

"Oh, Adam." I drop onto the couch. What have I done? And why? There's nothing I can say that excuses my behavior. Not Doug's affair. Not the alcohol. Not my distant parents. Not my depression or my anxiety or the divorce that tore me apart. There's no justification in the world that excuses such a lie.

Zach glances at me and then crouches next to Adam and works to absolve himself. "You're right," he says. "I should've told you years ago. I can only beg for your forgiveness. I'd be humbled if you'd give me that."

"You can beg all you want," Adam says, "and tell me you're sorry for the rest of your life. But it's never going to change what I've been through. And it won't change what I've become. Fact is, you're a goddamn coward. You should've told the truth from the start." Adam staggers to his feet with a look of disgust. "I thought you were my friend, but you're a fraud just like my mom."

"That's not true," Zach says, standing with a groan.

"I hate you. I hate both of you. And I'm out of here, man. For good this time. Come on, Ember. Let's go."

"Are you going home?" I ask in the smallest of voices.

Adam makes a guttural sound like he's getting ready to spit. "I'm sure as hell not going to *your* home. I want nothing to do with you."

Ember gazes at me with the saddest of eyes. "I'm sorry," she mouths. Then they turn and rush from the house. I wait in silence until I hear my son's car zoom off before I get up and head for the front door.

"I'm sorry," Zach calls out. "I didn't mean for things to end like this."

I don't turn. I can't bear to see his face. "Yes, you did. You always wanted this. Seems you were right all along. My lie destroyed my son's life."

"Our lie."

"Whatever." I stumble down Zach's steps and stumble up mine. I unlock my front door, head straight to my bedroom, kick off my shoes, and climb into bed.

My mind flashes back to that horrible year: Doug's affair. Hunter's drowning. Tina's fiery death. Then I pause on the day Doug left me. We were having dinner at the Sojourner Restaurant, and for the first time in months, we seemed to be getting along. But midway through the stir-fried vegetables, he cleared his throat and said he needed a change.

A change? *A change?* What type of change? A new car? A pet? Different cereal? Better gym? Oh, no. He wanted a new life. Said it wasn't me but him, and it had nothing to do with his affair with the young intern at work. It would've happened anyway. And the kids? Our kids? His kids? Alice and Adam? He said they'd adjust to their new life. Then he reached out and took my hand and told me he would always be my friend. I held tight for a moment before I let him go. Then I walked out of the restaurant and staggered the long mile home, where I sobbed into my pillow until I couldn't breathe.

Eventually I fall sleep and slip into my nagging nightmare in which I morph into an oak. But this time my leaves don't fall, my branches don't shrink. Instead, I'm rooted to the ground as a wildfire closes in. The flames surge up my trunk until all that's left is a pile of ash.

My eyes open, and I leap from my bed, pulse racing. *It was a dream,* I repeat, but no matter. I feel a terrible closeness to death. I flick on the house lights and walk in circles until my breathing slows. Then I sit on the couch with my favorite photo album in an attempt to stave off sleep.

The photos are from the year we took a family vacation to Kauai. Alice was seven. Adam five. We rented a house near the end of the road, across from a white sand beach lapped by turquoise waters. We were still in love then, Doug and me. You can see it in our eyes. The kids are golden and sandy, holding rocks and shells. I remember watching them frolic in the warm ocean water, sure I had found the secret of a good life. That I had shaken off the sadness of my childhood. How naïve I'd been not to have known the truth: there is no escaping the past.

Two

Monday. September 30

I took a sick day on Friday, but now it's Monday, and I've dragged myself back to work. I had no choice in the matter. Stacks of problems await me here. It was a long weekend. The longest ever. Just me and my depressing thoughts. The only interruption came from Zach, who stopped by on Sunday morning and pounded on my front door. I hid in the interior bathroom until he continued on his way. I didn't want to see him. Hear his words. I needed some time to reflect.

My Fitbit buzzes, and I frown, thinking it's become a symbol of my flaws. Critical. Unyielding. Judgmental. It kept buzzing me all weekend long, reminding me of my missing steps. But what do ten thousand steps matter when I'm all alone in the world? No friends. No family. No future. A life built on a lie. I'm not a vessel of perfection. I've only been acting like I am.

Over the weekend I thought a lot about Zach's insightful words. How we each dealt with Hunter's death in our own wretched ways. Zach became an alcoholic; Adam found drugs. Alice embraced solace on the road. And me? The instigator? I wrapped myself in a self-righteous cloak so I could look down on everyone else. Who could ever live up to my expectations? No one. Not even me.

I want to change. Have to change. Learn to accept my past. See myself for who I am. But where to start? Should I reach out to Adam? Contact Alice? Tell my ex-husband the honest truth? Should I call Carlyn and beg for forgiveness for not standing by her side?

With a sigh, I turn to my computer, where hundreds of emails await. I whip through several dozen until I reach one that gives me pause. There was another death this weekend. The fifth destitute in as many weeks. And not just any destitute. Eleanor Kingsley, the guest Kai forced to move to a studio to make room for the ex-governor's wife. She was found on the ground next to her bed, a sheet twisted around her neck. A bizarre accident that occurred sometime late in the night.

I retrieve Eleanor's file from the cabinet and scan the pages for a contact number, but there are no relatives left in her life. And without a penny for a burial, I'll have to refer her case to Pastor Sam.

I place the file with the stack of the recently deceased. Is there anything unusual in the numbers? Something sinister behind the uptick? Could someone be targeting the destitutes, or is this just a strange run of bad luck? No Post-it Notes have surfaced with the bodies, so it's doubtful the prankster is involved. I stare hard at the files, as if by doing so the truth will make itself clear.

"Morning." Detective Ruiz steps inside my office, his wide eyes begging forgiveness. "Have a moment?"

"A quick one," I reply, standing and forcing a smile.

"I'm Detective Ruiz," he says, holding out his massive hand.

"Yes, I know." I give his hand a quick shake. "I've seen you around campus."

He settles into his seat, and I do the same. "I have a few questions about your employees." His gentle voice contrasts with the intensity of his size. "I'm interested in their whereabouts on the morning of Milo Kushner's death."

The smile fades from my face. "I'm sorry. I'm really backed up. Can we do this another time?"

He straightens his tie. "Just give me ten minutes," he says. "Then I'll get out of your hair."

Out of my hair? I don't know why, but the phrase gets stuck in my head. It's obvious I'm exhausted and not thinking straight. This is no time to be speaking to the police. "Ten minutes max," I say. "If you need more time, then you'll have to schedule a meeting."

"No, ten minutes is good." He goes on to ask me about several employees who were parked in the lot on the morning of Milo's death. I answer all his questions, and then he taps his pencil on my desk. "What about your son?" he asks, looking up. "Adam Mosby? He is your son, correct?"

I nod. "Yes. Adam is my son."

"I see the resemblance."

"In a way . . ." In truth, he resembles his dad.

"He's been working at Serenity for how long?"

"Several weeks now . . . actually over a month."

"It must be nice to have your son living so close. Is he your only child?"

"I have a daughter."

"She live here too?"

"No." What is the chitchat for? Is he trying to soften me up?

"Then where . . . ?"

"When she's not touring, she lives in Hollywood."

"Touring? An actress?"

"A singer."

"You must be proud."

"I am." I fix my eyes on my computer. "Now if you're done with your questioning, I have a lot of work to do."

"I'm almost done." He peers at his notes. "Just a couple more questions. Can you remind me again of your process for hiring new employees?"

I never told him about our process. He must have met with HR. "We work with several online employment sites and advertise in the local papers."

He shakes his head. "I mean, your process for vetting your employees. Criminal background checks. That sort of thing."

I shift uncomfortably in my chair. "What do you want to know?"

"Do you run background checks on everyone?"

"I don't. HR does."

"But you review them?"

"Sometimes."

"And what would . . . hmm . . . the word's on the tip of my tongue. *Exclude.* Yes. That's it. What would exclude a candidate from working here?"

"I'm not sure what you mean."

A hint of frustration darkens his face. "I assume HR runs the background checks for a reason. If a candidate had a felony on his record, for example . . . ?"

"We still might hire them. It depends on their crime."

"So what kind of ex-criminals would be excluded?"

"Pretty much anyone involved with theft, drugs, or violence." He doesn't say anything, so I continue on. "We also wouldn't hire anyone with a hit-and-run. Or more than one DUI."

"How about a history of spousal abuse or drug possession? Would you exclude someone like that?"

I finger my Fitbit. "Yes. Quite possibly, we would."

He nods and flips through his notepad. "How about your son, Adam? Was he subject to a background check?"

I picture Adam's file hidden deep in my desk. "Of course."

"Where is it?"

"I'll have to look."

"Should I assume it's clear?" His eyes have grown hard, and it dawns on me he knows the answers to his questions before he asks. I force my next words from my mouth.

"Not quite."

He nods in a knowing way. "I didn't think so."

"Look, I'm fully aware of my son's history, but he's a changed man. He's fine."

"What about his recent felony charge? Know anything about that?"

Hell. "It's a personal matter between him and his wife. He's pleaded not guilty to the charge."

The detective fingers his tie. "And he met his wife . . . where?"

I clear my throat, bite my lip. When I say the words, they sound bad. "In rehab, but . . ."

"But?" He studies me, and I get the feeling the man is reading my mind.

"It shouldn't matter to you where he met his wife."

"In this case, it might."

"He had a short-lived problem with addiction, but he's now clean."

"He's been arrested, though." The detective flips through his notes. "In his senior year of high school? I believe he was arrested on campus."

"The charges were dropped."

"Because he didn't commit the crime or because you hired a good lawyer?"

"What are you insinuating?"

"How about the recent incident in Palmdale?"

"That had nothing to do with drugs."

The detective scours his notepad. "Are you sure?"

"As far as I know. Why are you asking?"

"Just interested. I'd like to take a look at Adam's personnel file."

"That's impossible."

"Impossible?"

"Without a warrant, I mean."

"I hate to go there."

"Our procedures require you request his file from our executive director. If Kai agrees, then we'll hand it over."

"I'll do that."

"Fine." I swipe my hand across my forehead. "Now, I really need to get back to work."

"Just a few more questions; then I'll be done here."

I breathe deep. "All right."

"Can you tell me if Milo Kushner's background check was clear?"

"I believe so."

"No history of violence or drugs?"

"We wouldn't have hired him if he had a questionable history."

He nods, his eyes scouring my face. "But you hired your son."

"That's different."

"In what way?"

"He successfully completed his treatment."

"Three times?"

"Yes," I reply, the words wrenched from my mouth. "Three times."

He jots down a note. "Who do you report to?"

"Kai Gilchrist."

"The boss man. Hmm." His eyes spark. "So you discussed your son's history with him?"

"No." I carefully choose my next words. "I discussed my son's history with our HR director. She was comfortable that his past problems had been resolved."

"You're referring to Molly North?"

"Yes."

"Is Ms. North a friend of yours?"

"Our relationship had nothing to do with the decision," I fib. "Now if you'll excuse me . . ." I peer at the door, inviting him out.

"Ah, yes. You've got work to do." The detective gets to his feet, and I do the same. "Forgive me for being a nuisance," he says.

"You're not being a nuisance. I'm just busy."

"Aren't we all?" He backpedals toward the door and pauses beneath the doorjamb. "One last question. Any idea why your son would have parked on the far side of the parking lot the morning Kushner was killed?"

I stare at him, working my way through an answer. Does he know about the Adderall? About Zach's and Adam's lie? If so, he must think I'm involved. "I don't know," I say. "You'll have to ask Adam."

"I did. He said he likes to walk. That true?"

"It is." The detective stares at me, and again I get the feeling that he knows exactly what I'm thinking. I wait until he leaves the room, and then I drop into my seat, stomach churning. I feel guilty. But what have I done? I didn't actually lie, just sidestepped the truth.

Three

I leave my office shortly before five and head to the auditorium, where Kai has called a sudden mandatory all-hands staff meeting. I arrive to a standing-room-only affair and take my place against the back wall. I scan the sea of uniforms and spy my son seated beside Ember near the front of the room. She's whispering something in his ear. Should I warn him about the detective? If I do, will he cause a scene?

I turn my attention to the stage, where Kai sits between Finn and an unknown woman. Pastor Sam rounds out the pack. My attention focuses on the stranger. She's young and seems enamored by Kai, giggling at something he says. Finn, on the other hand, sits stone faced, hands in lap, back as straight as a rod. Pastor Sam is dressed in her characteristic black, her eyes fixed on the heavens above.

I nervously finger my Fitbit, another problem gnawing away. I've never been relegated to the audience. How come I'm not onstage? I jump at a tap on my shoulder.

"You doing okay?" Except for his vivid blue eyes, Zach looks as wretched as I feel.

I nod. "Yeah. I guess."

"I was worried. I didn't mean for things to spiral like that."

I gesture at the crowd pressing around us. "I don't want to talk about it here."

"After?"

I nod, wondering if Detective Ruiz might still be out and about. "I'll meet you at the memorial garden after this meeting wraps up."

"Okay." Zach leans over and rubs his knee a couple of times. "Shouldn't you be up on stage?"

I don't answer. Just work my hands together until it feels like my fingers might break.

Pastor Sam opens the assembly with a blessing and asks everyone to bow their heads. She gives a short tribute to Nurse Milo, talking about his legacy as a nurse and a man. Kai follows up with some quick remarks about the importance of communication and teamwork. He's dressed in shades of pink and purple, a bandana wrapped around his head. He concludes with a quote from the Bible. It sounds odd coming from his hipster mouth.

"Yea, though I walk through the valley of the shadow of death, I will fear no evil: for thou art with me; thy rod and thy staff they comfort me."

There's a smattering of applause, and Kai returns to his seat. Then Finn takes the mike and, with military precision, gives a security update. He talks in generalities for a while and then gets specific.

"In the wake of Nurse Milo's death, corporate will be implementing additional controls." He leans forward, his features set in a scowl. "In November, we will be issuing updated ID tags with a tracking feature. We will know where you are and what you are doing each and every moment of your shift. All prescriptions will be logged in with their contents recorded daily." He pauses, seemingly for effect. "And there will be random drug testing beginning tomorrow. If you are asked to give a sample, you must consent or face the loss of your job."

An unhappy murmur runs through the crowd, and Finn makes an ugly face. "You all signed waivers at the time you accepted your positions. They are held in your personnel files. If you have any questions or concerns, you are welcome to discuss with HR."

Kai jumps up when the grumbling continues and signals that Finn should take his seat. "Remember," Kai says in a persuasive voice. "These new rules are for your own protection. In fact, we've collaborated with the local police department on many of our proposed changes, including the need for drug testing." The grumbling only gets louder. "It's for your safety," Kai says, his face growing red, "and the safety of our guests." He waits until the crowd settles down before continuing.

"Moving on, I'd like to announce an exciting change in staffing. After nearly a quarter century of dedicated work, our wonderful head of HR, Molly North, has made the difficult decision to retire. She's a private person and didn't want a lot of fanfare, so she requested we keep her decision confidential until after her departure at noon today. Molly plans to spend her time traveling and visiting her grandkids. She wanted me to pass on her good wishes to the staff."

What? I almost choke. That's a lie, pure and simple. I recently had lunch with Molly, and she had no plans to retire. In fact, she spoke about her husband's long battle with cancer and how Serenity's benefits were the only thing keeping them financially afloat. What did Kai do to her? How'd he pull that off? I pause at a worrisome thought. Did her leaving have anything to do with me? With Adam's background check? I never would've pushed her to ignore his infractions if I had thought she might lose her job.

"We'll miss Molly," Kai continues, "but I'm excited to announce we have her replacement waiting in the wings. Charlese, come greet your new family." The newcomer gets to her feet and totters to the mike on three-inch heels. Kai shakes her hand and then turns to face the crowd. "Staff, I'm pleased to introduce our new head of human resources, Charlese Baker. She comes direct from headquarters with an unparalleled background in her field."

Unparalleled background? Are you kidding me? If the woman is even thirty, it would be a shock. Molly's experience must run rings around hers.

Kai rambles on. "Charlese has trained in the latest management techniques and has exciting plans for their implementation. Now, please stand, and let's give her a warm Serenity Acres welcome." He raises his hands and begins to clap, and most of the employees do the same. I glare at Zach when he joins in. He gives me a sideways glance that asks, "What else am I supposed to do?"

Charlese swivels back and forth as if her waist is detached from her hips. "Hello, Santa Barbara," she calls, gracing us with a beauty queen wave. "I want you to know I'm *absolutely* over the moon in love with Serenity Acres and *so* excited to be given the opportunity to join your marvelous team." Charlese speaks in a high-pitched, perky voice in which every sentence is part melody. "And to be living on the glorious American Riviera? Wow. Isn't this the most beautiful place you've ever seen? I think so, and I've traveled to some pretty nifty places." She glances back at Kai before continuing. "But I'm sure you'd like me to get to the point so you can get home to your loved ones, right?"

"Right," someone yells, and there's a smattering of laughter. Charlese acts like a good sport and joins in.

"Okay, then," she says once it quiets down. "I want you to know we've spent weeks examining our health-care offerings and have concluded that it's time for a change. We are ready to acknowledge here and now that we have gotten things 100 percent wrong."

We have?

"It's high time we empower you, our fantastic, brilliant employees, with your God-given right to freedom of choice. We are embarking on a program that will allow each and every one of you to take control over your own lives."

There's a smattering of applause. The crowd mostly seems confused. But that doesn't seem to bother Charlese. She beams in an awkward way and bobs her head several times. Enough of the sleight of hand, I think. Let's get to the point.

"So today, I'm here to announce that *all* of you will be receiving a 3 percent raise beginning January 1." She's quiet for a moment while thunderous clapping ensues, underscored by several shouts and whistles. "On that same date, you will have the freedom to choose your own health care. We will no longer force you onto a company plan."

What?

Her words speed up. "We will assist you in setting up a health savings account at the bank of your choice. In fact, we will contribute a full $1,000 to each of your accounts." There's another round of applause here that includes a few whoops. Oh my God. Are you kidding me? Can't you see the spin?

"In addition," Charlese continues, "we've hired a consultant that will assist each and every one of you with finding the health-care plan of your dreams."

I take a deep breath and look around me. Does the staff understand what they've lost? Serenity Acres will no longer be offering health care to their employees and families. No 3 percent raise or $1,000 bonus will ever make up for that. Then it dawns on me. Not only will the staff be losing health care, I'll be losing mine too. I can't afford that. No one can. But how is this possible? Isn't it counter to the federal health-care laws? I have to speak to Kai. Convince him this is wrong.

"Is she saying what I think she's saying?" Zach whispers, leaning close.

"I'm afraid so."

"But what about my knee? My operation is scheduled for January."

"Could you move up the date?"

"I already tried, but the clinic refused. They said it wasn't an emergency."

"Maybe you should make it one."

"You mean hurt myself?"

"You never heard that from me." I focus my attention on Kai, who looks like he's swallowed the proverbial canary. "Let them eat cake," I mutter.

"What?"

"Nothing. Let me talk to Kai. I doubt he's thought through the ramifications of this decision. He's never even discussed the issue with me."

"Or maybe he *has* thought through the ramifications, and it's all about his bonus and the goddamn bottom line."

I open my mouth to argue but then shut it. Of course. Zach is absolutely right.

Four

I push through the throngs of employees and make my way to the stage. While a handful of staff members are celebrating, many others appear dazed. A few are speaking angrily, and I can't say I disagree. There is no jackpot at the end of this rainbow. Management has pulled a con.

I climb the steps to where Kai and Charlese are chatting like the oldest of friends. I barge right in and tap Kai on the shoulder. "I have to speak to you."

"Hello, Ruth," Kai says, grinning at Charlese. "This is the one I've been telling you about. Our VP of operations."

This?

Charlese nods and holds out her hand. Close up she's not so pretty. And she's definitely not so young. Her face looks like it's been frozen by Botox. "I look forward to working with you," she says in her singsong voice.

"Me too." I reluctantly take her hand before turning my attention to Kai. "Why wasn't I seated with the management team?"

Kai acts bewildered. "I'm sorry. Did you feel left out?"

"Left out?" I want to strangle him. "You know I'm part of senior management. What do the employees think?"

He takes on a thoughtful tone. "Gosh. I'm sorry. You were sick on Friday, so I thought you might want to catch up on your work. I didn't think about the visual. I apologize."

For a moment his apology confuses me. But then I get back on track. "Can I speak with you in private?"

Kai tugs his cell phone from his pocket, scrolls, and shakes his head. "Love to," he says, "but let's make it tomorrow. Don't want to be late for Kali class."

"But I need to speak with you *now*." That last word bursts from me like a gunshot. I try to ignore Charlese's surprised look.

Kai shrugs, looking unhappy. "I guess we can talk on the way to my car."

"That's fine."

I follow Kai down the steps and across the auditorium, a new leather knapsack bumping against his back. Once we step outside, I dig in.

"I should've been included in such a momentous decision."

"Momentous decision? What are you talking about?"

"Ending health care for our employees."

"Well, if you'd been here on Friday . . ."

"Are you serious?" I just might slap him. "I miss one day in ten years, and that's the day you eliminate key benefits?"

Kai places a finger to his lips, signaling I should keep my voice down. We hurry by several clumps of anxious-looking employees and then sidle by Adam and Ember. Adam turns away with a pinched expression, but Ember offers us a sweet smile. "Nice program," she says.

"Thank you," Kai replies. He lowers his voice as we pass. "You should get rid of that girl."

"Who? Ember?"

He chuckles. "That's her name? Wow. Anyway, I'm serious about letting her go. She doesn't fit in with our brand."

"Because of her looks?"

"Why else?"

"So everyone who works here has to be attractive?"

"No, but they shouldn't be horribly disfigured. It's really hard to take."

"You know what you're suggesting is illegal?"

"Not if it stays between us." Kai picks up his pace, and I try to focus my thoughts as we dash along the path to the parking lot. I've got a lot of questions to ask. I'll deal with his Ember comment later.

"Who made the decision to fire Molly?" I ask.

Kai slows his pace. "She wasn't fired."

"I happen to know she had no intention of retiring."

He straightens his bandana. "Truth is, we came to realize she wasn't a team player."

"We?"

"Corporate."

I try to keep my voice calm. "I'm guessing she didn't agree with the decision on health care."

"You're guessing right."

"Well, I disagree with you too."

Kai lets out a frustrated sigh. "You heard Charlese. The employees will get a raise and a thousand dollars in the bank."

"That won't begin to cover their health-care costs."

"Not our problem."

"But it is."

"In what way?"

I think of Zach and his failing knee. "We have a responsibility to our staff. We . . . we can't treat them like . . . like rubbish."

Kai smirks. "Since when do you give a damn about the staff?"

"I always have."

"Bullshit."

"Well, I do now. Anyway, I know of at least one employee who has an operation scheduled in January. The loss of coverage will be disastrous."

"She can up the date."

"Maybe *he* can't."

"Well, then, *he'll* have to figure it out."

"But we're talking tens of thousands of dollars."

"I think you're exaggerating to make your point."

"I'm not." I fumble for the right words to make my case. "I believe dropping health care is a bad business decision."

"How so?"

"We'll lose our best people. They'll go elsewhere."

"Where to?"

"To Peaceful Pastures, for example."

"No, they won't."

I open my mouth to argue, and then I think back on Kai's meeting with the Doughboy. Could he be colluding with the local retirement homes? I try another tack.

"I believe what you're doing is illegal."

"Well, I'll pass that on to the corporate lawyers who have determined otherwise."

We arrive at Kai's shiny black BMW, where he dons a pair of reflective sunglasses before turning to me with a frown. "Look," he says, "if we lose a few disgruntled employees, that's not the worst thing that could happen. It'll only make us leaner and meaner. And the improvement to the bottom line from reducing our health-care expense is almost magical in its immediacy."

I say the next words knowing they'll cause trouble. "Aren't you supposed to be a Christian? Care for others and that kind of thing?"

Kai's cheeks flame red. "Don't involve my religion in this." He throws open his car door and slides into his seat. "The point is, we're a corporation, not a nonprofit. You need to get that through your head."

"But . . ."

"If it's your own health care you're worried about, you needn't be. Level fives and above will retain benefits."

"This is bigger than me."

"Well that's noble of you. Now, I've got to get going."

"So there's no chance you'll reconsider?"

"None."

"Well, I'm . . ." Kai slams the door shut on my words. He guns the car motor and then rolls down the window. My face reflects oddly in his glasses. "You should know that Molly resisted change, and now she's gone."

"What're you saying?"

"I'm reminding you that as a member of the management team, you're expected to support corporate decisions. And along those lines, I'm still waiting on that list."

I pretend to not know what he's talking about. "List?"

"The list of destitutes ranked by what they owe? You couldn't have forgotten. I've sent several requests."

"No, I haven't forgotten."

"So where is it?"

"It's just . . . well, I've been busy."

He scowls. "I asked you for that information weeks ago, and now corporate is asking me. Every day you lag results in the loss of thousands of dollars. That will have a direct effect on both your bonus and mine."

"You understand you're evicting them. Or what's left of them."

"What do you mean by that?"

"Does it seem strange that five destitutes have passed away in as many weeks?"

"Are you insinuating something?"

I straighten and place my hands on my hips, aware I'm out on a limb. "We may need the coroner to investigate."

"Investigate? Are you crazy?"

"No, I'm not. There's something weird going on."

"Weird?" Kai slaps his steering wheel. "That's enough. I don't want to hear anything more about your crazy theories. And I *do not* want the coroner notified, understand me? We are going to be facing enough bad press due to the Milo situation. We don't need you to add fuel to the fire."

"But . . ."

"But nothing. You work for me, remember? I'm your boss. You can either keep your thoughts to yourself, or you can resign. Your choice." Kai revs his motor and zooms off. I'm about to shout after him when my cell phone chimes and Alice's face lights up the screen. I haven't spoken to her in weeks. Just a few texts here and there.

"Hi, sweetheart," I say. "How are you? Is everything okay?" There's stone silence on the other end. "Are you there, Alice?" My pulse races as I remember the awful call I received from the Miami Police Department a few years ago. A drunk bandmate had tried to rape Alice, but she'd been able to fight him off. She escaped with a broken wrist and a cut on her neck that needed two dozen stitches to close. She'd been a changed person after that, her confidence swept away. It took a year for her to regain her singing voice. God, don't let history repeat. "Please talk to me," I say, gasping for air. "Or should I call 911?"

"Is it true?" she asks in a flat voice.

"Is what true?" My heart drops.

"You know what I'm asking." She sounds so harsh, I catch my breath. Of course I know.

"It was a long time ago, and your dad . . ."

"Don't even try to blame this on Dad."

"But . . ."

"How could you do that to Adam? How could you do that to me?" The screen goes dark, and I bow my head. I let a few tears flow before I swallow my guilt and stumble my way to the memorial garden, my heart heavy in my chest.

Five

Monday, September 30

"I'm sure you're pissed," Zach says as soon as I step into the garden. "But I think deep down you know we did the right thing."

I stare at him, trying to ascertain my feelings, something I've avoided for far too many years. "I *am* upset," I say. "But not at you." Nor Adam. Nor Alice. There's only one person I'm truly disappointed in, and that's myself. I drop onto the cement bench, hot and sweaty. The desert winds are blowing, and the temperature's been rising all day. Even the koi look sluggish.

"So, you're not mad at me?"

"No. You did what you had to do."

He nods and takes a seat on the bench and reaches for my hand. "I don't want to lose you as a friend. You're important to me."

I smile, but I don't look up. "I appreciate that. But life as I know it is over."

"Things may look bad at the moment, but I'm sure Adam will come around."

"Are you?" I gently tug my hand from his grip. "Because I'm not."

"I'll talk to him."

"I doubt that'll help."

"Maybe Alice could intervene."

I swallow a bitter laugh and tell Zach about her call.

"Too bad," he says, looking discouraged. "I guess it might just be you and me for a while." He crosses his arms. "At least I got rid of Tina."

"Tina?" I eye him like he's crazy. "What're you talking about?"

"I've never told you, but she's been in here all along." He thumps the side of his head. "She said she'd never leave until we told the truth about that day."

"She speaks to you?"

"She did."

"And you've been living like this for . . . ?"

"For twenty years."

"Is that why you drank?"

"In part . . . I also drank to forget."

"And she hates me, I suppose."

"Well . . ."

"That's okay. I'd hate me too." I take a shivering breath, thinking of the destruction I've wrought. "Is she gone now?"

"I hope so. I haven't heard a word since Friday."

"Thank God."

"Yes, thank God. Although . . ."

I glance at him sideways. "Although what?"

"I think I'm going to miss her. It gets lonely living alone."

"I know."

We sit quietly for several moments, and then Zach glances at his watch. "Anyway. I don't have much time. You ready to hear what I learned about the Goodnight Club?"

I pull my thoughts together. "If you're ready to hear about Detective Ruiz."

Zach snaps to attention. "Why? What happened?"

"He came to my office this morning, asking questions. I think he's on to Adam. I mean, he doesn't seem especially bright, but still . . ."

"Don't let him fool you."

"What do you mean?"

"He's smart. Exceptionally so. But sometimes he likes to play the part of the fool. He's outed a lot of criminals that way."

"Good to know." I think back on our conversation. Wonder if I said anything that could lead him to Adam and the truth behind his lie.

"So what kind of questions did he ask?"

"Mostly about Adam's background. History of drug use. Where he met Nikki. The fight in Palmdale. He even knew Adam had been arrested in high school."

Zach lets out a low whistle. "That record's been expunged. He would've had to dig hard for that information."

"Which means?"

"He's on to something."

I scour Zach's face. "What're you saying?"

"That I'm worried. Javier has a lot of leads to run down, so why focus on Adam?"

"Could he have learned that Adam was planning to buy drugs from Milo?"

"If he did, we're screwed. All three of us."

I get to my feet, feeling sick. "Oh, Zach, what're we going to do?"

"I'm not sure. I'll have to think on this. We may need to tell Javier the truth."

"But that could mean . . ."

"Jail, yeah. At least for me and Adam." He slouches low on the bench.

"Oh my God." I begin to pace.

"What I want to avoid is a murder charge."

"Murder?" I stop in my tracks. "Why would you be charged with murder?"

"If they don't find the perpetrator, the circumstantial evidence may lead them to Adam and me."

"No . . ."

"Yes. With Adam's history of drugs and the accusation of violence and my years of alcohol abuse, well . . . that's bad enough. Add in the fact that we lied . . . shit. I'd arrest us too."

I drop on my knees and take Zach by the shoulders. "You can't let this happen, understand? It would destroy Adam. It would destroy you." It would destroy me. I give him a shake. "For God's sake, you were a good detective at one time. You need to investigate this yourself."

His blue eyes search mine, and for the briefest of moments I think he might take me in his arms. Instead, he gets up and holds out his hand to help me to my feet.

"You're right. Let me think on this during my shift. Maybe I can dig up a lead or two."

"Maybe? Or you will?"

"I'll try my best."

"Should we say anything to Adam?"

"No. The less he knows, the better."

"All right. Please stop by my house first thing tomorrow morning. Okay?"

"I doubt I'll know anything by then."

"It doesn't matter. I'll be worrying all night, and you're the only one I can talk to."

He nods and glances at his watch. "Shit. I'm late. I'd better go."

"What about the Goodnight Club?"

"I'll tell you about that tomorrow."

It's dark by the time I leave my office for home. I'm exhausted, so I decide to take a shortcut to my car by taking the path that crosses the corner of the golf course. I hesitate when I see a shadow moving in my direction.

"Who's there?" I call, fingering my cell phone.

Pastor Sam steps into the feeble light of a street lamp.

"You scared me," I say.

"I apologize."

"No need. It's just, with the death of Nurse Milo . . ."

"Understood. We're all on edge."

"Very much so. Still working?"

She fingers her jeweled cross. "In my line of work, the day never ends."

"Problems with a guest?"

"I suppose. I stopped in to see the Harringtons."

"How is Kate?"

"Things have been rather difficult of late."

"Is she ill?"

Pastor Sam tilts her head, regarding me with interest. "You're aware Gordon Harrington resides with her?"

"Of course." Actually, I had nearly forgotten. He's not an official guest and rarely leaves their villa.

"Well, he's been doing poorly, and it's draining for a woman of her age. I offer support whenever I can."

I nod, thinking of the frozen man I haven't seen in well over a year. I should check in on him, or at least check in with Kate. I'm surprised he's lived this long. "And how is Gordon this evening?"

"Surviving. Not much more."

"That's sad."

"It is. Hopefully he'll meet his maker soon. Have a good evening." The pastor begins to walk away.

"Wait a moment."

She pauses. "Yes?"

"I'm wondering what you thought about the staff meeting today."

"Thought?" She regards me coolly.

"I mean, about the termination of health insurance benefits. Don't you find that concerning?"

She dips her hands deep into her jacket pockets. "It's not my place to interfere in administrative decisions."

"But what about the staff? Surely you're concerned for their welfare."

She stares at me, unblinking, her eyes pools of liquid black. "May I speak to you in utmost confidence?" she asks.

"Of course."

Her voice drops. "I've had my concerns about young Kai Gilchrist since the day he set foot on campus. And when he was promoted to executive director, well, those concerns quickly multiplied."

"What kind of concerns?"

"I'm not in a position to discuss, but on the most basic level, he has no empathy for our elderly guests, nor for the hardworking staff."

Her words are like a blessing to my ears. "I thought I was the only one troubled by his attitude."

"No. You most definitely are not." She pulls her cell phone from her pocket and eyes its glowing face. "I'm sorry. I must hurry off. One of our Catholic guests has taken ill, and she's asking for last rites. I'd like to support her until the priest arrives."

"Of course. Don't let me hold you up."

The pastor rushes off, and for a moment, I bask in a glow of validation. It's nice to know I'm not the only one who sees Kai for the unethical man he is.

I'm about to move on when I spy a slip of paper nearly hidden in the weeds. I pluck the pink Post-it Note from its nest and catch a whiff of a medicinal scent. I turn it over and angle the note so it reflects the watery light. *Gordon Harrington* is written across the top. Beneath it, *9.30.19.* I peer into the darkness, suddenly nervous. Should I head to the Harringtons' and check on Gordon? But how would I explain my sudden visit? I wouldn't want to worry Kate, and the pastor said Gordon was fine. I consider calling Zach to tell him about my discovery, but then I remember our bigger problem and decide it's best to wait. I'll show Zach the note in the morning, and we can decide how best to proceed.

Six

I drift through a valley of fog so dense I can hardly see. Alice and Adam are shrieking in the distance. *"Mommy! Mommy!"* Something is terribly wrong.

I fly after them down a ribbon of road. A masked man has grabbed hold of their arms.

"Stop! Release my babies."

But the man is running too fast; he seems to be floating on air. And my steps grow heavier and heavier until my feet are rooted to the ground. Then my body hardens into a trunk; my arms split into branches. I've morphed into an oak tree, with pink Post-it Notes for leaves.

"Mommy, help!"

I sit up in bed, heart pounding.

"Ruth!" The clock says it's not yet seven, and there's a banging on my front door. *"Ruth!* It's Zach. Open up."

Zach. That's right. I asked him to stop by. I climb out of bed and stumble to the door. "Give me a moment," I call.

After hurrying back to my bedroom, I pull on leggings and an old sweatshirt. Then I brush my teeth and remove the traces of mascara shadowing my sleepy eyes. All the while, I hear Zach's heavy steps pacing on my porch. His nervousness makes me anxious. Did he learn something last night?

I fling open the door, and Zach stands before me dressed in his olive-and-black uniform. He looks tired, his eyes rimmed in red, a frown gripping his worried face.

"Did something happen?" I ask.

"Coffee, please? Before we dive in?"

"Sure. Follow me." I brew a pot while he waits at the breakfast nook, working his hands together. "Here you go." I set down two white mugs of steaming black coffee and take the adjacent seat. I can't hold back any longer. "So what is it? What have you found?"

He clears his throat. "Gordon Harrington is dead."

"Dead?" The memory of the pink Post-it Note flashes before my eyes. "How? When?"

"Not sure how, but he died sometime last night."

"Of natural causes?"

"I don't believe so."

"Then how?"

"It has to do with the Goodnight Club." Zach runs a hand through his disheveled hair. "I've learned what it is and who is involved."

"Tell me."

"Kate Harrington is their unofficial leader."

"Kate?" I picture the elegant elderly woman with the flaming red hair. "I don't understand. Does this have something to do with Nurse Milo?"

"I'm not sure. Could be. Let me explain." He goes on to tell me about his nighttime visits with Kate. About the camaraderie on their front porch. About sharing a glass of whiskey, which he acknowledges is a fireable offense. Then he moves on to her husband. About a night he helped turn Gordon in his bed. How he pitied the man who was entirely helpless and looked like a frozen corpse.

"That's sad, but . . ." His meaning begins to come clear. "Are you suggesting he didn't die from natural causes?"

Zach nods. "I'm fairly certain the Goodnight Club had a hand in this."

"Kate told you this?"

"She implied."

"So you're saying they killed him?"

"Not exactly."

"Then what?"

"I'll tell you, but you've got to promise to keep this a secret. You can't spew to anyone else."

Spew? I get to my feet and begin to pace. "I prefer not to agree to anything until I know what we're talking about."

Zach kneads his knee with a pained look on his face. "At least promise not to pass judgment before you hear me out."

"I'll try . . ." I grab a kitchen towel and wipe my hands, and then I wipe my brow.

"You feeling okay?" Zach asks.

"It's early, Zach. And it's warm in here. Just tell me what's up."

Zach focuses his gaze on his feet. "Well . . . a few years ago a bunch of guests decided not to leave the end of their lives to fate. They were searching for not only quality of life but for quality of death. They formed a club to take control of their destinies. They called it the Goodnight Club. They meet in secret once a month."

"At Serenity Acres?" What he's saying is not making sense.

"Yes."

"But how is that possible?" I sag onto my chair, wondering how I wouldn't have known.

"They're adults, Ruth. And most are quite sharp. They may look old, but I'm guessing many are brighter than us."

"So this group meets to . . . ?"

"To support each other in their decision to end their lives."

The caffeine doesn't seem to be working. I can't grasp the meaning behind Zach's words. "So they support each other's plans for suicide? A version of the Hemlock Society?"

"Sort of." Zach leans forward, hands on knees. "They support each other's plans to die on their own terms."

"I'm not following you. If it's not suicide, then . . ."

He grips his hands together and gazes at me with his startlingly blue eyes. "A professional helps them complete their mission."

"A professional? Someone helps them to die?"

"Yes."

"Then you're talking murder."

"Not murder. Assisted suicide."

"Which is murder in this state."

"Maybe our society calls it that, but ethically . . . ?"

"Ethically?" I stumble to my feet and fumble over my words. "It's . . . it's murder, plain and simple."

"I don't know . . ."

"What do you mean? You were a detective once. You know right from wrong."

He shakes his head. "I guess I stopped seeing things in black and white when Hunter and Tina died. Life isn't goddamn fair. Things don't always make sense. And I gave up being judge and jury when I saw the curveballs God serves up."

"And Gordon? He was part of this Goodnight Club?"

"In a way, yes."

"And this *professional* helped him to die?"

Zach nods. "I believe he administered the drugs."

I lean back, appalled. "But Gordon couldn't speak. Couldn't write. Couldn't move. So, he couldn't have given his consent."

"Except that he had a wife who loved him and understood his needs."

"Or, he had a wife that was tired of caring for him and took the easy way out."

Zach shakes his head and groans in frustration. "You told me you wouldn't rush to judgment."

"This is no rush. This is reality. You're not thinking straight." I resume pacing, trying to wrap my head around this mess. "Did Kate give you any more details?"

Zach drops his head in his hands. "God, I'm tired. I need to get some sleep."

"There's no time for that. I need to know everything you know."

He looks up. "All right. I'll tell you what I know. The Goodnight Club meets monthly in various locations to discuss ways to end their lives. They get down to the nitty-gritty details. They research end-of-life drugs and that sort of thing, although they leave the method of their passing in the hands of the professional."

"So how does this 'professional' know who and when?"

"When a guest decides he's ready, he fills out his name and chosen date on a pink Post-it Note. Then he gives it to Kate, and somehow it makes its way to an ambassador, who then passes it on to the person Kate calls the Angel. This Angel is the professional, the one who administers the drugs."

"So they call the professional an angel?"

"*The* Angel, yes."

"Did Kate tell you who this Angel is?"

"She says she doesn't know."

"What about the ambassador?"

"She's never met either one."

"Well, I may have." I grab my purse and search through the contents and whip out the pink Post-it Note. "Check this out."

Zach takes the note from my trembling hand and looks up at me in surprise. "Where'd you find it?"

I tell him about my encounter with Pastor Sam. About finding the note on the ground.

He shakes his head. "I'm guessing it's just a coincidence that the pastor was at the Harringtons'. I can't believe she'd be involved."

"Why not?"

"Wouldn't it go against her faith?"

My eyes narrow. "So you admit what's happening is murder?"

"Maybe in society's eyes, but not mine. I understand what it's like to suffer so deeply you no longer want to live."

I fold my arms together. "You've laid a terrible problem at my feet, haven't you? Think of the Post-it Notes I've collected without reporting them. And there could be many more that died in the hands of this 'angel.' I mean, what if he isn't so benevolent? What if he's a killer? A serial killer? For instance, the destitutes have been dying at an unusually high rate. Could he be involved?" I pause, getting excited.

"You're speculating here," Zach says.

I can't keep my voice from rising. "What else am I supposed to do?"

"Try to figure this out. Calmly."

"How do we do that?"

"To start with, I can ask Kate if the destitutes were part of the club."

"Better we tell the authorities."

"By the 'authorities,' do you mean Javier?"

"Yes."

"And tell him what? We don't know for sure who the Angel is, or the ambassador for that matter. And if we bring this story to him without evidence, who knows how it'll go down? It could focus the wrong kind of attention on us. On Adam."

I consider his words. "Then what do you suggest we do?"

"Investigate further. See what we can find out. Speak to Kate and to the pastor."

"And what if the pastor is this Angel? What if she's dangerous?"

"I doubt she's dangerous," Zach says. "Maybe misguided, but not dangerous. The more facts we have to this story, it may make our next step clear."

I hesitate. "All right. I'll text the pastor and set up a meeting. Let's see what we can find out."

"Good. But I really need to get some sleep. I've got to be thinking straight."

"Fine. Go ahead and sleep. Let's plan to meet this afternoon."

Seven

Tuesday, October 1

Zach and I arrive at the pastor's office shortly before five in the afternoon. That's the earliest she could meet, which gave Zach a day of sleep and me some time to clear my head.

I visit the chapel fairly often, but its beauty never gets old. The altar is framed by flower bouquets. Lemon oil scents the air. Stained-glass windows paint vibrant rainbows across the polished wood floor. Church services are held Friday through Sunday, and funerals dot the week. There's even the occasional wedding when an amorous guest ties the knot. You would think those would be happy events, but many are definitely not. Some family members dread losing control of parents; others worry about diluted trusts. We even broke up a fistfight once between an elderly groom and his middle-aged son.

The pastor's office is located down a flight of steep stone stairs, tucked behind the altar in the back corner of the chapel. The light is dim, the air musty. Ventilation comes from a fan. The room was originally built for storage, but when the pastor arrived five years ago, she had it converted to her office.

At the bottom of the steps, I tap on the thick wood door, and it opens with a creak.

"Come in," the pastor says. She must have recently showered, because her gray hair is plastered to her head. Her skin is more sallow than usual, as if she's recovering from the flu. We follow her inside the musty-smelling office, where she takes a seat behind an antique desk and we settle onto two straight-backed chairs. There's no sign of a computer, printer, or landline, but hundreds of books line the walls. Most of them appear quite old, especially the ones tucked behind a large glass bookcase.

"Welcome to my home away from home," the pastor says, patting a thin leather-bound book resting on her desk. "May I offer you something? Coffee or tea?"

"No, thank you," we answer in unison. You wouldn't know it from our vantage point, but there's a tiny kitchen and half bath tucked behind the back wall. There's also a small bedroom not much larger than a closet. I'm told she sleeps there now and then.

"I apologize for the smell," the pastor says, fingering her cross. "Old books go hand in hand with mildew, and as you can see, I've collected quite a few. What started as a hobby has developed into a passion. In fact, some might call it an addiction."

"Rare books?" Zach asks, eyeing the glass bookcase.

"Some date back to the sixteenth century. You can have a look, if you like."

"Another time. I'm scheduled to work the night shift." Zach clears his throat. "Do you meet with many guests down here?"

She shakes her head. "Not many. I typically engage with them in the chapel or the central conference room. But some of my more agile guests prefer the privacy of my office. You can't hear a thing through these thick walls. They find that comforting when they're spilling their secrets."

"Secrets?" Zach leans forward. The detective has come alive.

"Yes. Most people have them. And at this point in their lives, many like to share them. It gives them a sense of relief."

I gaze at the woman, thinking how odd she is and that it's time we get on with our mission. I glance at Zach, but he doesn't take the lead, so I start in. "We'd like to ask you a few questions."

"About?"

"About this." I pluck the pink Post-it Note from my pocket and place it on her desk. "Do you recognize it?" She takes the slip of paper and gives it a good look. "Should I?"

I scour her face for a clue. "I found it on the ground where we met last night. Remember? You had just left the Harringtons'?"

She sets down the note. "Of course I remember. But this isn't mine."

"And now Gordon is dead."

"Yes, I heard. Poor, unfortunate soul. It's a gift that he's moved on."

"It's a bit of a coincidence, don't you think?"

"What do you mean?"

"Was he alive when you visited earlier in the evening?"

"Very much so."

"Did you see him again after that?"

"I did not."

Zach jumps into the conversation. "Did you help him to pass?"

"To pass?" Pastor Sam tilts her head. "What exactly are you accusing me of?"

"We know about your involvement with the Goodnight Club," he says in a firm voice.

"You do?"

"Yes."

"Interesting. Why don't you tell me what this Goodnight Club is?"

"I think you know."

"Pretend I don't."

"All right. I'll play along." Zach fills her in on what he learned from Kate. The pastor shows no emotion while he winds his way through his tale.

"So let me get this straight," she says as he finishes up. "You believe I'm the . . . ?"

"The Angel."

"No. I'm not that."

"But you're involved?"

She settles back with a hint of a smile. "I suppose I am."

"In what way?"

"I'm the ambassador."

"So you know about the Post-it Notes," I say.

"I suppose I do."

"And you work as a team with this Angel?" Zach asks.

"I don't know if you'd call us a team, as I've never met the man. But yes, I help coordinate the crossings with the Goodnight Club. I'm an intermediary of sorts."

"So you were involved with Gordon's death."

"With the arrangements. Yes."

"But you weren't there?"

"No." Zach and I glance at each other, unsure of what comes next. The pastor continues without our prompting. "I'm fairly certain you guessed about my involvement, and I could just leave it at that. But I need your help with an issue that has cropped up, so I'm willing to tell you what I know in exchange for your assistance."

Zach turns to me and lifts his eyebrows as if saying, *Are you okay with this?* I nod. I'm willing to hear her out. "Okay," he says. "We won't do anything illegal, but we will consider providing help if you supply us with information."

"Fair enough. But first, let me tell you a story about how I came to believe in assisted suicide. Maybe it'll help you understand my outlook on life."

"All right."

She folds her hands together as if in prayer. "I won't drag you through my pathetic childhood and all its moments of angst and hurt.

Let's just say I was never happier than the day I left Idaho for Yale. It was as if I had entered a whole new world, one where I could truly be myself. My freshman college roommate became my first lover. Stacy. Dear Stacy." The pastor closes her eyes and smiles. "So beautiful. So pure. She was from California and as different from me as night is from day. She was the sun to my moon, the sugar to my salt. People flocked to her like bees to blooming roses. I loved her with all my heart."

The pastor pauses, and her eyes turn misty. "And then, as the story often goes, my day turned into night. Stacy had a little mole on her face, right above her lip. A *beauty mark*, she used to call it, just like Marilyn Monroe. But one day, the mole started changing. It seemed to double in size overnight. By the time Stacy was diagnosed with melanoma . . . well . . . let's just say it was too late."

The pastor plucks a tissue from her desk and takes a swipe at her nose. "Melanoma is a wretched disease that destroys every facet of a person's life. For Stacy, it began with the disfigurement of her face. Soon great tumors appeared on her body, balls of boiling black cells that covered her arms and her legs. Near the end they clogged her lungs, slowly suffocating her to death. She asked me to help her end her life, but there was nothing I could do. I watched the love of my life slowly choke on the tumors pressing against her throat. I would've given my soul to help alleviate her pain. But all I could do was hold her hand while the light dimmed from her eyes." She takes a shuddering breath. "Her death remains the most tragic moment of my life."

"I'm sorry for your loss," I say, meaning it.

"Me too," Zach adds, squirming in his seat.

"Thank you. As you can imagine, I spun into a terrible depression, from which it took years to emerge." She looks up, her eyes now steeled. "But when I did, it was with a mission: I would never again allow a poor soul to undergo such horrible suffering. If a person wanted help to ease their passage, I would do so with God's blessing."

"So that's when you became an ambassador?" Zach asks.

"Not exactly. For many years I worked in a hospice facility, where I could assist patients facing the end of their lives."

"And when you arrived here?"

"I did nothing more than bring comfort, until one day I was recruited."

"By whom?"

"By the Angel, of course."

"But you don't know who this Angel is."

"No. We communicate by notes. That's how I was first contacted. The Angel left a note in my mailbox, and I agreed to help."

I lean forward, eager to learn more. "So, Loretta Thomas was targeted?"

"Not targeted. She chose when and where to cross."

"And Mary Panini?"

"We helped her too."

"What about Simon Appleton?"

She shakes her head. "No. He died a natural death."

"But he was scheduled to cross?"

"Yes, but he changed his mind. That's not unusual, mind you. Many of our Goodnight Club disciples are all bark and no bite. They enjoy the camaraderie of the group, and it often brings them enough hope, so they no longer want to die."

"So what do you need our help with?" I ask, trying to move this along.

She places her hands flat on her desk and takes a deep breath. "Something odd is going on. It began with Nurse Milo, followed by some unusual deaths in our destitute population."

I nod. "Too many of them have died in too short a time."

"But why target the destitutes?" Zach asks.

"Think about it," the pastor responds. "They're the perfect victims. For the most part, they have no family and few if any friends. And, of course, our new administration is more than willing to look the other way."

Zach nods. "So you believe your Angel has . . . what? Gone on a killing spree?"

"No. I don't believe my Angel would ever do such a thing. What I do believe is there is a serial killer on the loose."

"A serial killer?" I take a deep breath. "That's a frightening thought."

"It is." She fixes her gaze on Zach. "You were a detective once, yes?"

"Years ago."

"Good enough." She turns to me. "And Ruth, you have access to inside information. Employee files. Things like that."

"Well, yes, but that doesn't mean—"

She speaks over my words. "Then what we need to do is investigate. Determine who the murderer is and bring him to justice. The killings must end."

I nod. "You're right. The killer must be stopped. But this is not a time for amateur sleuths. We need to involve the police. You must tell them everything you've told us."

She shakes her head. "Impossible. They will see me as an accessory to what they believe are the Angel's crimes. I could end up in jail."

"But if you don't, the murders will continue." I look at Zach. "We have no choice, right? We must inform Detective Ruiz."

"You can't." The pastor gets to her feet. "You promised you'd help me."

I fold my arms. "Yes, but not if it means another innocent person might die."

Her lips thin. Her eyes narrow. "It appears my personal story didn't move you."

"Of course it moved me, but that won't stop me from doing the right thing."

"What would stop you?" she asks, fondling her cross.

"What do you mean?"

She tilts her head. "What if I deny everything I've told you and instead tell the story of how an afternoon tryst led to a little boy's death? And how the two adulterers allowed unwarranted guilt to consume a young man's life. And how that young man tried to purchase drugs from a dealer who was later found dead. And how that young man was encouraged to lie by a former detective with a history of alcohol abuse. And how his mother has known of a series of killings but kept her suspicions to herself. Would any of those words cause you to reconsider your next step? For your sake and Adam's, I hope so."

VI. LUST

But I tell you that anyone who looks at a woman lustfully has already committed adultery with her in his heart.

—Matthew 5:28

The Angel

When I was a child, my father and I played a daily round of chess. My father was not a pleasant man, especially when he was drunk. A foolish move sent me to bed without dinner; an imprudent loss brought a thump to my head. My mother watched these antics from the kitchen; she rarely became involved. Preferred to spend time with her books and magazines and dream of a better world. She was the one who taught me about secrets, how important they can become. She ran off one day when I was at school, never to return. Later, I found her journal, which told the story of a woman I didn't know. Frightened, beaten, depressed, she left my father for a kinder man. Kept her problems close to her heart until the day she walked out the door. That's when I became attached to the world of secrets and began to worm them from my friends.

I don't condemn my mother for leaving her abuser; I condemn her for leaving her child. Years later when she begged for forgiveness, I turned my back on her as she had done to me.

I may not have cared for my abusive father, but I am grateful for the years of chess. The game taught me about patience and strategy, when to hold back and when to attack. I'm considering my options now, as the walls begin to close in. Do I design a cunning ambush or pack my possessions and disappear? Setting a trap is not an easy task; it can involve a high level of risk. I may have to sacrifice a pawn or two to avoid forfeiting my advantage. And if my opponents discover my intentions? I risk succumbing to checkmate. But if my attempt at a trap succeeds, I walk away with the ultimate win.

God works in mysterious ways; his intent is not always clear. By handing Ruth the errant pink slip, he led her straight to the pastor's door. I had to pray on that for a moment. Understand the meaning behind the move. Was the Lord testing me with an outing? Teaching me a noteworthy lesson? Or was he offering me a solution? An answer to my prayers? I spent hours on my knees before I gleaned the answer from Saint Olga: take matters into your own hands and use your iron fist.

ZACH RICHARDS

One

It's so quiet in the room I can hear the ticking of an unseen clock. And breathing. Lots of breathing. Pastor Sam's. Ruth's. Mine. But not a word from Tina. I reach up and tap the side of my head. Come on, Tina. Tell me what to do. The musty stench clogs my nose; my head is beginning to ache. It's hard for me to think of anything besides bolting from the room.

"Please take a seat," the pastor repeats.

I hesitate and then drop into my chair, and Ruth follows my example.

"Good." The pastor licks her lips.

"Are you threatening us?" I ask, trying to buy some time.

"Threatening?" Pastor Sam closes her eyes and leans back, the tips of her fingers touching as if in prayer. She leans so far back I think she might tip the chair and tumble to the ground. Maybe that would cause a concussion, and she'd forget everything she knows. Yes, that would make things easy. Unfortunately, she opens her eyes.

"Threatening?" she repeats. "Yes, I suppose I am." She sets her hands down and leans forward, her jeweled cross clanking on the desk. "I need you to understand the ramifications of your actions. Of what exactly might happen should our secrets escape into the world."

"How do you know . . . ?" Ruth asks in a trembling voice. "How did you find out?" Ruth's face glows red and glistens with a steamy sweat. It *is* warm down here in the pastor's pit. My shirt is sticking to my back.

"How do I know about *your* secrets?" A smile lights the pastor's face. "Well, you may not know this, but dear Ember is like a daughter to me. The daughter I wish I had had. She views me as her confidant, the person she trusts more than anyone else in the world. She's estranged from her parents, so she can't reach out to them. And she has a hard time making friends. It's sad but not a surprise that her scars scare them off. So, the truth is she tells me her secrets, and I know more than I probably should. For instance, did you know your son has fallen in love with Ember, and she's beginning to feel the same way? He's fallen quite hard, in fact. She let him move in with her this week. And Ember? As an empath, she takes on the pain of others, and your son has filled her cup. She believes he has been misunderstood, that he's a diamond in the rough. A young man who made many bad choices and now yearns for a better life."

"What's an empath?" I ask.

"People like Ember and me who take on other men's crosses. Carry them on our backs. It can be a source of strength, and it can be a curse. Of course the greatest empath of all was our Lord, Jesus Christ. He carried the weight of the world on his shoulders, and look what happened to him." She works her bony hands together. "Some are born with the power. Others develop it from a tragic event. I became an empath the year I lost my Stacy, but Ember, like Christ, is the real thing. She was born an empath, and the loss of her children only heightened her perceptive powers." Her gaze slides from me to Ruth. "Do you know the story of her loss?"

"Yes," Ruth replies. "She told me."

"Interesting. She must trust you. And you, Zach?"

I hesitate. "I heard she lost her kids."

"That, she did. In a most horrible way. They died in a fire set by her ex-husband, Bodie." She pauses and stares at me, knowingly. My throat goes dry; my hands tremble. The scent of burnt flesh taints my nose.

"Anyway," she continues, "one of her daughters passed quickly; the other suffered for months. That is why Ember believes in our mission to bring comfort to those in pain."

I force my thoughts off the children. "So, Ember knows about you and the Angel?"

"Yes, she does. In fact, she helps us on occasion."

"Helps? In what way?"

"She ensures the Angel has his privacy when a crossing has been arranged."

"*Jesus*," I mutter under my breath. Who isn't involved in this mess?

"Have you spoken to my son?" Ruth asks in a demanding tone.

Pastor Sam tilts her head. "Of course. I met with Ember *and* Adam. They sat in front of me, like you two. They requested a joint counseling session, and how could I tell them no? They are so sweet together. I wouldn't be surprised if they got married one day." She gets to her feet. "Are you sure I can't offer you anything to drink?"

"No, thank you," Ruth says.

"Nothing for me either," I add.

"All right then, give me a moment."

Ruth and I sit quietly while the pastor is gone. There's a rattling of dishes, and soon after, she returns with a mug of steaming coffee, which seems a strange choice given the temperature in the room. "Now where were we?" she asks, settling into her chair.

"You were telling us about Ember and Adam," I reply.

"Oh, right. Yes." She takes a sip of coffee. "Adam is quite lovely. So very handsome and polite. The poor man has been through the wringer. He's searching for answers, and I believe it's my duty as a pastor to assist him in his journey to become a better person. But he's in somewhat of a quandary. I mean, not only are there the rather grim accusations from his battered ex-wife, but he also lied about his motive as well as his whereabouts the morning of Nurse Milo's death. Add in his history of drug use . . . well . . ." She shakes her head.

"He didn't *batter* Nikki," Ruth says angrily. "And they aren't yet divorced. That woman is a liar. Adam never laid a hand on her. He's not that kind of man."

The pastor takes another sip of coffee and seems to savor the taste before setting down her mug. "My dear, I'm afraid you sound like an overly protective mother not willing to face the truth. Adam acknowledges he pushed his wife, and it caused quite a bruise."

Ruth makes a choking sound.

"If it makes you feel any better, he insists his wife hit him first. But she's not admitting to that, and, unfortunately, there's no evidence to support his claim. He's gotten himself into quite a mess. But he could get off on probation unless his involvement with Nurse Milo comes to light."

"There was no real involvement," I insist.

"Of course there was. That was one of the issues we discussed. Ember is helping Adam to come to terms with his life, and she believes he must start by being completely honest. So, he told me the truth about Nurse Milo. Not that he hurt the poor man, but that he lied about where he was and what he was doing there." Her dark eyes fix on mine, giving me a chill. "What I find interesting is that you, a former detective, not only urged him to keep quiet but lied on your own account."

"I . . . I didn't actually lie . . ."

"My understanding is you did."

I tighten my hands into fists. Why the hell would Adam spew? "I was only trying to protect him."

"Protect? Of course. I understand. You and Ruth must be horribly guilt ridden by what you did to that poor boy. But in assisting him in such a manner, you may have caused more harm than good."

"It was only Adderall," Ruth blurts out.

The pastor shakes her head. "But it was an illegal attempt to purchase a drug, was it not?"

Ruth doesn't answer.

"Anyway, I think we can all agree, we don't want Adam to go to jail. When I think of all he's been through . . ." She pauses and wipes her eyes. "The years he shouldered all the blame for Hunter's death. No wonder the poor man's a mess. I'd like to find a way to help him, if only for Ember's sake. I owe it to the poor girl." The pastor leans back and strokes her cross.

"So, what do you want from us?" I ask, feeling boxed in every which way.

"Haven't I made myself clear? I want you to keep my secret so I can continue with my life's work." She pauses. "Don't make a face. I don't plan to stay here much longer. In fact, I will be giving my notice next week."

That's a surprise. "Where will you go?" I ask.

"I'll be doing missionary work in the slums of Mumbai, where there are thousands of poor souls that could benefit from my work."

I fold my arms tight against my chest. "Anything else you want from us?"

She nods. "You're not to reveal anything about the members of the Goodnight Club. They've done nothing wrong, and they deserve their privacy."

I glance at Ruth, who sits stone faced. I can't get a read on her feelings. Is she pissed? Scared? Deliberating? "Is that it?" I ask.

"One more thing. I'd like your help in exposing the serial killer. I can't leave here with a clear conscience if this monster isn't stopped."

"You think it's a him?"

"Yes. I do. But the gender doesn't matter. At heart, he's a sadistic murderer, pure and simple. I'm sure he killed Nurse Milo and possibly

Simon Appleton, and then there are the poor destitutes." She pauses to wipe her eyes. "Now, then. Will you agree to my demands?"

"I don't know." I glance at Ruth. "We need to discuss this in private."

"I'll give you until tomorrow afternoon."

"Before?"

"Before I set events in motion that will forever ruin your lives."

"I don't like threats."

"It's not a threat. It's reality."

Ruth interrupts. "Wait a moment. I have a question." She sets her hands on the desk and leans forward. "Do you have any idea who this killer could be? Even the slightest guess?"

The pastor nods. "I do."

"Tell us."

She taps her fingers on her desk. "The thing is, I have no real proof, just a lot of circumstantial evidence that points to one man . . . Kai. Gilchrist."

"Kai?"

"Yes." The pastor takes a moment to drain her coffee. She then pulls a tissue from her drawer and dabs at her lips before continuing. "For one, there's the financial motive. The man has been supporting his expensive lifestyle by accumulating a mountain of ruinous debt. But there's more. He reeks of evil. I honestly believe he's the devil incarnate. A bloodthirsty beast."

I picture Kai's face, his behavior, his demeanor. "Kai? Evil? I'm not sure I agree." Although I can't help but recall the knife he waved in my face.

"Well, I do." Ruth says. "I think it makes sense."

The pastor grins. "It does. He's the missing piece to the puzzle, but we'll need to find evidence, of course."

"So if we help you," I say, not wanting to reveal my thoughts, "how will you help us?"

"Well . . . your secret will be safe. Ember's assistance won't be exposed. I'll find a way to divert attention from Adam, which should be easy to do once Kai's malicious actions are brought to light. And to add icing to the cake, I'll counsel Adam to forgive both his mother and mentor, and I'll suggest he keep Ember in his life."

Once again the room goes quiet, and I hear the ticking of the clock. I glance at Ruth. She's staring at me with a question in her eyes. I nod quickly and return my gaze to Pastor Sam.

"All right. Give us twenty-four hours."

"And you won't say anything in the meantime."

"We won't."

"Then swear on the Bible." She pushes the leather-bound book in our direction.

"That's a Bible?" I ask, eyeing the thin volume.

"It's my Bible, yes."

I shrug, and we place our hands on the cold leather and proceed to give her our word.

Ruth and I leave the chapel and enter the gates of the adjacent herb garden. Shadows fall across the lawn; the scent of wisteria blooms. I'm due at work in fifteen minutes, and I'm tired and feeling sick. Ruth, on the other hand, looks energetic. She's ready to put up a fight.

"I knew it," she says, pacing back and forth like a trapped cat. "I knew there was something wrong with Kai."

"I'm not so sure. We should be careful not to jump to conclusions."

She stops in her tracks and eyes me in disbelief. "*I'm* not jumping to conclusions. *I'm* agreeing with Pastor Sam. And she's right. It's the only scenario that makes sense."

"I don't know . . ."

"What don't you know?"

I work to clear away the fog. "It's just that . . . Kai doesn't seem to fit the mold of a serial killer."

"How would you know?"

"I studied them back in the day. I mean, I agree he's a liar. And a backstabber. And a lowlife sneak. But a killer? No. I don't think he has it in him. He's way too much of a wimp."

"A wimp?" She places her hands on her hips. "And wimps don't kill? Is that a scientific fact?"

"No . . . but . . ." I think about the night Kai brandished his knife. About his Kali classes and his venture into martial arts. Is it possible he wasn't just dabbling? Is it possible I've been played? "I probably should've mentioned this before." I tell Ruth about my encounter with Kai and his slice-and-dice karambit. Her face screws up in anger.

"*Why didn't you tell me?*" she screeches, rousting a flock of starlings.

"Tell you what? That some idiot millennial has a hard-on for a prepper's workout class?"

"Workout class? Are you kidding me? He flashed a knife at work."

"He didn't flash it."

"No? Then what the hell did he do?"

Well, he did flash it. But not in the way she thinks. How can I explain? Especially to a by-the-book stickler like Ruth. "Maybe it's something. Maybe it's not."

"Well, I think it's something, and obviously the pastor does too." Ruth nervously taps her Fitbit. "If we can prove he killed Milo and the others, wouldn't that clear Adam's name?"

"Of course, but . . ."

"But nothing. We need to take our theory to Detective Ruiz. He can arrest Kai, and this whole mess will be over."

Now it's Ruth who's not thinking straight. "You heard what the pastor said. We go to Javier now, we'll have to tell him everything. That includes what we know about the Goodnight Club and the Post-it Notes. And if we spew, the pastor will out us. We could end up in even more trouble than we are in now."

Her eyes narrow. "Then what do you suggest?"

"Well . . . as far as I can tell, we're in a catch-22. Damned if we do and damned if we don't."

"So do nothing?"

"Of course not."

"Then what?"

"We need to gather more evidence before approaching Javier. Something that firmly incriminates Kai."

Ruth nods. "All right. I can't argue with that. How? When?"

I think for a moment. "What if I talk to Kate again? Maybe she knows more than she told me the first time around. And you can work on Ember."

"Agreed. But I have another idea. What if you also have a look around Kai's office? Search for that knife. He might've used it to kill Milo."

"I don't believe Milo's wound came from a karambit knife."

"Why's that?"

"Because of the way it's curved—it's better for slashing, not stabbing."

"Maybe he used another kind of knife."

"If he did, I doubt he'd be stupid enough to leave it in his office."

"He was stupid enough to show one to you."

"Another reason I doubt he's the perp."

Ruth shakes her head in frustration. "So look for something else. Hard evidence. Notes. Or an incriminating email."

I eye her like she's crazy. "You understand you're asking me to break into his office?"

"No, I'm asking you to investigate a noise."

"A noise?"

"Isn't that what security guards do?"

"That's breaking and entering, Ruth. We—*I*—could get in a shit-load of trouble."

Ruth begins to pace again, arms folded, back straight. "So you're worried about yourself? Not Adam?"

"Of course I'm worried about Adam. I just don't know if I'm ready to break the law."

"Well, it sounds to me like you only give a damn about yourself."

"I'm just asking you to slow down. Think clearly."

Her voice goes shrill. *"Do what?"* She stops pacing and moves close enough to poke a finger in my chest. *"You're* the one that spent all those years moaning about what we did wrong. What we should've said. And you know what? You were right. We should've copped to the truth the day Hunter died. And now? Now that we have a chance to help my son, you want me to think clearly. *Clearly?* To slow down? Don't ask you to do anything illegal? Well fuck that. Yes. I said it. *Fuck that.* I'm going to help my son, and you're going to help me to help him. We are going to clear Adam of any suspicion. And *you . . ."* She jabs her finger hard for full effect. *"You* are going to stop worrying about doing something wrong." She jabs again. *"You* are going to investigate Kai, starting tonight." She stakes a step back, breathing hard. "Now I'm going home. I need some food and to sleep. I'll expect a report from you first thing in the morning."

"You understand if we go that route, we'll have to tell Javier everything we know."

"So?"

"Including what you knew about the pink slips. And why you never spoke up."

Ruth takes a deep breath and exhales as if clearing the past from her lungs. "I don't care what happens to me. I just want to help Adam. Understand?" She turns and marches off, head held high.

I watch for a moment before sagging onto a nearby bench. I'm exhausted. Completely beat. But I'm a long twelve hours from climbing into my bed. What I need is a strong cup of coffee. Maybe two. Because deep down, I know Ruth is right. She might've been the one to tell the first lie, but I got Adam into this mess. I have to get him out.

Two

Wednesday, October 2

"Evening, Kate."

"Evening."

It's past midnight when I find Kate resting on the veranda in her lounge chair. She's dressed in all black tonight, her hair pulled back in a bun. A candle flickers in the darkness, sending up a sweet, musky scent.

"I've been waiting for you," she says. "Have a drink?" Her face is paler than usual, her eyes rimmed in red.

I settle beside her with a thud. "Not tonight." I need to keep my head clear. Ask the right questions. See if I can glean enough information to help clear up this self-made mess.

"Please?" she says in a small voice. "For me? Consider this my husband's wake?" She downs half her drink, the ice clinking hard against the glass.

"You're shaking," I say. "Are you cold?"

She sighs. "Not cold. Depressed, I suppose. It's been quite a day."

"I bet." I reconsider and pour myself a stiff one, thinking I'll only take a sip. "I'm sorry about Gordon . . ."

"It was time. Still . . ."

"You regret how it happened?"

"Not in the least."

"You don't feel guilty?"

"Why would I?"

"Your Angel was involved, right?"

She hesitates for the longest time before answering. "Right."

"I thought so."

"It was time. You saw Gordon. He was in horrible pain. I just couldn't bear it anymore."

I nod. "I'm not here to judge you. I just want to ask you a few questions."

"About . . . ?"

"The process."

"Why?"

"I have my reasons."

She eyes me warily. "You're not going to have me arrested, are you?"

"Of course not."

"Then fire away."

I wet my mouth with a few drops of whiskey. "Were you here when the Angel came?"

She shakes her head. "I was in my room. That was our agreement. The Angel tapped on the door when he or she was done. I waited five minutes and then . . . well, by then Gordon was gone." She sighs. "I hope you don't mind the scent. I lit the candle in Gordon's honor. It reminds me of the cologne he wore when we first met. It was at a party in the Hamptons; I was living in New York. That was the first time I laid eyes on Gordon, and I knew he was the one. He was by far the handsomest man in that room that night, and the nicest one for sure."

"Love at first sight?"

"Corny, I know, but true. Our relationship started off a little rocky, but it quickly smoothed out. I can't believe our life together is over. That I'll never see him again." She makes a choking sound, which might be the closest she gets to crying. I reach out and take her hand.

"I'm sorry."

"Don't be." She grasps my hand tight before releasing to finish off her drink. "I have a lot to be thankful for, and I'm going to focus on that. Once his boys arrive, my peace and quiet will be gone." She holds out her drink, and I fill it up without her asking, the amber liquid splashing back and forth. "They never liked me, you know. The boys, I mean. They believe I stole Gordon from their mother."

"Did you?"

"Steal him? Well, yes, in a way I suppose I did. Their marriage was over by the time I met Gordon. They were living like brother and sister. A brother and sister who didn't get along. And then, well, something terrible happened. Once we made it through that, Gordon left his wife for good. We were married the following year." She sighs. "You don't find men like Gordon anymore, present company excepted."

I down half my drink, enjoying the warm sensation. "I wouldn't compare myself to your husband. I haven't been so honorable. I'm not that good of a man."

"Oh, but you are. You must know that."

"I've made a lot of mistakes."

"So have I."

"Like?"

"Well to start with, in society's eyes, I'm an accomplice to murder."

And I'm an accomplice in my son's death. I think on those words for a moment, and then I drain my whiskey and set my feet on the ground. My knee is throbbing like a bitch tonight. I give it a rub and eye Kate. "Back to the subject at hand. What can you tell me about Pastor Sam's involvement with the Goodnight Club?"

"Pastor Sam?"

"Yes. My understanding is that she's the Angel's ambassador. That she acts as some sort of go-between, delivering Post-it Notes to her master. That sort of thing."

"Her master? That's an interesting choice of words."

"Why?"

She finishes off her drink and sets it down with a clank. "Where did you get this information?"

"It doesn't matter. Let's just assume I'm right."

"Hmm. If so, then I've been wrong all along."

"What do you mean?"

"I had come to believe the pastor was the Angel."

The pastor? I think back on our conversation. Could she have been telling a pack of lies? "Why'd you think that?"

"Through the process of elimination. The Angel had to be knowledgeable about the campus, with the ability to secure and dispense the appropriate drugs. At first I thought it might be someone on the medical staff. I had my eye on a nurse or two. Early on, Nurse Milo came to mind. But it also needed to be a compassionate person. I swiftly ruled him out."

"So you believe the Angel's motives are good ones?"

"Absolutely. Why else would she put herself in jeopardy to help us if her motives weren't pure? It's not like she was paid to take on the risk. She only asked that we reveal a precious secret, and all of us were willing to give her a peek into our pasts for the promise of a peaceful end. I'm sure you realize if she's ever caught, she'll spend the rest of her life in jail."

I nod. "So you never spoke to, or met, the Angel."

"I repeat. No. It was safer that way. The first time a club member ever laid eyes on the Angel was the night of their crossing."

I think about that for a moment. "But how would the member identify the Angel if they had no idea who it was?"

"What do you mean?"

"How would they know who would show up at their door?"

"Um . . . well. I guess we never thought about that."

"How about this ambassador? Did she attend the crossings?"

"Not that I know of. Why? Is there a problem?"

"What about the night Gordon died? Did you see anyone?"

"Outside of the pastor earlier in the evening, no. No one. Why are you asking?"

I consider how much information to share. "There seems to be a problem."

"What kind of problem?"

"You know that Nurse Milo was murdered."

She swats at a mosquito. "Of course. That's old news."

"Well . . . the same person may be responsible for the deaths of several destitutes."

"Deaths? You mean murders?"

"Yes."

"Are you talking about a potential serial killer?"

"I am."

She raises her hand to her throat, her eyes growing wide. "Who told you this?" she asks in a voice just above a whisper.

I hesitate. "Promise to keep this confidential?"

"Of course."

"Pastor Sam."

"Really." She's quiet for a while, working her hands together. The crickets grow louder. A breeze ruffles the leaves. "Well, this is quite concerning," she finally says.

"Agreed."

"Does the pastor have any idea who this killer might be?"

"She has an unproven theory that it's Kai."

"Kai? Kai Gilchrist? That mealymouth suck-up?" She laughs. "Honestly, I can't believe it. He'd be scared of a bug."

"Looks can be deceiving."

"I suppose. Still . . . I find it hard to believe."

"Honestly, so do I. But could you do me a couple of favors?"

"Anything."

"First, don't repeat what I've told you about a potential serial killer to anyone. I don't want to cause panic."

"Of course. I promise. What else?"

"Can you poke around a little? See if there are any rumors out there that might help us find this killer. Or even identify the Angel. That person may have access to information we need. I don't have to tell you this is a life-or-death matter."

She nods, a smile brightening her face. "I promise I'll make a few calls first thing in the morning."

"Thanks. And lock your doors tonight. If there truly is a killer out there, you could be in danger."

"Me? In danger? How very exciting." She rubs her hands together. "I must say this is a thrilling turn of events. Murder and mayhem at Serenity Acres. They'll make a movie about us one day."

"Hopefully the good guys win."

"Hopefully. Now, before you leave, be a gentleman and refill my glass."

"I thought you were tired."

"I was, but not anymore."

An hour later, I'm working my way through administration, wondering how the hell I'll get into Kai's offices, when I catch a lucky break. A housekeeper steps from his lair and offers me a tired smile. "Hola," she says.

"Hola . . ." I scan her name tag. "Maria."

Maria is young and pretty, a Latina woman. Something about her face reminds me of Tina, and I tap the side of my head. "You can leave that door unlocked," I say. "I've been asked to inspect the room."

She screws up her forehead and stares at me, and I realize she doesn't understand. So, I fumble through my terrible Spanish, making it clear I want to go inside. I finish up by patting my security badge like I'm someone in a position of power. I feel a tinge of guilt when it works.

"Bueno," she says in a tiny voice, pushing her heavy cart down the hall. I wait until she's rounded a corner and then step into the outer office, shutting the door behind me with a click.

The lights are off, so I fumble for my flashlight and wave it around the outside room. Everything is perfectly organized; there's not a piece of paper in sight. I quietly cross to Kai's inner sanctum and gently open the door. I hear voices in the hallway and freeze, heart pounding, until they fade away.

What the hell am I doing? I wonder. *What could I possibly find?* But I think of Ruth's and the pastor's theory and grit my teeth and continue on. I search through Kai's drawers and rifle through his files, but the sharpest thing I come across is nail clippers. I open the top drawer of his desk and discover a pad of paper covered in what looks to be passwords. I aim my cell and take a photo and almost laugh at what he's written on top. *KaiRocksIt.* Kai Rocks It? Are you kidding me? That *has* to be his computer password. Further proof the guy's an idiot and a jerk on top of that.

I stare at his computer, tempted to conduct a quick search. Do I dare log in? Will I be caught? My heart rumbles like a train in my chest. What if every keystroke is monitored? I wouldn't put that past Finn and his corporate thugs. Still, it's late, and I'm guessing they don't work all night. I decide to give it a try.

I take a seat and wiggle the mouse until the computer screen glows bright. I enter *KaiRocksIt* and wait while the icon scrolls round and round. And then? Damn. I'm in.

Taking a deep breath, I log into his email and begin to search. I type in the word *destitute*. A few trivial memos pop up. Then I try *murder*, but that only leads to a long thread on how best to suppress the news of Milo's death. I try to think of other search terms and then recall Ruth using the word *insolvent*. I type in the nine letters and find an email with an interesting attachment—a nasty memo, yes, but nothing close to a murder confession. Still, I decide to forward it to Ruth. At least she'll know I tried. I read it a second time before hitting "Send."

I want to emphasize that I've been using every means at my disposal to eliminate the insolvents from our rolls. Luckily, we've recently had an unusually high number of deaths that have thinned the ranks of the defaulters from forty to thirty-five. That alone has allowed us to bring in new guests resulting in $5 million in down payments with an additional $75 thousand in monthly cash flow. I hope that will alleviate some of your concerns. I expect to have more good news in the near future . . .

"Zach?"

I look up into a shadow, thick and dark. I shut down the program, but it's too late.

Three

Finn didn't say a word when he walked me to security. He motioned that I should follow, and I did exactly as I was told. He ordered me into the back office and told me to wait until he returned. It's a windowless room used for storage that stinks like metal gone to rust. It's lit by one flickering fluorescent light that drones nonstop. Boxes are piled high in one corner, old computer equipment in the other. The decrepit wooden desk I'm seated behind is covered in layers of greasy dust.

I get up and slowly pace until my pulse stops racing and exhaustion creeps into my bones. Then I settle into a chair and tug my cell phone from my pocket. It's 5:30 a.m. Should I text Ruth and tell her what happened? No, stupid. Your phone could be confiscated and used for evidence. How about I give her a quick call? Another stupid idea. The best thing I can do is nothing. Stay calm and let the situation unfold.

As the minutes tick by, my nerves ratchet up, and I try focusing on what I've learned. I think back on the pastor's accusations, on Kate's assumptions, on the wording of Kai's memo. Do the puzzle pieces fit together, or are we just shoving them into place? And if Kai isn't the killer, who is? How about Finn? He has the skill and the demeanor, but what's the motive? Did corporate hire him to cull the herd? Maybe, but most likely not. How about a nurse? A doctor? A caretaker? Selena sure gets around. And what about Pastor Sam? Maybe she's not the ambassador. Maybe she's the Angel, like Kate believes. But if so, why is she lying? Who is she trying to protect? I shake my head. I spent too many years drowning in the bottle. My brain is no longer sharp.

Just when I've had enough of the solitary confinement, the door rattles open, and Finn steps inside. He holds two Styrofoam cups of coffee and offers me one. "It's black," he says.

"Black works." I take a nip and grimace. The liquid is hot and bitter. Black as black can be. But I keep on drinking, hoping it will help to clear away the fog.

Finn shuts the door, pulls up a folding chair, and glares at me, stone faced. "Well?" he says after a few moments. He doesn't blink, just stares at me with his creepy lashless eyes. He reminds me of a wolf. A wolf who has cornered his prey.

"Well what?" Two can play the waiting game. It's from Interrogation 101. If he's not the serial killer, maybe he's somehow involved in the crime. I scan his face for clues, but the military has served him well. He shows no expression at all except for a slight twitch of his upper lip.

"You want to talk about it?" he asks.

"Talk about what?"

"About breaking into Kai's office."

"I didn't break in."

"You lied about your purpose to the housekeeping staff."

"It wasn't a lie." Not exactly.

"You told the housekeeper you were asked to inspect the room."

Guess little Maria was neither as sweet nor as dumb as I thought. "Just doing my job."

"And what part of your job was that?"

"The part where I look into anything suspicious."

"And there was something suspicious going on?"

"I thought so."

"Like . . . ?"

"Thought I heard something."

Finn drains his coffee in one gulp, even though it's close to boiling hot. He then crushes the cup with his hand and tosses it into a pile of trash. "Time to cut the crap," he says, leveling his eyes on mine. "What were you doing on Kai's computer?"

"Messing around."

He folds his arms and leans back. "You can make this easy, or you can make this hard. As soon as our tech guy gets in this morning, he'll scan Kai's computer and know exactly what you were up to."

"Be my guest." I say those words nonchalantly, but that's not how I feel. It was stupid of me to forward that email to Ruth. Now they'll know she was involved. If I can get to her, I can at least warn her, and she can come up with some sort of cover. I stumble to my feet, and a lightning bolt shoots from knee to spine, the pain ragged and raw. "Shit," I mumble, leaning against the wall. "You can't hold me here. I'm an employee, not a soldier, in case you're confused."

"Sit," Finn orders, and after a few quick beats of my heart, I do what he says. I fold my arms, willing my knee pain away, and stare into his narrowing eyes. He stands, his gaze locked on mine. "You may not be willing to speak to me, but try copping that attitude with the police." He yanks open the door and calls out, and a moment later, Javier steps into the room.

"Morning, Zach," he says.

"Morning." I slump in my seat.

Javier turns to Finn and nods. "Mind if I take over from here?"

"Be my guest."

Finn steps from the room, slamming the door behind him.

"That man has quite the temper," Javier says, settling into Finn's chair, which creaks under his weight. "So tell me," he says. "Why am I here?"

I stare at Javier, knowing his game. He'll be friendly, try to get me to talk. And there are some things I want to tell him. But I have to carefully pick and choose what I say. "Finn claims I broke into our CEO's office."

"Did you?"

"No."

"But you were in the room . . . ?"

"Yes."

"And on the computer . . . ?"

"For research."

"On what?"

"A potential crime."

Javier rubs his chin. "What crime?"

I think on that. The memo may be evidence of management behaving badly, but it doesn't confirm a crime. I've got to do a little more sleuthing and take the time to build my case. "I'm not ready to talk about that."

He nods, considering, then sets his hands on his thighs. "Okay. So you just happened to be in the CEO's office, and somehow you came across his password, and you were perusing his computer, and . . . help me here, Zach. It kind of sounds like breaking and entering. And this Finn guy is demanding we press charges."

"Jesus." I shift in my chair to ease the pain. "They can fire me. I'll go away. No need to involve you or the police."

"Except . . ."

I don't like the way he says that. Nor the way he fixes his eyes on a point above my head. "Except what?"

"There have been some developments in the Nurse Milo case . . ."

"You found the killer?" I feel a sudden surge of optimism that this mess could get resolved.

"Maybe the killer. More likely witnesses. Or possibly accomplices." He pauses to straighten his tie.

"Tell me."

"We've received information that confirms two men were at the scene of the crime that morning. Both employees. One younger, one older. One a security guard. One a kitchen worker who was there to purchase drugs." He gazes at me, his eyes unyielding, and I can't stop the heat from creeping up my face. I've never been good at poker. The truth is, I suck. I lick my lips, thinking I'd give anything for a shot of whiskey. "I can explain," I say.

"Be my guest." Javier crosses his legs and leans back in his chair, pressing his fingertips together. "But do us both a favor and make it the truth."

I work my thumbs into my throbbing knee. "You've got to believe me. There's nothing sinister about this. Maybe stupid, but not sinister."

"I'll buy that. Now go on." He's watching me closely, not like a friend but like a cat getting ready to pounce.

"Adam had gotten himself into a bit of a mess."

Javier pulls a pen and a pad of paper from his pocket. "Adam . . . ?"

"Adam Mosby."

"Ruth Mosby's son?"

"Yes."

He writes something down. "Isn't that the kid who was supposed to be watching Hunter the day he drowned?"

I nod, refusing to look him in the eye. "It is."

"And you were willing to help him out?"

"I was."

"Well, you're a far better man than I am."

Tell him, Tina says. *He deserves to know the truth.*

I tap the side of my head. What is Tina doing here? I thought she'd left for good. "Not now," I mumble.

Yes, now.

I fix my gaze on Javier's questioning eyes. "The thing is, I owe him."

He frowns. "I don't understand."

"Ruth and I . . . well, we told a lie that day."

301

"The day Hunter died?"

"Yeah."

Javier's eyes narrow. "What kind of lie?"

It takes a moment for me to answer. "A chickenshit one. Adam wasn't the reason Hunter drowned. It was us. Me and Ruth." I take a few deep breaths before continuing. "That afternoon Hunter was having a blast in his pool, and the thing is, the water was only a few inches deep. And Adam was out there watching, so . . ."

"So?"

"So . . . we kinda disappeared into Ruth's bedroom for a while."

"You mean . . . ?"

"Yes."

"Shit." Javier sags like he's been gut punched. Then he throws his shoulders back. "And to think I felt sorry for you all these years. I've been an idiot."

"You have to understand . . ."

He raises his hand. "No," he says coldly. "Actually, I don't."

"But Javier . . ."

"And don't call me Javier. From now on, it's Detective Ruiz." He scribbles in his notepad.

You did the right thing, Tina whispers.

"Go away."

"I'm not going anywhere," Javier says. "Not until you answer all of my questions."

"I wasn't speaking to you."

He shakes his head at that. "Let's go back to what you were saying. What kind of 'mess' had Adam gotten into?"

Of course Javier already knows the answer. "He had a spat with his wife."

"Define *a spat.*"

"She accused him of battery."

"When?"

"Couple of months ago."

"And Adam has a history of . . ."

"Of narcotics abuse. So does his wife. But that's over, at least for Adam. He's clean, I promise."

"Then why was he meeting Milo?"

"He needed some Adderall."

"An illegal transaction, correct?"

"Yes, but nothing terrible. His drug days are over."

Javier lifts his gaze from his pad of paper and works me over with his eyes. "You sure?"

"Yes," I say with a lot more conviction than I feel.

"Huh. That's interesting." He flips back through his pad and stares at it close. "When he was arrested, they found a stash of opioids in the house. His wife claims they were his. Neither of them had a prescription."

"They didn't belong to him," I say firmly.

"Of course not."

"I'm serious. His wife's the dopehead." Why the hell didn't Adam tell me about the opioids? What else don't I know?

"And you?"

"What about me?"

"You clean?"

"What kind of question is that?"

"The kind I have to ask."

Anger simmers in my gut, low and hot. "The hell you do."

He nods. "Maybe it would be best if I read you your rights."

The anger subsides and is replaced by panic. The office light flickers and dims. "You're going to arrest me?"

"Looks that way."

"But why . . . ?"

"You lied to me, Zach. And I'm pretty damn sure you're lying to me again."

I sputter through my next words. "I lied to you because I was trying to keep the kid out of more trouble. Stupid, I know, but my intentions were good. Adam's mistake was to skip a doctor and go direct to Milo for his Adderall. And when he came across Milo's body . . . well, he panicked and called me for help."

Javier writes something down, probably a reminder to subpoena our cell phones. "And that's when you told him to lie."

"I didn't *tell* him."

He rolls his eyes. "You agreed you would help in a cover-up."

I want to slug Javier in the face. This is why he's so good at interrogation. He pokes and prods his suspects until he gets them to say or do something that incriminates their asses. Adam would never survive under questioning. His temper would get to him first. I take a deep breath to calm myself before I continue. "I know this looks bad. I really do. But it's all a coincidence meant to deflect you from the truth. You know Nurse Milo was a dealer, right?"

He nods. "We have evidence that Milo stole meds from the nurse's station and the patients. It's really no surprise. He'd been previously charged with a number of small crimes involving use and possession and even spent a year in jail for burglary."

"So how'd he get a job here?"

"The old-fashioned way. He changed his name and applied for the position with forged paperwork. We now believe he's also behind a string of campus thefts that have gone unreported. Stolen drugs, jewelry, and artwork. That kind of thing. The local pawnshop identified him as a regular customer. We're tracing some of his sales as we speak."

"But why wouldn't the crimes have been reported?"

"I don't have an answer for that, but I'm guessing that management wanted to keep their problems to themselves. Wouldn't look good for potential clients to hear of a high crime rate when they're set to spend millions on this place."

I think about that. "So, you believe Nurse Milo might've been killed by an accomplice?"

He hesitates. "I'm not at liberty to discuss . . . you in any kind of financial trouble, Zach?"

It takes me a second to get what he's insinuating. "That's a ridiculous question."

"Is it?"

"It's dumb."

"Dumb?" He taps his finger against the side of his head. "I never said I was a genius. But here I have two men that lied about being on the scene of a crime."

"I didn't lie about being at the scene."

"Correction. Here I have a security guard who lied about who *was* at the scene of a crime. And this security guard has a history of alcoholism and possible financial problems. And the guy he lies about also has a history of addiction and is facing felony charges of opioid possession and spousal abuse."

My hands harden into fists. "This is all bullshit."

"Is it? Because in my world—and let's be clear, it's one that you once occupied—it begs all sorts of questions, and I think you know it. Now then. It's time for us to go." He pulls out a pair of handcuffs, and I almost puke my coffee.

"*Jesus*. Are you kidding me?"

"I'm not. You're under arrest."

"You're charging me with murder?"

"No. At this point you're being charged with making a false statement at the scene of a crime."

"Don't do this."

"I have no choice."

"At least do me a favor and skip the handcuffs."

He stares at me for a moment before returning the handcuffs to his belt. "All right. Now let's go."

"What about Adam? What will happen to him?"

"He'll be arrested when he steps on campus."

"Today?"

"You bet."

My stomach drops like a stone down a well. "Can't you give him a break?" I plead. "Arrest me but not Adam."

"Get up before I cuff you."

I get to my feet, knee rebelling. "Tell me one thing," I say. "The cameras weren't working, so who told you we were there?"

"No one told me."

"Then how?"

"We received photos late yesterday."

"Photos? Who from?"

"No idea. Anonymous package with a half dozen or so."

"Maybe they were sent by the real killer."

"Right," he scoffs. "Now get moving before I use the cuffs. I'll be following close behind."

I take a step and almost collapse. My knee doesn't seem to be working; it's like the tendons have given out. But I don't want to look like a total failure, so I do my best to hobble through the main security office.

Finn gives me the evil eye as I pass close to where he stands. I wonder if he's gloating. Or plotting. Texting Kai with their next step. His bitch boy Barnet barks something on his phone. He covers the mouthpiece with his hand, and his eyes shift from me to Javier. "Code black," he says to Finn.

"Shit," Finn says. "You kidding me? That's the third one in two days."

"This is different. Someone's been stabbed."

"Stabbed? Who?"

"Kate Harrington."

I whip around. *"What?"*

306

Barnet listens to more on the phone and then sets it down and glares at me. "Seems she's identified the killer. Written his name in blood."

"Whose name?" Javier asks.

Barnet points at me. "Zach's."

Javier grabs my arm and spins me around. A bolt of fire zaps my leg. "Where were you last night?" he asks.

"Here," I reply, pulse racing. "Doing my normal rounds."

He sticks his face in mine. I smell onions on his breath. "Were you at or near the victim's apartment?"

I clear my throat and swallow. "I don't think I should answer that."

"Then we'll do this the hard way." He pulls out a set of handcuffs. "Turn around," he orders.

I twist and my knee gives way. I drop to the ground with a groan.

VII. WRATH

A gentle answer turns away wrath, but a harsh word stirs up anger.

—*Proverbs 15:1*

The Angel

I've made the difficult decision to leave, or I suppose the decision's been made for me. I can no longer operate behind the scenes when suspicion could turn on a dime. So I'm feeling melancholy tonight as my date of departure nears. I pack a box of sacred possessions and then pause to sip on a flute of port. Listen to Albinoni's sweetest of adagios while I page through a lifetime of precious work.

I linger on Loretta's day of torment; on Mary's frigid years in bed. On Simon's theft of millions from his corporation, on Milo's rape of a teenage girl. And the addition of the destitutes? Well, they were an interesting lot. All they needed was a little encouragement, and most jumped at the chance to cross. Eleanor Kingsley was my very favorite, and her secret didn't fail to impress. In a fit a childish anger, she pushed her sibling down a stairwell the day the girl turned twelve. Her sister spent months living as a near vegetable until she caught a cold and expired. Death by strangulation was my idea. I doubt Eleanor would have agreed.

Kate harbored a surprising secret; I required her to write it down. How else could I justify assistance to Gordon, a man with a shuttered mind? Seems they weren't the perfect couple they presented to the world. There was a hit-and-run in Gordon's past, and his mistress was in the car.

Kate a deceitful adulteress? I never would've guessed. The couple spent their decades together assuaging their collective guilt. Sent money to the wronged family, spread their wealth around like manure. Still, I wouldn't have given up the pawn if I hadn't needed to save the queen. But Kate's death provided the perfect ploy to turn away any threat of suspicion. Now what to do with my final problem? I must wrestle my mind around that.

My thoughts return to packing. There's so much I have to do. I will be moving to the city of Catania, a lovely port set on Sicily's east coast. A humble church has requested my services, and I'm loath to turn it down. It's a region saturated with sacred history that includes the life of my favorite saint. A young and virtuous noblewoman, Saint Agatha refused the hand of a powerful man. When he ordered her body to be mutilated, Saint Peter intervened. She was then rolled naked upon shards of pottery until she expired in excruciating pain.

How exquisite her final suffering; how she agonized in the name of her Lord. As a devotee of the loveliest of saints, I plan to seek justice for all who are harmed. Expose the evil of men who hurt women and crucify them in their beds. Solidify my work as my Lord's avenger and wreak vengeance on the land. But first I must compose my final move. It's time to close out the game.

RUTH MOSBY

One

It's nearly eleven when I arrive at my office, massaging my still-numb jaw. I had a dentist appointment this morning to replace a long-crumbling crown. I tried to cancel, but the receptionist threatened I'd be charged, and I can't afford the additional expense. So I went to the appointment, and while the dentist worked, I tried to bring clarity to my thoughts.

The pastor confirmed what I've come to believe: Kai is involved in the destitute deaths. Maybe he's not the actual killer, but he could be directing someone that is. Finn? Barnet? A staff member? All possibilities. And Milo? It seems likely his killing is related. But how? And why?

I need to speak with Zach. See if he was able to gather enough evidence for us to present our case to Detective Ruiz. But this morning he seems to have gone AWOL. He's not at home, and he's not answering my texts.

Where are you, Zach? Please, surface. Of all times to disappear, this is the worst. Are you avoiding me, or did you fall asleep in your car? And please, don't tell me you're drinking. That would be the absolute worst. I rev up my computer and scan my emails. Among the dozens in my in-box is one from Kai sent at four a.m. That early-bird message is almost stranger than an AWOL Zach. Since when does Kai climb out of bed before eight? And what would he be doing at his office at that hour? Did he send this, or did someone else? I tap out another text. Call me! Now!

After opening Kai's email, I scan the attachment, and my pulse begins to race. This is it, the motive behind his madness. Of course Zach would say it's not proof of a crime, but isn't there something called *circumstantial evidence*? I mean, if all the clues point to Kai, can't he be charged? That would get Adam off the hook. But who sent the email? Obviously Kai wouldn't forward it. Did Zach somehow break into his computer? If so, was he caught? I have a sudden, horrible thought. Maybe he's been murdered too.

I call Zach for the umpteenth time and once again get sent to his voice mail. "Where are you, Zach?" I nearly yell into the phone. "This is crazy. You need to get in touch."

"What's crazy?"

I look up to find Kai slouching in the doorway, his face fixed and pale. He saunters to my desk and slides into a guest chair. He's not wearing his usual jeans and button-down but is clad in sinister black. I scan his face and see evil there. He's the one. The serial killer. A madman hiding behind an innocent face. I steel my shoulders and finger my phone. One false move, and I'll call 911.

"I asked you a question," he says, his left eye twitching.

"Private conversation," I reply.

"With our employee Zach?" He studies me with a look of such utter hatred it almost feels like a blow to my head. My face grows warm, and sweat drips down my back. Will he use his knife? Can I stop him? How to protect myself?

"I wanted to speak with him about his hours," I say, trying to control the trembling in my voice.

"Work hours?"

"Yes." I ease my purse from the floor onto my lap and blindly search through the contents. When I come across Adam's faux credit card, I slip it into my pocket.

"Why would you have anything to do with his hours? The guy works for Finn."

"Well, yes, but . . ." But what? "Anyway, do you need something? I don't have much time. I'm off to meet a potential guest."

"I'll walk with you," he says.

"No need. I can handle her myself."

His gray eyes narrow to slits. "Why don't we cut the bullshit?"

I look away. "I don't know what you mean."

"I think you do." He gets up from his chair and shuts the door. Then he turns to me, arms folded. "Now tell me about you and Zach."

I shrug, feigning calm. "Zach Richards? The security guard? Well . . . he works for us."

"Come on, I'm not an idiot. I know about you two."

I hesitate, my mind fumbling for words. "We're neighbors; that's it." I ease the knife from my pocket and onto my lap and fold it like Adam instructed.

"I don't believe you."

With the knife in hand, I feel a little less frightened. "Not my problem," I reply. "Now if you'll excuse me, I have to go."

He thumps the door with his hand. "If you try to leave here, you're as good as gone."

Good as gone? I hold the knife tight, wondering where best to strike. His neck? His heart? "What do you mean?"

He makes a sound like he's choking. "The director of world operations is on her way. She wants to meet with us."

"About?"

"About all the shit that's been going down. Corporate's worried about their investment, and I don't blame them one goddamn bit. A murderer stalking guests at an old folks' home? Not a great look for our brand." He throws his head back and laughs. I wonder if he could be drunk, but it's a little early for that. Maybe he's crazy. That's it. He's a madman. I grip the knife tighter as he continues. "I'm guessing we'll both be fired," he says. "But at least *I'll* get my two years' severance, while the only thing you'll get is a free jail cell."

"I don't understand." He's sounding less like a serial killer and more like my loser boss.

He waves off my words. "What I don't get is how you could surround yourself with such scum. I mean, you're OCD when it comes to policy and procedures. Always harping on the rules. And then you hire your druggie son and squash his background check after employing the neighborhood drunk."

A warm wave washes over me. "I can explain," I say.

"I wouldn't want you to incriminate yourself, but I'd like to understand. What were they after? I mean, I understand Nurse Milo. That's just some drug deal gone bad. But old lady Kate?" He shakes his head. "That totally stumps me."

"Kate? Kate Harrington?"

"Who else?"

My hands turn cold and clammy; my heart hammers in my chest. "What happened to Kate?"

Kai sighs and rubs his twitching eye. "Look at you playing all innocent. Detective Ruiz may not have arrested you yet, but I'm betting he'll get there soon."

"I don't know what you're talking about."

"Really? You want to play that game? All right. Kate Harrington has been murdered, stabbed in the neck."

Drums pound in my ears. "I don't believe you."

"Well, it's true."

My world tilts to the left and then to the right. "My God. When?"

"Early this morning."

I reach for my throat, the room spinning. Kate murdered? Impossible. Did Zach go to her villa as we discussed? Is that what this is about?

"And then your buddy breaks into my computer and forwards you a memo on the destitutes. Do you want to tell me about that?"

We eye each other like two boxers circling. Something in his manner tells me he's the killer. He's just trying to mess with my head. I picture thrusting the knife at his heart. Or his neck. Yes, his neck would be better. "Maybe he was gathering evidence," I say.

"Evidence of what?"

Here goes. "Of your horrific actions towards the destitutes."

"My what?"

"You know what I'm talking about."

"I don't." Two spots of color bloom on Kai's pale cheeks. "The only thing I've been doing is my job. And unlike you, I've been doing it very well."

I glance at my computer and scan the memo, gaining strength from its words. "Exactly. And you've been helping the destitutes along."

He eyes me like I'm crazy. "What're you talking about? Everything we've done is perfectly legal."

"Including killing them?"

"Killing?" His bad eye twitches wildly. He tugs at his bun.

"Yes. Killing. You're in debt, and you've been killing them off to up your bonus." I search his face as I say those words, delving for the truth.

His eyes grow wide. He's faking innocence, I'm sure. "Why would you say that?"

"Because it's true."

His mouth drops open. "You think *I've* been murdering the guests?"

"You or one of your henchmen."

"Henchmen? What is that? Something from an old movie?" He throws open the door. "You're crazy, lady. I'd never go so far as to kill someone for this miserable job. I hate it here. In fact, I'm glad I'm

319

getting fired. It'll put me out of my misery." His voice drops to just above a whisper. "Want to know a secret? I never wanted to be executive director. *Never.* I only applied so I could wreck your miserable little dream. You've been riding my ass ever since I got here. In fact, you've been a complete goddamn bitch. If you had gotten the ED job instead of me, you would've fired me in ten seconds flat. Right? Am I right? Come on, answer."

I don't answer because, of course, he *is* right.

"Thought so. Well, you'll be happy to know I'm getting out of this place. I'll be heading north to San Francisco, where I plan to find something, anything, that's more interesting than this pile-of-shit job."

Kai is working hard to throw me off, but I won't let him. I get to my feet. "You can't leave before the bodies get exhumed," I say. "The coroner will need to pinpoint the exact causes of the destitute deaths."

He points his finger at me. "There's only one person that's been accused of killing, and that's your good friend, Zach. The police have arrested him for the murder of Kate Harrington."

That knocks the breath out of me. "Impossible," I whisper.

"Is it? Because before she died, old Kate Harrington wrote Zach's name on the ground in blood."

"I don't believe you."

"You don't need to believe me. A fact is a fact."

"I'll call Detective Ruiz to confirm."

"You do that. But you might not get him right away. I believe he's busy interrogating the two suspects as we speak."

"*Two* suspects?"

"Yeah. Two. He also arrested that loser son of yours."

My heart skips a beat. "He arrested Adam?"

He nods. "Happened this morning in the parking lot. Quite a scene. Your kid was crying like a baby. If he hadn't created such a disturbance, I'd say it was fun to watch."

My mind bumbles this way and that, caught in a trap of fear.

"I suggest you pack up your desk," Kai says. "No matter which way this goes, neither of us will be working here much longer. You and your entourage have taken care of that. By the way, what's that in your hand?"

I glance at the knife peeking through my fingers and slip it into my pocket.

"Yeah. I thought so. I'll pass on that sweet morsel of information to the police."

Kai turns and leaves my office, and I drop into my chair, stomach churning. Dear God. Could things get any worse?

Two

Ember stands in the shadow of the memorial slab looking like a lost waif. If it weren't for her sky-blue uniform, she might be mistaken for a child. I sent a text requesting we meet in the garden before the start of her evening shift. I assumed she would've heard about the arrests, but she must have slept through the day's events.

"Adam's been arrested." I repeat.

"You said that. But how is it possible I wasn't told?" She wrings her delicate hands together. "I mean, isn't Adam allowed one phone call, or does that just happen in the movies?"

"He called his father." I know that because Doug left me an angry voice mail. Said there was a good chance Adam was going to be charged with murder, and he wanted nothing to do with him. He was tired of his son's screwups and wouldn't offer a cent for his defense. That he had his own family to consider. *His own family.* Like Alice and Adam were throwaways. I could throttle him for that.

I tried contacting the jail for information, but I kept running into dead ends. Eventually my call was forwarded to an ill-tempered woman who insisted all my questions would be answered if I attended an eight a.m. meeting with Detective Ruiz. Something about her tone told me this was an order, not a request. I hung up the phone, panicked, wondering if I should give a lawyer a call. I dug through my purse until I came across Leo Silverstein's battered business card. But I had never followed through on Carlyn's request for support, so it seemed awkward to reach out now. I tried googling local criminal lawyers and even gave one a call. But he wanted five thousand just to speak with me, more if he accompanied me to the precinct. I couldn't see spending that kind of money since at any moment I might lose my job.

"Why was he arrested?" Ember asks, her voice shaking. "What are they accusing him of?"

I try to organize my thoughts. "They know about Adam's meeting with Milo."

"But he didn't do anything bad. He just told a stupid lie."

"They also arrested Zach. They believe the two of them are in collusion."

"Collusion? I'm afraid I don't understand."

"Why don't you take a seat?"

"What's wrong?"

"I'll tell you, but I think it's better if you hear this sitting down."

She opens her mouth to argue and then eases onto the bench. Taking a seat next to her, I catch a whiff of her lemon scent.

"Okay," she says in a frightened voice. "Go ahead."

"There's no easy way to say this." I swallow, my throat gone dry. "Kate Harrington is dead."

"What?"

"She was murdered early this morning."

"Murdered?" Ember starts to tremble, and I reach out for her hand. "I don't understand," she says. "How could anyone hurt Kate?" She pulls her hand from mine, gets to her feet, and begins to circle the koi pond. "It's impossible. She was a wonderful woman. Who could do such a horrible thing?" She pauses and runs her hands across her stubbly blonde hair. "Are you telling me they think Adam and Zach have something to do with her death?"

"Unfortunately, yes."

Despite the warmth of the evening air, I, too, begin to shake. "They're saying Kate wrote Zach's name in blood on the villa floor."

She throws up her hands in frustration. "That's crazy. It makes no sense."

The same thought has been nagging at me all day. "I agree. I believe whoever murdered Kate is trying to implicate Zach in the crime."

"That's frightening. Do you have any idea who it could be?"

"No. But we need to figure this out, and quick. I don't have much time. There's a chance I'll soon be fired, or even arrested."

"You?" She eyes me in disbelief.

I nod. "Last night Zach broke into Kai's office and forwarded me a private email. It's thrown suspicion my way."

She raises her hand to her mouth. "Oh my God. Is there anything I can do to help?"

I level my eyes on hers. "You can start by telling me the truth."

"I don't understand."

"I want to know about the Goodnight Club."

Ember's cheeks flush red. "The what?"

"The Goodnight Club."

"I don't know what you're talking about."

"Yes, you do. And it's important you explain. I think the secrets surrounding the club might be wrapped up in what's happening to Adam and Zach."

She sits cross-legged on the grass, her mouth shut tight. I continue on. "I know you were working with the ambassador."

She hesitates. "Who told you that?"

"Pastor Sam."

Her forehead wrinkles. "She told you I worked *with* the ambassador? Are you sure?"

"Absolutely. Zach and I confronted her with Gordon Harrington's pink slip, and she told us about the club. She said she was the ambassador to someone she called the Angel and that you assisted from time to time."

Silence falls between us. Ember rocks back and forth. Crickets chirp in the hedges, filling the empty void. She takes a deep breath and speaks in a halting voice. "I don't know why, but the pastor is not telling you the whole truth."

"In what way?"

"She is *not* the ambassador."

"Then who is?"

Ember nibbles on her lower lip. "I am."

"You?" I feel like a rock has struck my head.

"Yes."

"But then . . . . what is the pastor's role?"

"Pastor Sam is the Angel."

"*What?*" I jump to my feet. "She's the one helping our guests to kill themselves?"

Ember shakes her head. "No. Pastor Sam is an angel of mercy. She assists her disciples with their crossings."

"What are disciples?"

"Members of the Goodnight Club."

My mind works back and forth. "I don't understand. Why would she lie about your roles?"

Ember gets up and begins to pace. "She probably wanted to keep her identity a secret, and I'm guessing she also wanted to protect me. Some people think what we do is wrong."

"It *is* wrong. It's against the law."

She pauses and looks at me. "I don't happen to agree."

"Obviously not." I try to organize my thoughts. "How involved were you in the . . . the crossings?"

"I never attended one, if that's what you're asking."

"Not even as a witness?"

"No."

"Then what was your job?"

She works her pale hands together. "I acted as a liaison between the club and the person they only knew as the Angel."

"Which means?"

"When a member was ready to cross, Kate would leave their pink slip under that small rock beneath your bench. My job was to retrieve the notes and deliver them to the pastor."

"Did you ever meet the pastor here?"

"Yes. We'd rendezvous to discuss logistics or to smooth out potential problems. Like the time Dario Panini threatened to have a coroner examine his mother's body. We stopped soon after Zach arrived. He nearly caught us a couple of times, and the pastor was adamant our relationship be kept secret."

I consider that. "Did the club members know your identity?"

"No. We felt it was safer that way."

"Not even Kate?"

"We never told her, but I'm fairly certain she guessed the pastor and I were involved."

"Why's that?"

"She'd hint around every now and then."

I lean over and pick up the rock.

"You won't find a pink slip. Gordon Harrington was the last crossing. The club has been disbanded, and the pastor has suspended her services. She'll be leaving town soon."

"She told us she was moving to Mumbai. That true?"

"I thought she mentioned someplace in Europe."

I move close to Ember, my eyes searching her face for the truth. "I need you to be 100 percent truthful with me. Did Pastor Sam ever mention anything about a serial killer?"

"A serial killer?" She looks confused. "No. Never. She *was* worried about a *copycat* killer."

"Copycat?"

"Yes, because of Simon Appleton."

"But he died of a heart attack, didn't he?"

"The pastor believed someone intervened, and she was angry because she knew he hadn't wanted to die."

"Did she do anything about it?"

"I'm not sure. But eventually she told me I wasn't to worry . . . that the problem had been solved."

I watch her closely. "Was that before or after Milo's death?"

Ember screws up her face in thought. "After, I think. Why?"

"I don't know. I'm just trying to put pieces of this puzzle together." I lick my lips. "What about Kai? Did she ever suggest he might be involved?"

"Mr. Gilchrist? No. Never. Why would you ask?"

"So, she never mentioned him in connection with the suspicious deaths of several destitutes?"

"No."

"That's strange. She told us she believed Kai was a serial killer. That he killed Milo and at least five of the destitutes."

Ember's good eye widens. "She *never* said that to me. And I wouldn't believe it if she had."

"Why not?"

"I don't believe Kai's evil, just self-involved. And besides, the pastor was the one working with the destitutes."

"What do you mean 'working'?"

"A dozen or so had become disciples."

"You mean they joined the Goodnight Club?"

"No. She worked with them separately."

"Worked with them?"

"Counseled them."

"About?"

"Their options. A number of the destitutes were devastated at the thought of having to move. They . . . they told her they would rather die than leave the campus."

"And you helped with this . . . this counseling?"

"No. I refused to. Many of the destitutes were healthy. They were just sad at the thought of losing their homes. I thought we should help them in a different way. Find them nice places to live."

"And the pastor didn't agree?"

She looks at me sadly. "No. She didn't."

I try to make sense of this new information. "And did some of these disciples cross?"

"At least five that I know of."

Five? I stare at Ember. The pastor was behind their deaths? But why would she lie to us? Not once but all over the place. What game is she trying to play?

"This is so confusing," Ember says, raising her hands to her head.

"Agreed." I think for a moment. "In fact, the only way we can clear this up is by speaking to the pastor in person. Right now. Before another moment goes by."

Ember takes a step back. "I don't know . . ."

"She's probably in her office. We can confront her together with her varying versions of the truth. Make her tell us what really happened so we can get to the bottom of this mess."

Ember takes another step back. "I don't think that's such a good idea."

"Why not?"

"Sometimes she has . . . well, she can get into these dark moods. I mean, occasionally she gets really angry and . . ."

"So you're telling me you're scared of her?"

She nods, looking paler than ever. "A little."

"Well, you needn't be. Nothing is going happen. We'll do this together, you and me."

Ember glances at her watch. "I'm sorry. I can't. I'm already late for my shift, and we're short-staffed tonight. Maybe tomorrow morning?"

"This can't wait until morning. We need answers, and we need them now. If you won't come, I'll just have to meet with her on my own."

"Are you sure you want to do that?"

"I have no choice. I can't bear to think of my son spending time in jail. And I feel terrible about Zach. I've got to find a way to help them both. It can't wait."

"All right. But can we talk later tonight? I want to hear what she says."

"What time?"

"I have a break at nine."

"Okay. I'll meet you at my office."

"You'll be here that late?"

"I need to start packing my things. Even if I'm not arrested, I doubt I'll keep my job."

"Okay." She gives me a quick hug. "Good luck."

"Thanks." She releases me and turns to leave.

"Wait a moment," I say. "Can I ask you one thing?"

"Yes?"

I take a deep breath. "Do you . . . do you think Adam will ever forgive me for what we . . . what *I* did to him? For telling that awful lie?"

Her face softens with a smile. "I do."

I nod. "Thank you for that."

"He's still angry, but he's coming to terms with his life. He knows he can't blame all of his poor choices on the events of that one terrible day. I will say it's a relief for him to be able to share the burden, to know that Hunter's death was not just his fault." She pauses and hugs me again. This time I feel the peaceful humming she emanated when she touched me months ago. "The important thing now is for you to forgive yourself."

"I'm not sure I can do that."

"If I can find a way to forgive myself, so can you."

"You? You didn't hurt your children."

She releases me, her shoulders drooping. "Not directly. But my burden is that I provoked Bodie that night in Big Sur when I knew he was on the brink. I should've gone to bed, discussed the issue when he was sober. If I had, there wouldn't have been a fire. Ella and Emma would be alive, and there'd be another baby or two." She closes her eyes; her face turns wistful. "We'd be living together as a happy family. I know it. I dream about it all the time. If only . . ." She wraps her arms around herself as if she's searching for her own inner peace. Then she opens her eyes, her dream over. "You see, we all have our regrets. Our wounds. What matters is how we live today. How we treat others. And how we find the strength to go on." Her gaze fixes on mine. "Now go speak to the pastor and get our men out of jail."

Our men. If only Adam could be so lucky as to spend his life with Ember. She would make up for everything that's ever gone wrong in his life. She would make up for me and my lie. I watch her slip into the evening shadows, thinking of our first meeting in the garden. *"I love watching the koi,"* she'd said. *"They never argue or fight. We can learn a lot from them, don't you think?"*

Yes. I do.

Three

Wednesday, October 2

I hurry to the chapel, my back dripping with sweat. I'm not sure if it's due to nerves or because at six in the evening, it's hotter than it was at midday. The Santa Ana winds are blowing; the campus trees are bent nearly sideways, and leaves race past my feet. Fire trucks wail in the distance, and I pause to scour the mountains. The last thing this town needs is another wildfire. We've had more than our share of bad luck.

It's a relief when I step from the heat of the evening into the cool of the shadowy chapel. I clatter across the flagstone floor and down the back steps, focusing on what I'm going to say. But when I knock on the pastor's door, there's no answer. I turn to leave and then change my mind. I'm hoping she'll soon return. She has to. I don't have the luxury of time. I need answers, and I need them now. I test the doorknob. The office is open. I'll wait inside until the pastor gets back.

I flick on the overhead light, and the room shivers in iridescent shadows. I don't like this windowless room with its claustrophobic feel. After taking a seat on one of the two straight-backed chairs, I anxiously wait. The musty smell rankles my nose; the shelves of old books loom like threats on all sides. The lights are flickering on and off, the winds wreaking havoc up above. God forbid the electricity goes out and I have to feel my way out of this place.

I check my cell phone. *Damn it!* My battery has gone dead. How could I be so stupid? What if Ember needs to reach me? I stand for a moment and then sit. Cross my legs and count to ten. My stomach does a few double flips. *Jesus.* My nerves are making me sick. Out of habit, I tap my Fitbit. I'm short five thousand steps. *Five thousand?* I'll never get to ten today. I frown at the absurdity of the thought. Who cares how many steps I take? I don't. Or maybe I do. I wait a few moments and get up and begin to pace back and forth. *One, two, three, four.* It's not for the steps, I tell myself. The rhythm helps me to focus.

Five, six, seven, eight. My gaze falls across the leather-bound book centered on the pastor's desk. I remember she'd called it her Bible, but it's much too thin for that. I pause and look over my shoulder and then gingerly pick up the book and flip it open to the first page. Just like I thought, it's not a Bible. In fact, it's not even a book but rather some kind of journal written in perfectly scripted longhand.

I skim through the first few pages and recognize the names of guests who have recently departed. Karen Crawley. Tim Taylor. Loretta Thomas. Mary Panini. Each entry has a common theme. Name, date, age. The method used to cross. That's followed by the telling of a secret. Most seem to be about clandestine lovers, hurts held close, sexual preferences suppressed. The saddest story comes from Loretta Thomas, who on her fourteenth birthday was raped by a pack of rabid college boys. I gloss over these entries quickly, not wanting to be a voyeur. Then I come across several entries that cause my stomach to constrict. The first is Simon Appleton's, which seems strange as the pastor claims she didn't help him to cross. And then there's an entry on Nurse Milo. But he couldn't have confessed his secrets to the pastor if he was felled by the serial killer. I scour the pages, seeking the truth.

Milo's entry is unlike the others. It wasn't whispered at the time of death. It's a listing of criminal activities. Drugs stolen, monies pinched, champions tortured. Even the rape of an undocumented kitchen worker, who was then threatened with deportation if she ever spoke out. This is followed by an accusation of blackmail but no further explanation of that particular crime.

I flip through more pages and come across the names of the five destitutes who died in recent weeks. Their entries support Ember's claim that the pastor had a hand in their sudden deaths. The final entry is Kate Harrington's. But that's impossible. She was murdered just this morning. How could she have relayed her secret? Unless . . . ? I almost drop the book.

"May I help you?"

"Pastor Sam," I say much too loudly. "I didn't hear you come in." The woman looks as tense as a coiled snake, her jaw clenched tight like a fist.

"Windy night," she says, holding out her hand. "May I?" The light above us shivers and fades, casting shadows across the pastor's waxen face. I hand her the book, my hand shaking.

"What're you doing in my office?" she asks, her eyes boring into mine.

I take a few steps back. "I . . . I wanted to speak with you."

"And snoop?"

"I'm sorry; I thought . . ."

The pastor settles at her desk and positions the book exactly where it sat before. "No need to explain. My fault. I shouldn't have left the door unlocked. I didn't expect to be gone so long. Mrs. Harrington's stepsons have arrived, and they are quite distressed, as you can imagine." She nods at my chair. "Will you please take a seat?"

I wave my cell phone. "I'm sorry, something's come up. I need to leave."

She eyes the phone with a thin-lipped smile. "No, actually, you don't."

I consider and then slip the phone back into my pocket and perch on the edge of my chair.

"Thank you. Now, what is it you wanted to speak to me about?" She fingers her jeweled cross.

"Nothing important," I lie. "I mean, it can wait."

"Really?" she says. "That seems strange. I thought you might be here because of Zach. He and Adam have gotten themselves into a bit of a mess, haven't they?"

I try to sound firm, but I hear my voice shaking. "It's all a mistake. They didn't do anything wrong."

She leans back and eyes me like I'm a puzzle she can't understand. "Unfortunately, the police don't seem to agree with your assessment, and I can't say I blame them. You have to admit that the evidence is quite strong. Photos have cropped up of their clandestine encounter with Nurse Milo. And poor Kate went as far as to write Zach's name on the ground in her own blood."

"You know as well as I do that Zach didn't commit murder," I say, feeling strength in my words. "You're the one who said there's a serial killer on the loose. He must be trying to frame Zach."

"You think?"

"Of course, *I think*. And you should too. Remember? You said this killer murdered Milo and possibly others. You need to give that information to the police."

She slowly shakes her head. "I'm afraid I can't do that."

"Why not?"

"My dear," she says. "You do understand any explanation to the police would implicate me in my work as the ambassador. And that's something I just can't have."

A spark of anger ignites my next words. "That's enough of your lies," I say. "I know you aren't the ambassador. You're the Angel. You're the one that's responsible for the deaths of the Goodnight Club members and more."

"That's quite an accusation," she says, narrowing her eyes.

"It's true. And if you won't help me, if you won't tell the truth, then I'll . . . I'll share what I know with Detective Ruiz. He'll get to the bottom of this."

"So . . . would you mind telling me who's accusing me of being the Angel?"

I hesitate but then decide it's best to lay my cards on the table. "Ember," I reply.

She nods. "Ah. My sweet little Ember? I'm surprised she'd tell such a lie."

"I don't believe she's lying."

"Actually, she is, and I can prove it."

I get to my feet. "Don't waste your time. Either way, I'm going to the police. They can be the ones to sort out the truth."

"You do understand they'll arrest the girl," she says in a calm voice.

"Maybe, maybe not."

"So you're willing to throw your son's lover to the wolves?"

"If it means saving my child and Zach, yes."

"What a selfish woman."

"I suppose I am." I turn to leave when the overhead light shivers and snaps off. I'm enveloped in a velvety darkness. I knock my chair backward trying to reach the door.

"Stay right where you are," the pastor orders. "I'll flip the circuit breaker. I wouldn't want you to trip and get hurt."

I hear her get up from her chair and tip-tap across the floor. "I think I've got it," she says. "Hold on. Let me check the light." The tip-taps start up again, and I fumble for the doorknob, propelled by a wave of fear. A hand grabs my shoulder, and something stabs my neck. I drop to the floor, wrenching my back. "Help me," I say. My tongue grows thick, and my thoughts cloud. There's a scratch of a match, and the light illuminates the pastor's devilish face. She begins to move, wobbling in circles like a drunken top.

"Sorry about the injection," she says. "I know it can be quite uncomfortable, but not for long."

"I can't breathe," I whisper. The light fades into darkness, and I slip into a deep sleep.

Four

Drip. Drip. Drip.

I awaken to the sound of water driving knives into my head.

Drip. Drip. Drip.

I'm locked in a musty darkness. Where? Why? Am I underground? In a grave? That's it, I'm in a casket. I've been buried. Please, God, I'm not dead. *No. No. No.* Wake up. You're in a dream. But no, I'm not. There's no air. I can't breathe. I can't open my mouth. My hands are stuck to my sides. It's a stroke. That's it. I've had a stroke. I can't move. My heart may blow through my chest. Gorge rises in my throat. *Stop!* If I puke right now, I'm dead.

I turn my head to the left. Light bleeds from beneath the door. Calm down. Now. Light. I see light. *Think!* I haven't been buried. I'm on the ground. I'm deadweight. It's a stroke. It must be. That's why I can't move. Can't speak. Can barely breathe.

Drip. Drip. Drip.

I stare at the light in search of calm. I time my breathing to the beat of the drips. My heartbeat begins to slow. Someone will find me. Soon. Yes. But where am I? Not at home. At work? Yes. I must be at work. But where? The drops sound like they're coming from a leaking sink. I concentrate on the light and begin to discern the texture of the floor.

Rock. Gray rock. Covered in dust bunnies. Flagstone? Yes, flagstone. Absolutely. And the musty smell? My memory is jogged just the slightest bit, and my body sizzles with electricity; I'm wired so tight it hurts.

The chapel. Dear God. I'm in the chapel. I'm in Pastor Sam's underground lair. The lights. The sting in my neck. She did this. She hurt me. I rock back and forth. The walls are closing in. Where am I? In a closet? There's barely enough room to move. This is no stroke. She's done something awful. I can't breathe. There's no air. I'm dying. This is the end.

Drip. Drip. Drip.

Breathe to the beat of the water. Work to gain control. I rock onto my side, my back seizing with pain. That's right. I fell. I remember that. That's good. That's okay. The pain will keep me awake, and that's what I need to save myself. I worm my way closer to the light until I can see the outline of my legs and feet. There's black duct tape wrapped around my shins. I peer closer. It's also wrapped around my waist. *Oh my God.* That means it's wrapped around my mouth. Please God, no! *I can't breathe.*

Nooooooooooo! The gorge rises fast; I can't stop it. A sour taste floods my mouth. This is it. It's the end. I'll suffocate. The most horrible way to go.

"Ruth?" a voice calls, sounding muffled and far away. "Ruth?"

I swallow. It can't be the pastor. She knows where I am. It's someone coming for me.

"Ruth?" The voice fades, and I hear a door open. No! Don't go! I bring my knees up to my chest and shove my feet against the door. Thump. Pain roars up my spine. Thump. I try again.

The door's thrown open, and there's a blinding light. *"Ruth?"*

All I can see is a melted face, but I've never seen anyone so beautiful in my life. Ember drops next to me. "What's happened? What is this?"

I moan as loud as I can.

She takes hold of the tape and rips it from my mouth. I gasp at the air. So happy to breathe I can't talk. I suck deep until it fills my lungs. "Hurry," I pant.

"Who did this to you?"

"The pastor."

"Pastor Sam? But why?"

"There's no time for explanations. *Cut the tape!*"

"Yes. Yes. Of course." She looks around. "I'll have to find something."

"No!" I hiss, hysteria mounting. "The pastor could be back any second. My pocket. Try my left pocket. You'll find a knife inside."

Ember reaches into my pocket and extracts the credit card knife. She stares at it a moment. And then she begins to saw at the tape that binds my arms until it snaps.

A shadow looms above Ember, but only a moan escapes my mouth. The shadow reaches between its breasts and yanks a knife from its hidden home. Oh my God. Her cross is a weapon. How could I have missed that clue? Pastor Sam raises her hand high.

"Move!"

The pastor drives the knife into Ember's neck. Ember's eyes open wide, and she whimpers like a puppy that's been hurt. And then she collapses onto me, blood running across my chest.

"Well, well. How sweet is that," the pastor says. "The saint helping the sinner."

"How could you hurt her?" I gasp. "You said you loved her like a daughter." My knife shines through her blood. I cover it with my hand.

"Did I?" The pastor shoves Ember aside with her foot and eyes me, her face pinched and worn. "I honestly did love the child, but she betrayed me in the end."

"Please," I beg. "She doesn't deserve this. Please, don't let her die."

The pastor shrugs. "Don't feel bad. She's a good person. God will cradle her in his arms."

The knife. How to use it? I'll only get one chance.

The pastor prods my stomach with her foot and then presses hard until I scream.

"That's what I love about the basement," she says. "No one can hear you down here." She drops to her knees, her jeweled cross reflecting the light.

"You used that cross to kill Milo?"

"Convenient, don't you think?"

"And Kate?"

"Of course." She holds up the shiny blade. "It's such a wonderful instrument. One part heaven. One part hell."

"By why Kate? What did she ever do to you?"

The pastor screws up her face. "She did nothing to me personally, although she was a sinner in God's eyes. An adulteress like you. She told a lie to save her man. So I had no qualms when I made the decision to divert suspicion to Zach. First I sent the damning photos. Then I iced the cake with Kate." She chuckles. "I like how that sounds."

"But we promised we wouldn't tell anyone."

"Of course I didn't believe you. I was just buying some time, and I assume you were doing the same."

"But we would've kept our promise."

"You threatened me, remember? You threatened to go to the police."

"I didn't mean it."

"Of course you did."

I rack my brain for words that might persuade the pastor to set me free. "But Zach knows about you. Kate told him everything and more. He'll tell Detective Ruiz."

"Tell them what? That I'm some angel's ambassador? I'll deny it all, of course. And with Zach's history of abuse and deception, no one will believe him anyway. I do have regrets about poor Adam. Wrong place. Wrong time. If only he hadn't purchased the Adderall. What a foolish choice. But who knows. Maybe they'll be lenient, and he'll get out of jail in five or ten years. I hope he does."

"Please . . ."

"Enough. I've got a lot of packing to do."

"I promise I won't tell anyone. Just let me go."

"And how would we explain poor Ember?" She holds her hand to her ear as if she's listening for my answer. "Exactly. Now, enough with the useless chatter. You understand I could've killed you with the injection, but that would've precluded a new entry to my journal. So I'll offer you two options for your crossing in exchange for a juicy secret. Would you prefer suffocation or fire?"

I position the knife between my fingers. I'll only have one chance. Aim for the eye? The neck? Could my stubby weapon pierce her heart? "You already know my secret. You told me so yourself."

"For your sake, I'm hoping there's something more." She moves away for a moment and returns with a roll of duct tape. "I think suffocation might be worse. Or a combination of both? What if I wrap this tape around your nose and mouth but don't seal it completely? I'll leave enough of a gap that you won't die, at least not right away. The fire will take care of the rest. Or I suppose I could stab you and end things quickly. That's not a bad way to go. But you must reveal your secret. The one that makes you tick. And please don't lie to me. It'll only make things worse."

"You already know my secret!"

She rips off a foot of tape. "Here we go . . ."

"How can you be so cruel?" Stupid question, but I'm trying to buy some time. "There must've been a point in your life when you were a good person. Remember your girlfriend? Stacy? How much you loved her? Cared for her?"

"Oh my." The pastor laughs and prickles my lips with the tape. "Wasn't that a sweet story? And I told it so very well, I almost believed it myself. But no, I'm afraid Stacy was not a good friend. I mean, yes, for a short time she was my lover, and we made all sorts of silly promises to each other. But the truth is, there was no melanoma. No sad story to end our love. It was something more crass than that. Like you, Stacy was a cheater. An adulteress. We had made promises to each other, and then she traded me in for a man." She caresses her cross. "In the end, she paid the price. The two of them died in a tragic accident at Grand Central. Tsk. Tsk. Someone pushed them in front of a moving train."

"Someone . . . ?"

"Her parents were suspicious, but they could never prove it was me. Anyway . . ." The pastor bows her head and sighs. "Now, that's quite enough of your stalling. We don't have much time."

The tape edges toward my mouth and nose. *"No!"*

"Go ahead," she says. "I'm listening."

"It's just . . ." I take a huge sobbing breath. "All right. I'll tell you. I hurt myself when I was a little girl."

The tape edges closer. "Hurt?"

My words spill out. "When I was ten, I fell down the stairs at my home, and I broke my arm."

Her face falls. She looks disappointed. "What kind of secret is that?"

"I didn't trip. I hurt myself on purpose."

"Why?"

"I thought it might make my parents love me."

"They didn't?"

"No," I say in a small voice. "They didn't."

The pastor makes a guttural sound. "So that's it? That's your big secret? God, spare me from boring people. On a scale of one to ten, your secret rates a zero." She tries to tape my mouth shut, but I jerk away.

"You won't get away with this," I say. "Kai knows I'm here. He'll know it's you that hurt us."

"I'm fairly certain you're lying but, no matter. I've already covered that angle. I've repeatedly told the housekeepers they must be more careful with the varnish. But they refuse to listen, and even now, there are oily towels piled up in the closet. They can combust on their own, you know, although in this case, I'll give them a nudge. Not right away, mind you; I want you to have time to contemplate your end. First, I'll write your final entry in my crossing journal, boring as it is." The pastor presses the tape against my mouth, and with every ounce of remaining strength, I plunge the knife deep into her neck. Her eyes grow wide, but she continues to struggle, so I stab at her eye and twist as hard as I can.

"Ruth!" a man's voice calls, and Detective Javier Ruiz appears overhead.

"Help me," I beg. "Help Ember." I don't remember much after that.

Epilogue

Labor Day Weekend
One Year Hence

Alice relaxes on one of the new lounge chairs I purchased last month. They match the new teak outdoor dining set that seats eight to ten. I'm excited to be hosting a Labor Day barbeque to show off my backyard remodel. It's nothing flashy, just a new fence, trimmed trees, and a resurrected lawn. I replaced the fountain, tore out the roses, and added a French kitchen garden. I paid for it with the bonus I received when Serenity's former owners begged me to return. The bad press had been too much for Lost Horizons. The company sold the campus back to the founders at a steep discount after the pastor's murders were exposed.

I think about Pastor Sam on occasion, especially when I come across a pink Post-it Note. Wonder what drove her to her killing spree— was she a Dr. Jekyll turned Mr. Hyde? Was there a good person locked inside her? Or was she a monster who used false empathy to mask her need to kill? If my knife hadn't nicked her artery, we might know the answer. Instead, she died in a pool of blood that night, her motive forever locked away.

"You need any help?" Alice asks.

"No. I think I'm good. The salads are ready, and Zach should be back any minute to light the barbeque." It's been nice having Alice pop into town every week or two. I'll miss her when she goes back on tour, but I'm careful not to bring the subject up. Touring is a part of her life, and she's been clear she wants my support. Voices spill from the front room, and moments later, Adam walks onto the porch, holding Ember's hand.

"Hi, sweetheart." I give my son a kiss on his lightly bearded cheek. He's looking much healthier these days. I turn to Ember. "How are you feeling?"

She smiles and strokes her bulging waist. "Good, but ready to have this baby. She's so active, she won't let me sleep. See? Here she goes again. She's dancing to the sound of your voice." Ember takes my hand and rests it on her belly. I feel the baby move.

"I think that's a foot," I say.

"Or a fist." Ember has let her hair grow; it almost reaches her neck. Soon there'll be no sign of the scar left by the pastor's knife.

Alice gets up and gives them both a hug. "Can't believe my baby brother's going to be a dad."

Adam rolls his eyes and smiles. "Crazy, right?"

She nods. "I'll put on some music."

I eye her warily. "What kind?"

She laughs. "I'll make it oldies just for you."

"Perfect."

"Alice doing okay?" I ask Adam once she's inside the house.

He nods. "Think so. There might be a boyfriend. She's been hinting around."

"There is," Ember says with a smile. "She's mentioned him a couple of times. He sounds wonderful, but she wants to keep him a secret for now. Make sure he's the right one before introducing him to the family."

Alice's reserve still hurts my feelings, but I work to swallow my words. It'll take time to repair my relationship with my children. I can't expect them to trust me right away. But the fact that we can have fun evenings together is more than enough for now.

"Is he a musician?" I ask.

"A writer. Mostly screenplays, I think."

I nod, pleased to hear the news.

"I'll break out the beer," Adam says. "Want anything?"

"No, thanks." I point to my glass of Pinot. "I'm good."

Adam steps inside, and Ember turns to me. "He loves his new job, by the way. He thinks so highly of the chef."

"I read a review of his restaurant. It's the biggest hit in town." I scan Ember's face. She's looking a little wan. "How about you?" I ask. "Still enjoying day care?"

She claps her hands together. "It's wonderful. I love little ones. And I'm learning the Montessori system. It makes a lot of sense."

"A lot easier than working with the elderly."

"Yes." Her voice drops the slightest bit. "But I liked working with them too."

I understand why Ember won't step foot on the Serenity Acres campus; the trauma of the knife attack will forever leave its mark. But I enjoy being in charge these days, making sure things run just right. No more targeting of the destitutes. They'll have their homes for the rest of their lives. And we've brought in a counselor to work with our elders on managing depression and loneliness. The Goodnight Club continues on, just in another form.

The side gate squeals opens, and Zach steps in with Carlyn on his arm. "Ready for the master to barbeque?" he booms, his blue eyes sparking bright.

"I sure am." I hurry down the steps and give them a quick hug. "How are you?" I ask Carlyn.

She waves her hand, and the diamond flashes. "I couldn't be more content." Carlyn has lost the weight she gained during the early months of incarceration. Thank God they gave her time served. With the support of Zach and me and a few old friends, the judge erred on the side of leniency. No additional jail time, just five years' probation and a commitment to volunteer. We're back to walking most mornings; it's almost like old times. Despite the terrible events of the past few years, we both seem much happier now.

I spend a few minutes raving over her engagement ring. Zach smiles like the proud husband-to-be that he is and then grabs a plate of hamburgers and gets to work.

Later that evening, after everyone has left, Alice and I sit out on the back porch, marveling at the stars. They're especially bright this evening—not the slightest hint of fog. She's had a little too much to drink, but truth is, so have I. There's a party raging nearby—lots of happy shouts and the ring of children's voices.

"I've always liked Labor Day," Alice says. "A family holiday without the pressure of gifts."

"Yes, but it means the end of summer. And you'll be leaving again soon."

"I'll be home by Christmas. That's not so very long. And I'm excited about touring in Australia. I hear it's an incredible place."

I nod, wanting to ask about the boyfriend, but tell myself, *Don't you dare.*

"What about you, Mom?" she asks, turning to me. "Won't you be lonely?"

"I'll have a granddaughter to fill my time."

She's quiet for a moment. "I know, but . . . does it bother you that Zach and Carlyn are engaged? I mean, somehow I thought you and Zach might hook up."

I finger my purple Fitbit. It stopped working the night of the attack, but I have yet to take it off. It's how Detective Ruiz was able to locate me after Zach filled him in on the Angel's antics, he discovered the pastor's fingerprint on the anonymous photos, and I was nowhere to be found. It's become my good luck charm. "Zach and I are exactly in the place we should be," I say. "We'll always be friends, and I'm happy for him and Carlyn. But for the time being, I need to work on myself."

"So you'll be taking those photography classes?"

"I started at City College last week."

"Good for you. And what about the therapist?"

"She's been marvelous. It really helps."

Alice reaches for my hand. "I'm proud of you, Mom. I really am."

I smile and gaze at the stars and think back on my dream from last night. Once again, I had morphed into an oak tree, but this time it was my nightmare in reverse. I began life as a budding acorn, and my trunk grew thick and strong. Soon my limbs pointed toward the heavens and were covered with verdant leaves. Squirrels feasted on my seeds, birds nested in my crown, and children frolicked among my roots. And as a full moon rose in a velvety sky, I fell into a deep and peaceful sleep.

ACKNOWLEDGMENTS

First and foremost, thank you to my family, Phil, Jessica, Ali, Peter, and now Soren and Sage. Your steadfast encouragement means more to me than a million five-star reviews. Thank you to my fabulous agent, Rebecca Scherer, who brings calm to any storm. To my insightful reader Cynthia Wessendorf, who smooths flaws from my early drafts. To Jessica Tribble and the Thomas & Mercer team for their unfailing and tireless support. To my good friend Laurie Leighty, who leads my local publicity team. To my unofficial weapons expert Ruairi Bateson for introducing me to the nuances of knives. And to my coworkers at Santa Barbara's Habitat for Humanity for reminding me of what is important in this world.

ABOUT THE AUTHOR

Photo © 2018 Linda Blue Photography

Catharine Riggs lives and writes on California's central coast. Before turning to fiction writing, Riggs worked as a business banker, an adjunct college instructor, and a nonprofit executive. *What She Never Said* is her second novel. Visit the author online at www.catharineriggs.com.